SONIC™
THE HEDGEHOG

ZETI HUNT!

SEGA®

IDW @IDWpublishing
IDWpublishing.com

Cover Art by
Abby Bulmer

Cover Colors by
Joana Lafuente

Series Assistant Edits by
Riley Farmer

Series Edits by
David Mariotte

Collection Edits by
Alonzo Simon
and **Zac Boone**

Collection Design by
Shawn Lee

ISBN: 978-1-68405-908-9

25 24 23 22   1 2 3 4

Originally published as
SONIC THE HEDGEHOG issues #41–44.

Nachie Marsham, Publisher
Blake Kobashigawa, SVP Sales, Marketing & Strategy
Tara McCrillis, VP Publishing Operations
Anna Morrow, VP Marketing & Publicity
Alex Hargett, VP Sales
Scott Dunbier, Director, Special Projects
Greg Gustin, Sr. Director, Content Strategy
Lauren LePera, Managing Editor
Joe Hughes, Director, Talent Relations
Keith Davidsen, Director, Marketing & PR
Topher Alford, Sr. Digital Marketing Manager
Patrick O'Connell, Sr. Manager, Direct Market Sales
Shauna Monteforte, Sr. Director of Manufacturing Operations
Greg Foreman, Director DTC Sales & Operations
Nathan Widick, Sr. Art Director, Head of Design
Neil Uyetake, Sr. Art Director, Design & Production
Shawn Lee, Art Director, Design & Production
Jack Rivera, Art Director, Marketing

Ted Adams and Robbie Robbins, IDW Founders

Special thanks to Mai Kiyotaki, Michael Cisneros, Sandra Jo, Sonic Team, and everyone at Sega for their invaluable assistance.

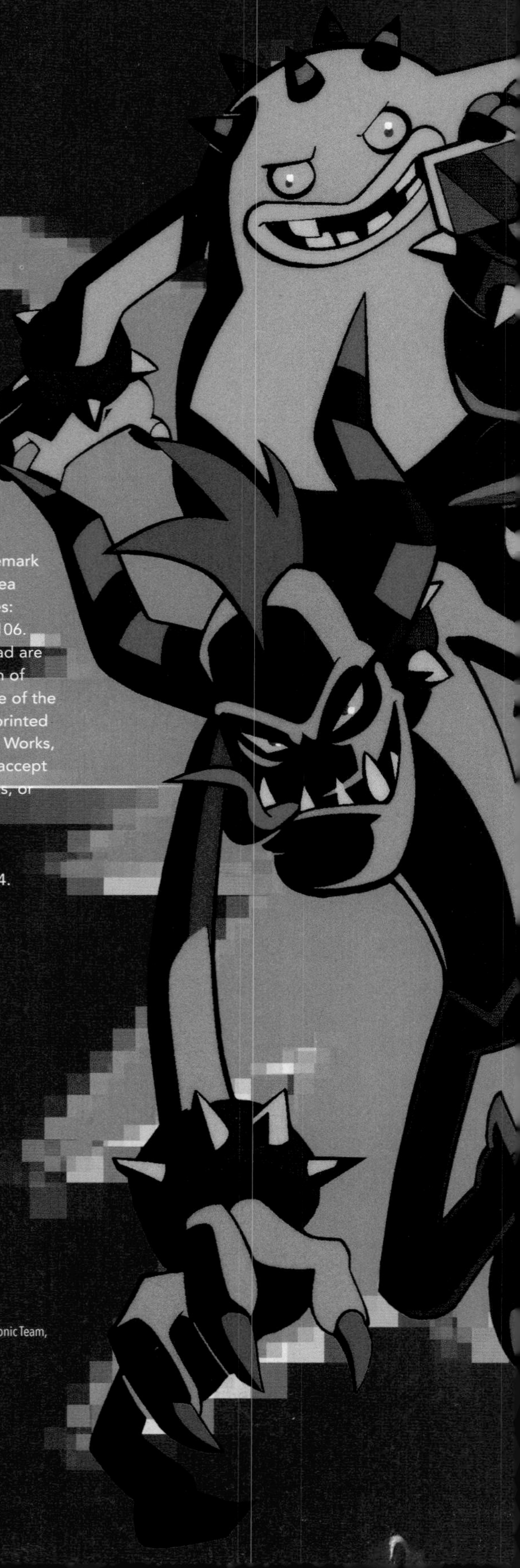

STORY **IAN FLYNN**

ART **ADAM BRYCE THOMAS** (#41)
TRACY YARDLEY (#42 & 44)
JAMAL PEPPERS (#43)
BRACARDI CURRY (#43)
THOMAS ROTHLISBERGER (#43)

ADDITIONAL INKS **MATT FROESE** (#42 & 44)
REGGIE GRAHAM (#43)

COLORS **MATT HERMS** (#41-42 & 44)
REGGIE GRAHAM (#43)
VALENTINA PINTO (#43)

LETTERS **SHAWN LEE**
NATHAN WIDICK (#43)

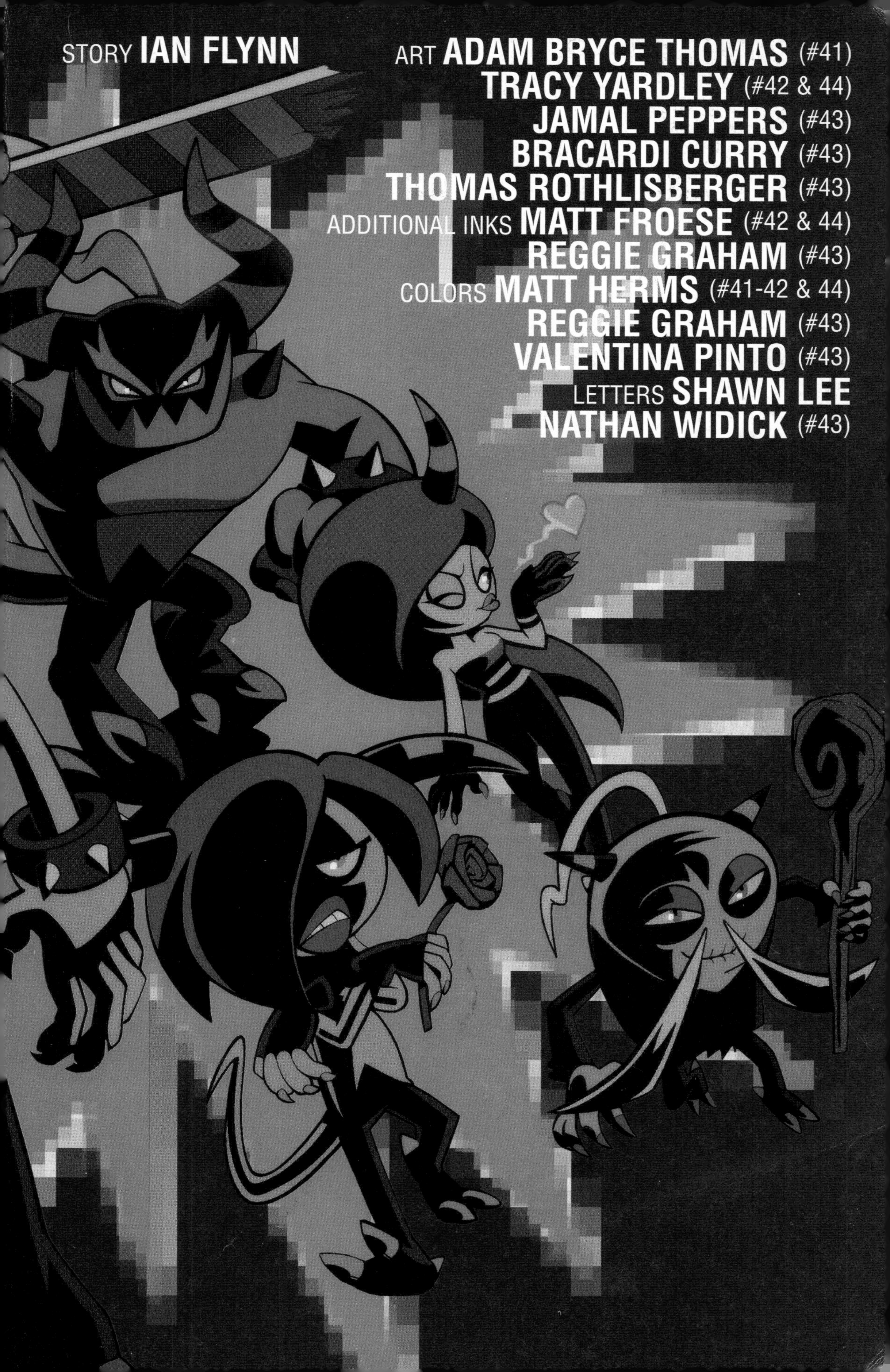

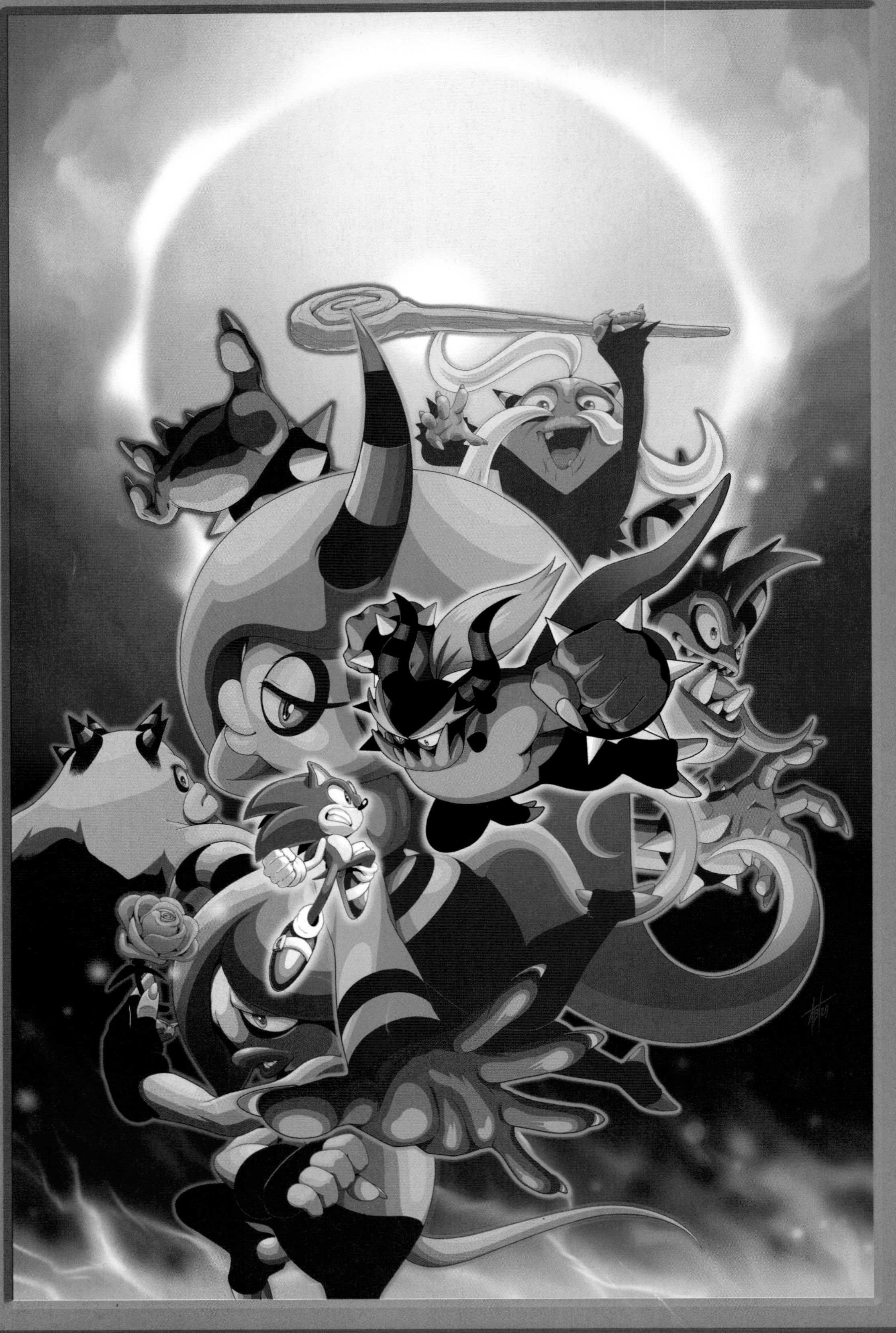

ART BY **ADAM BRYCE THOMAS**

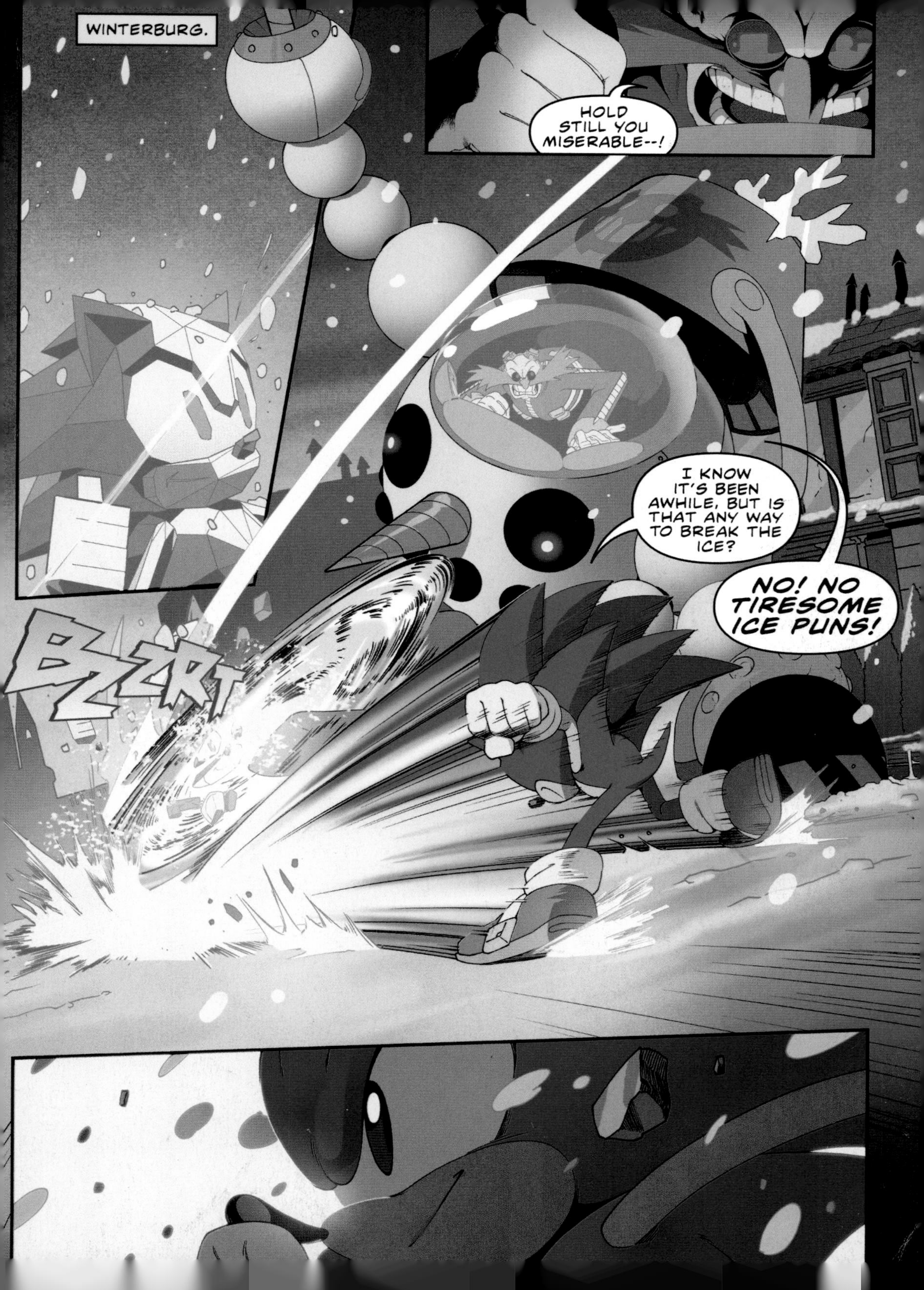
WINTERBURG.
HOLD STILL YOU MISERABLE--!
BZZRT
I KNOW IT'S BEEN AWHILE, BUT IS THAT ANY WAY TO BREAK THE ICE?
NO! NO TIRESOME ICE PUNS!

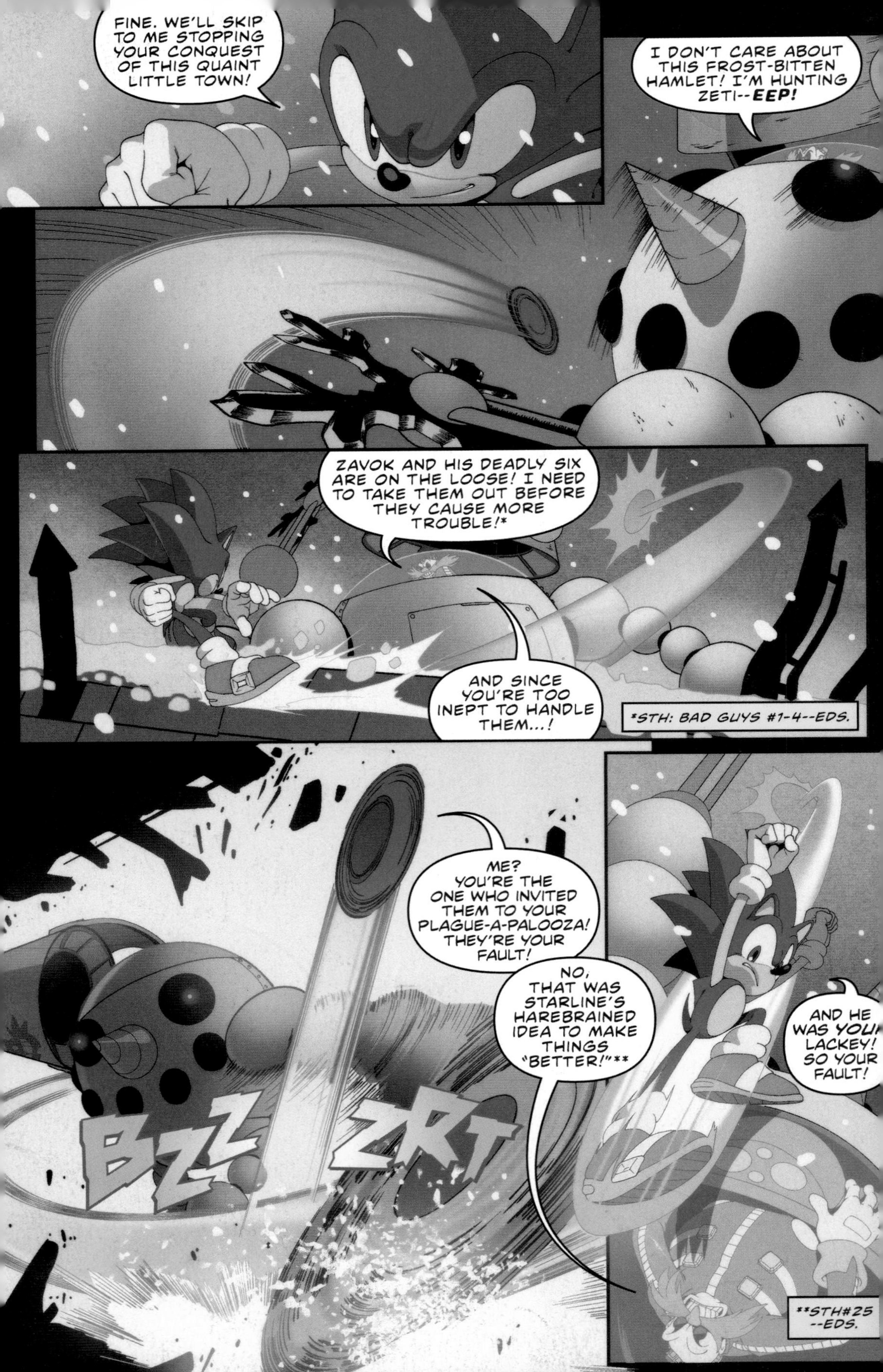
FINE. WE'LL SKIP TO ME STOPPING YOUR CONQUEST OF THIS QUAINT LITTLE TOWN!
I DON'T CARE ABOUT THIS FROST-BITTEN HAMLET! I'M HUNTING ZETI--EEP!
ZAVOK AND HIS DEADLY SIX ARE ON THE LOOSE! I NEED TO TAKE THEM OUT BEFORE THEY CAUSE MORE TROUBLE!*
AND SINCE YOU'RE TOO INEPT TO HANDLE THEM...!
*STH: BAD GUYS #1-4--EDS.
ME? YOU'RE THE ONE WHO INVITED THEM TO YOUR PLAGUE-A-PALOOZA! THEY'RE YOUR FAULT!
NO, THAT WAS STARLINE'S HAREBRAINED IDEA TO MAKE THINGS "BETTER!"**
AND HE WAS YOUR LACKEY! SO YOUR FAULT!
BZZZRT
**STH#25 --EDS.

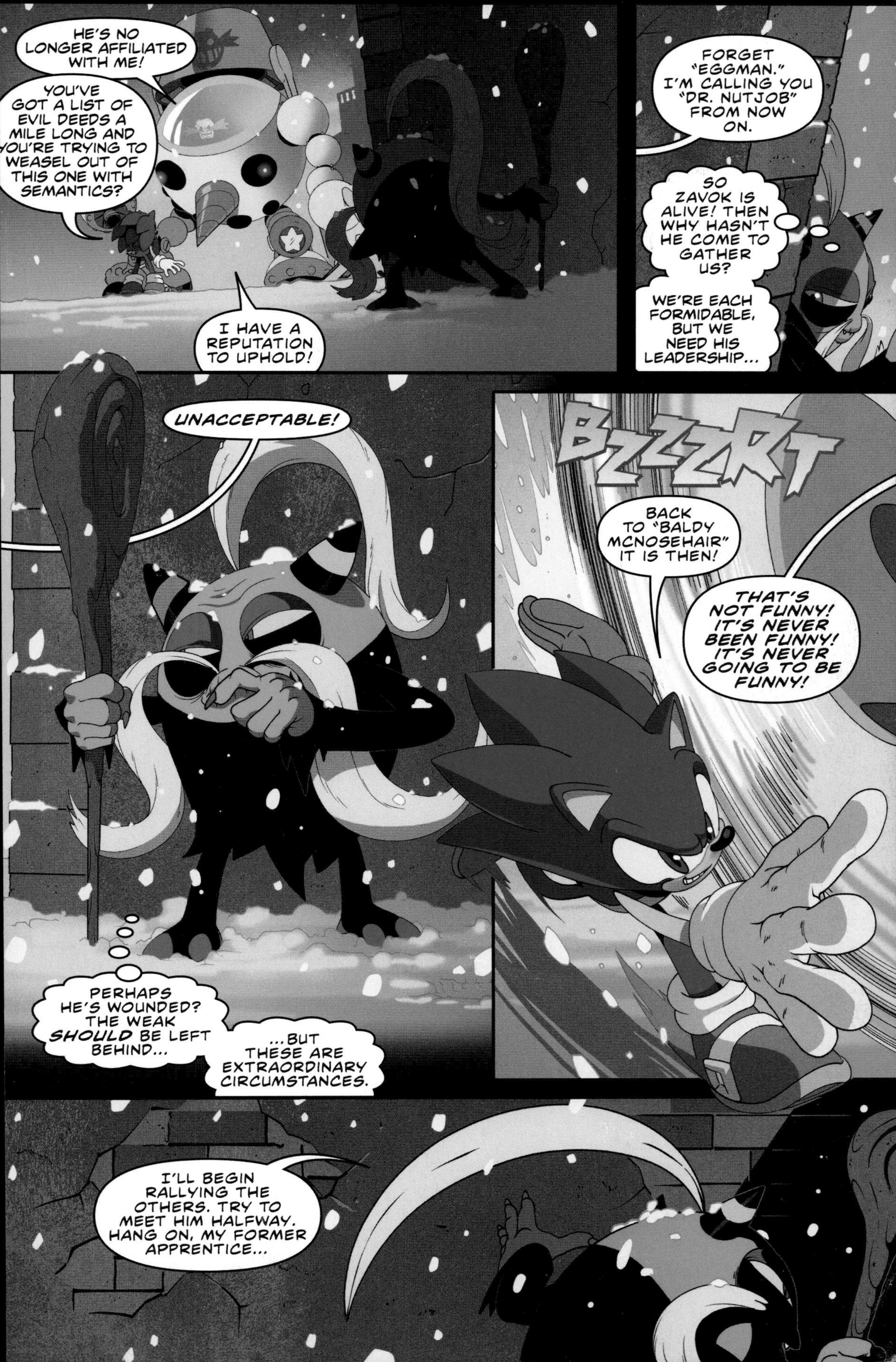
HE'S NO LONGER AFFILIATED WITH ME!
YOU'VE GOT A LIST OF EVIL DEEDS A MILE LONG AND YOU'RE TRYING TO WEASEL OUT OF THIS ONE WITH SEMANTICS?
I HAVE A REPUTATION TO UPHOLD!
FORGET "EGGMAN." I'M CALLING YOU "DR. NUTJOB" FROM NOW ON.
SO ZAVOK IS ALIVE! THEN WHY HASN'T HE COME TO GATHER US?
WE'RE EACH FORMIDABLE, BUT WE NEED HIS LEADERSHIP...
UNACCEPTABLE!
PERHAPS HE'S WOUNDED? THE WEAK SHOULD BE LEFT BEHIND...
...BUT THESE ARE EXTRAORDINARY CIRCUMSTANCES.
BZZZRT
BACK TO "BALDY MCNOSEHAIR" IT IS THEN!
THAT'S NOT FUNNY! IT'S NEVER BEEN FUNNY! IT'S NEVER GOING TO BE FUNNY!
I'LL BEGIN RALLYING THE OTHERS. TRY TO MEET HIM HALFWAY. HANG ON, MY FORMER APPRENTICE...

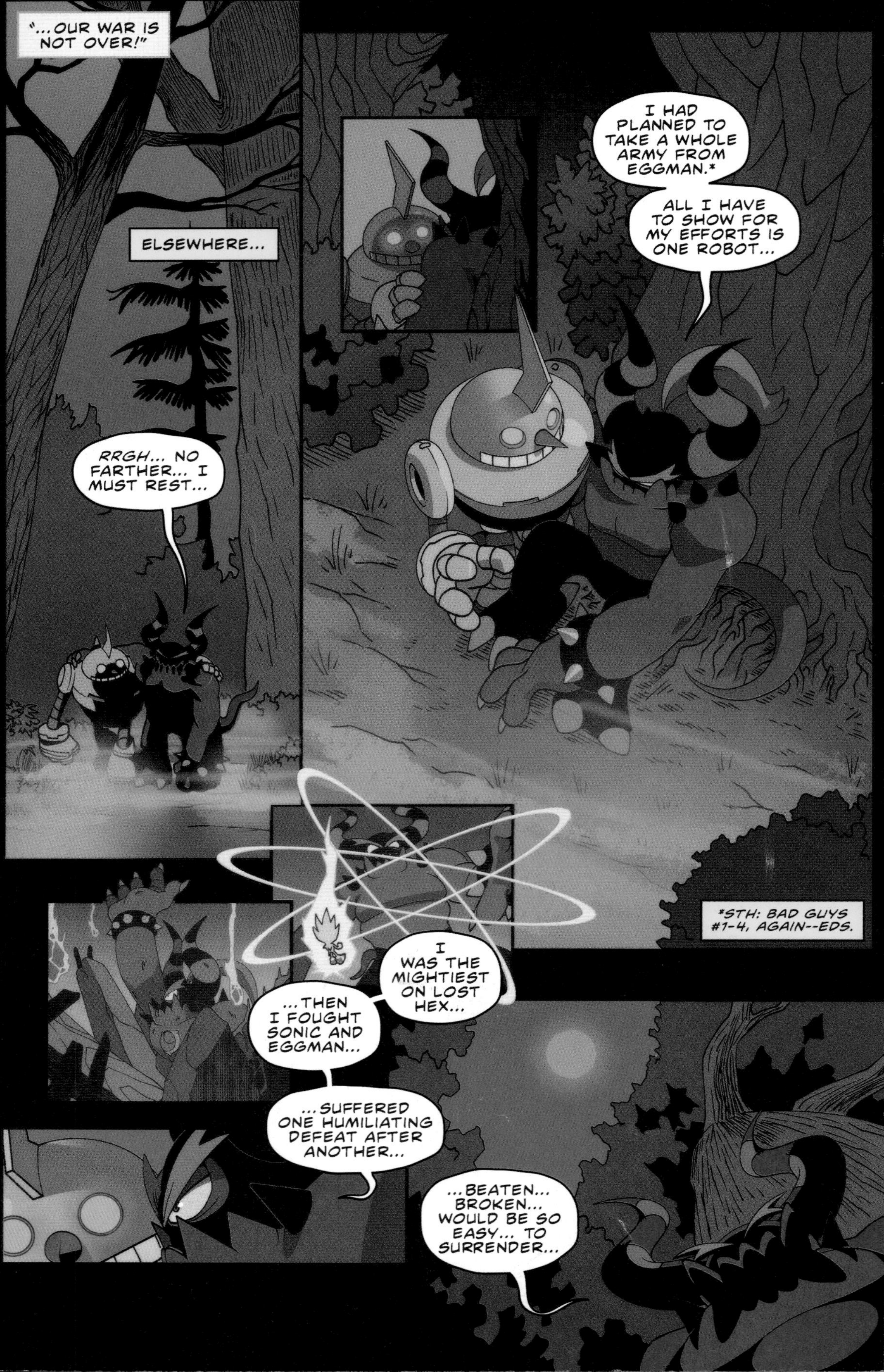
"...OUR WAR IS NOT OVER!"
ELSEWHERE...
RRGH... NO FARTHER... I MUST REST...
I HAD PLANNED TO TAKE A WHOLE ARMY FROM EGGMAN.*
ALL I HAVE TO SHOW FOR MY EFFORTS IS ONE ROBOT...
*STH: BAD GUYS #1-4, AGAIN--EDS.
I WAS THE MIGHTIEST ON LOST HEX...
...THEN I FOUGHT SONIC AND EGGMAN...
...SUFFERED ONE HUMILIATING DEFEAT AFTER ANOTHER...
...BEATEN... BROKEN... WOULD BE SO EASY... TO SURRENDER...

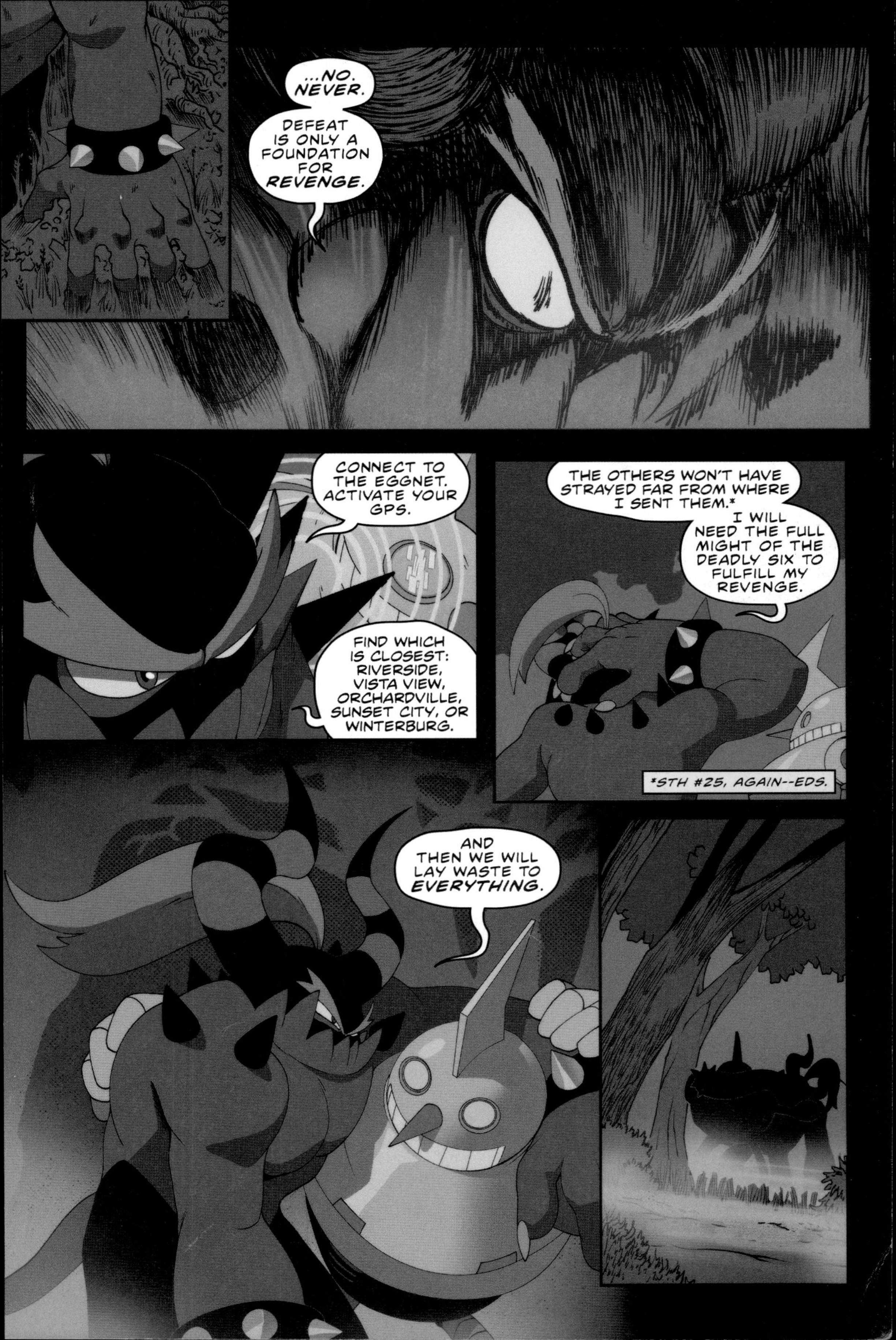
...NO. NEVER.
DEFEAT IS ONLY A FOUNDATION FOR REVENGE.
CONNECT TO THE EGGNET. ACTIVATE YOUR GPS.
FIND WHICH IS CLOSEST: RIVERSIDE, VISTA VIEW, ORCHARDVILLE, SUNSET CITY, OR WINTERBURG.
THE OTHERS WON'T HAVE STRAYED FAR FROM WHERE I SENT THEM.*
I WILL NEED THE FULL MIGHT OF THE DEADLY SIX TO FULFILL MY REVENGE.
*STH #25, AGAIN--EDS.
AND THEN WE WILL LAY WASTE TO EVERYTHING.

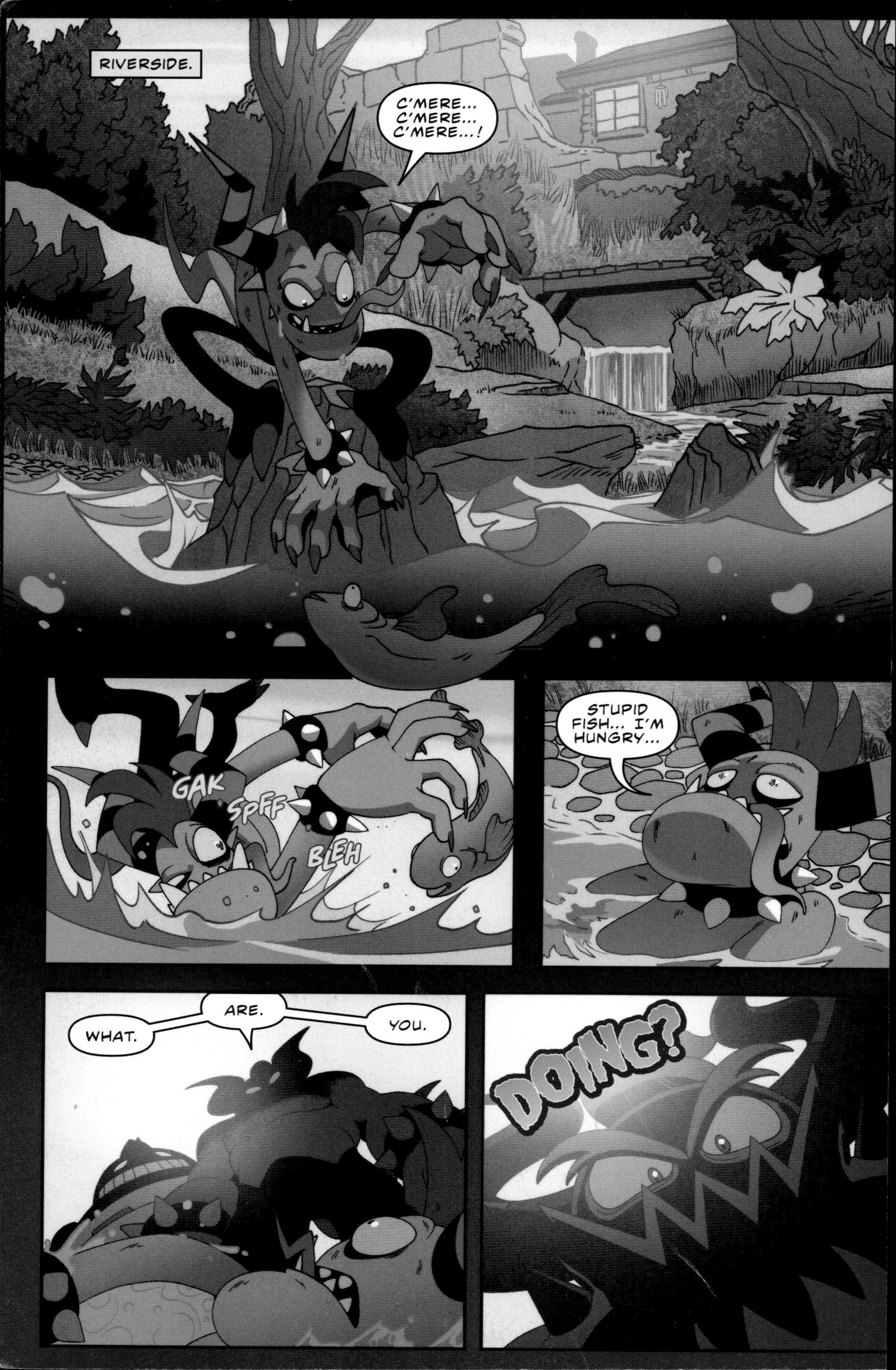
RIVERSIDE.
C'MERE... C'MERE... C'MERE...!
GAK
SPFF
BLEH
STUPID FISH... I'M HUNGRY...
WHAT.
ARE.
YOU.
DOING?

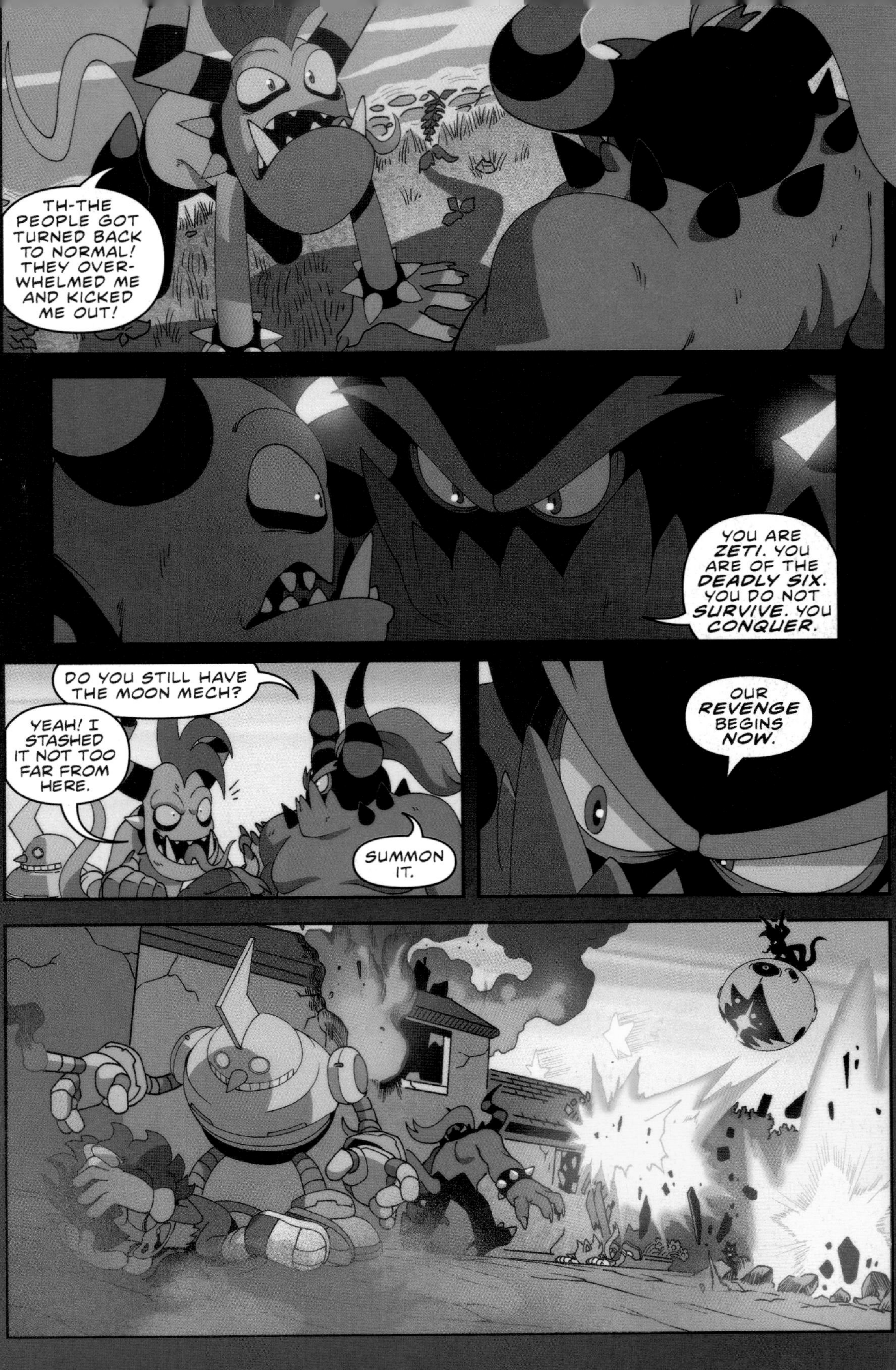
TH-THE PEOPLE GOT TURNED BACK TO NORMAL! THEY OVER-WHELMED ME AND KICKED ME OUT!
YOU ARE ZETI. YOU ARE OF THE DEADLY SIX. YOU DO NOT SURVIVE. YOU CONQUER.
DO YOU STILL HAVE THE MOON MECH?
YEAH! I STASHED IT NOT TOO FAR FROM HERE.
SUMMON IT.
OUR REVENGE BEGINS NOW.

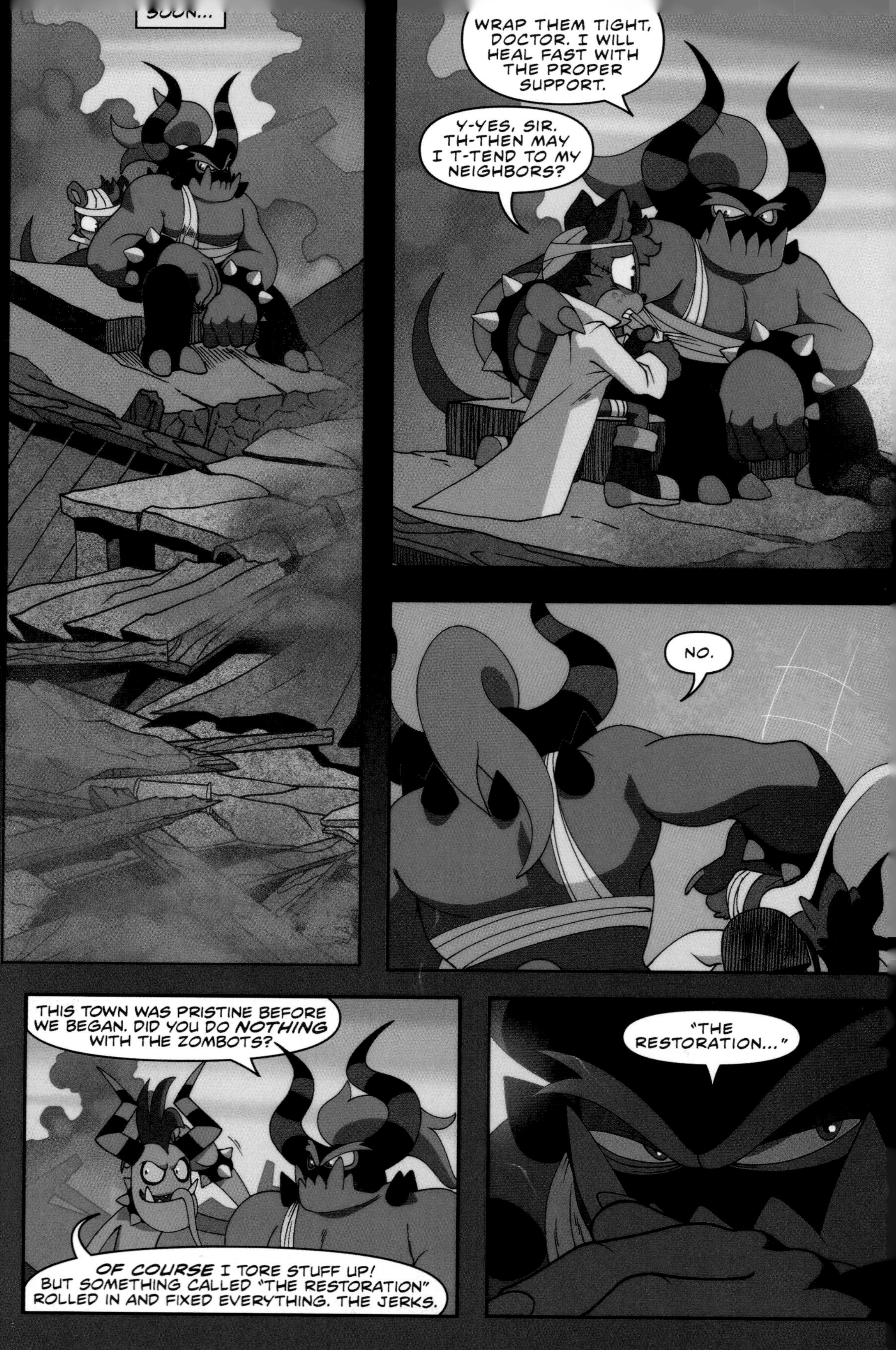

SOON...
WRAP THEM TIGHT, DOCTOR. I WILL HEAL FAST WITH THE PROPER SUPPORT.
Y-YES, SIR. TH-THEN MAY I T-TEND TO MY NEIGHBORS?
NO.
THIS TOWN WAS PRISTINE BEFORE WE BEGAN. DID YOU DO NOTHING WITH THE ZOMBOTS?
OF COURSE I TORE STUFF UP! BUT SOMETHING CALLED "THE RESTORATION" ROLLED IN AND FIXED EVERYTHING. THE JERKS.
"THE RESTORATION..."

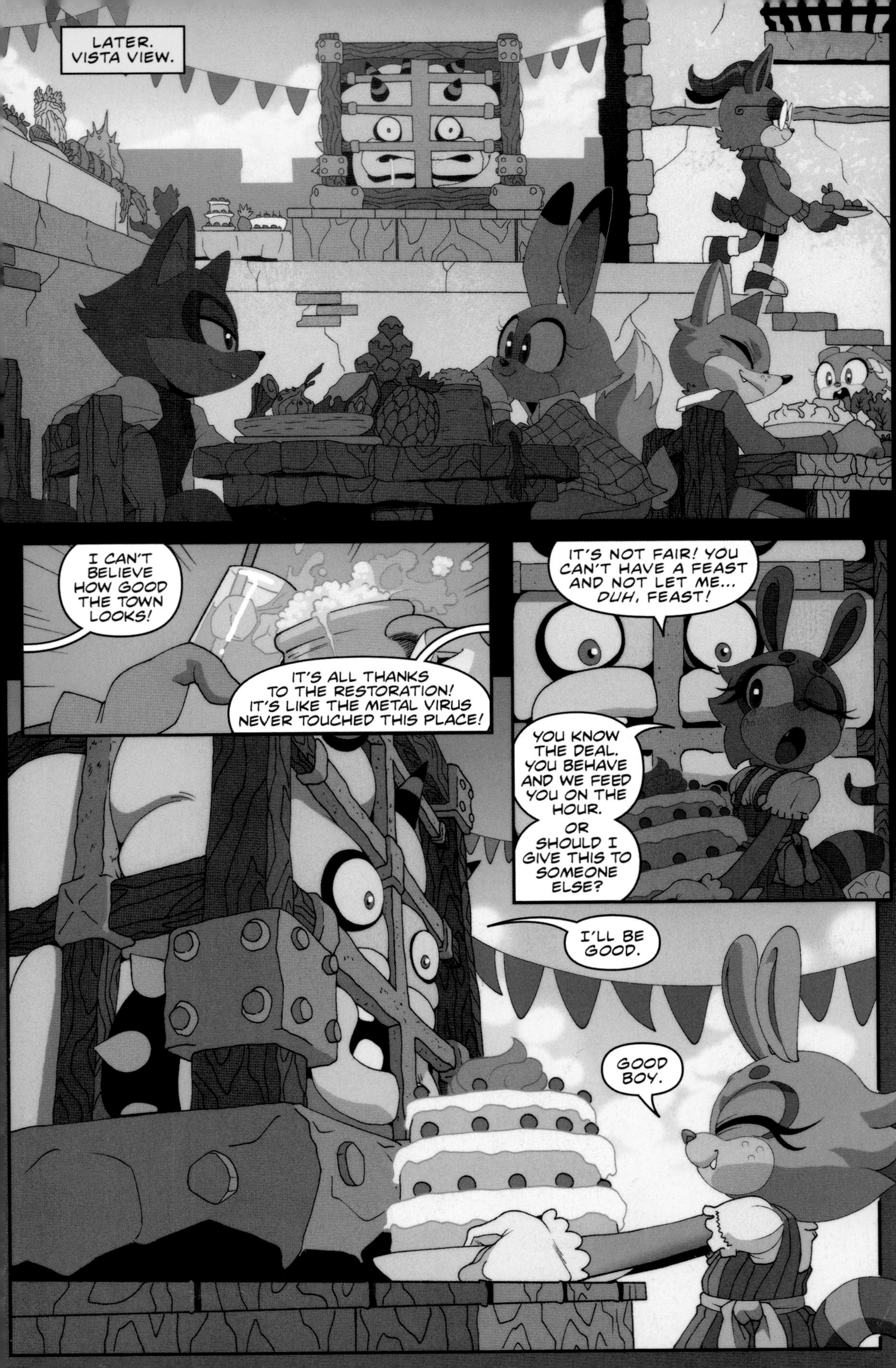
LATER. VISTA VIEW.
I CAN'T BELIEVE HOW GOOD THE TOWN LOOKS!
IT'S ALL THANKS TO THE RESTORATION! IT'S LIKE THE METAL VIRUS NEVER TOUCHED THIS PLACE!
IT'S NOT FAIR! YOU CAN'T HAVE A FEAST AND NOT LET ME... DUH, FEAST!
YOU KNOW THE DEAL. YOU BEHAVE AND WE FEED YOU ON THE HOUR.
OR SHOULD I GIVE THIS TO SOMEONE ELSE?
I'LL BE GOOD.
GOOD BOY.

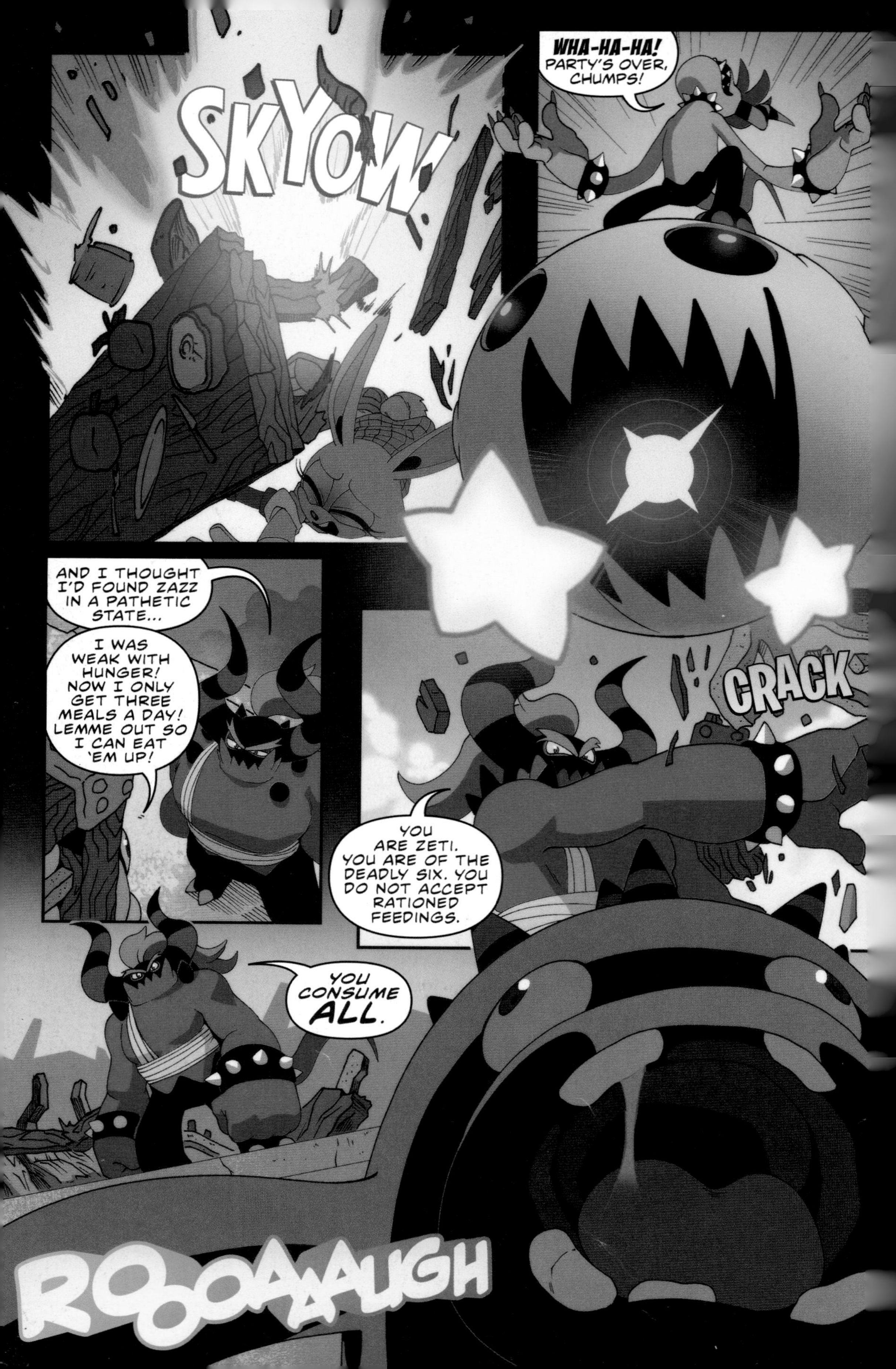
SKYOW!
WHA-HA-HA! PARTY'S OVER, CHUMPS!
AND I THOUGHT I'D FOUND ZAZZ IN A PATHETIC STATE...
I WAS WEAK WITH HUNGER! NOW I ONLY GET THREE MEALS A DAY! LEMME OUT SO I CAN EAT 'EM UP!
CRACK
YOU ARE ZETI. YOU ARE OF THE DEADLY SIX. YOU DO NOT ACCEPT RATIONED FEEDINGS.
YOU CONSUME ALL.
ROOOAAAUGH

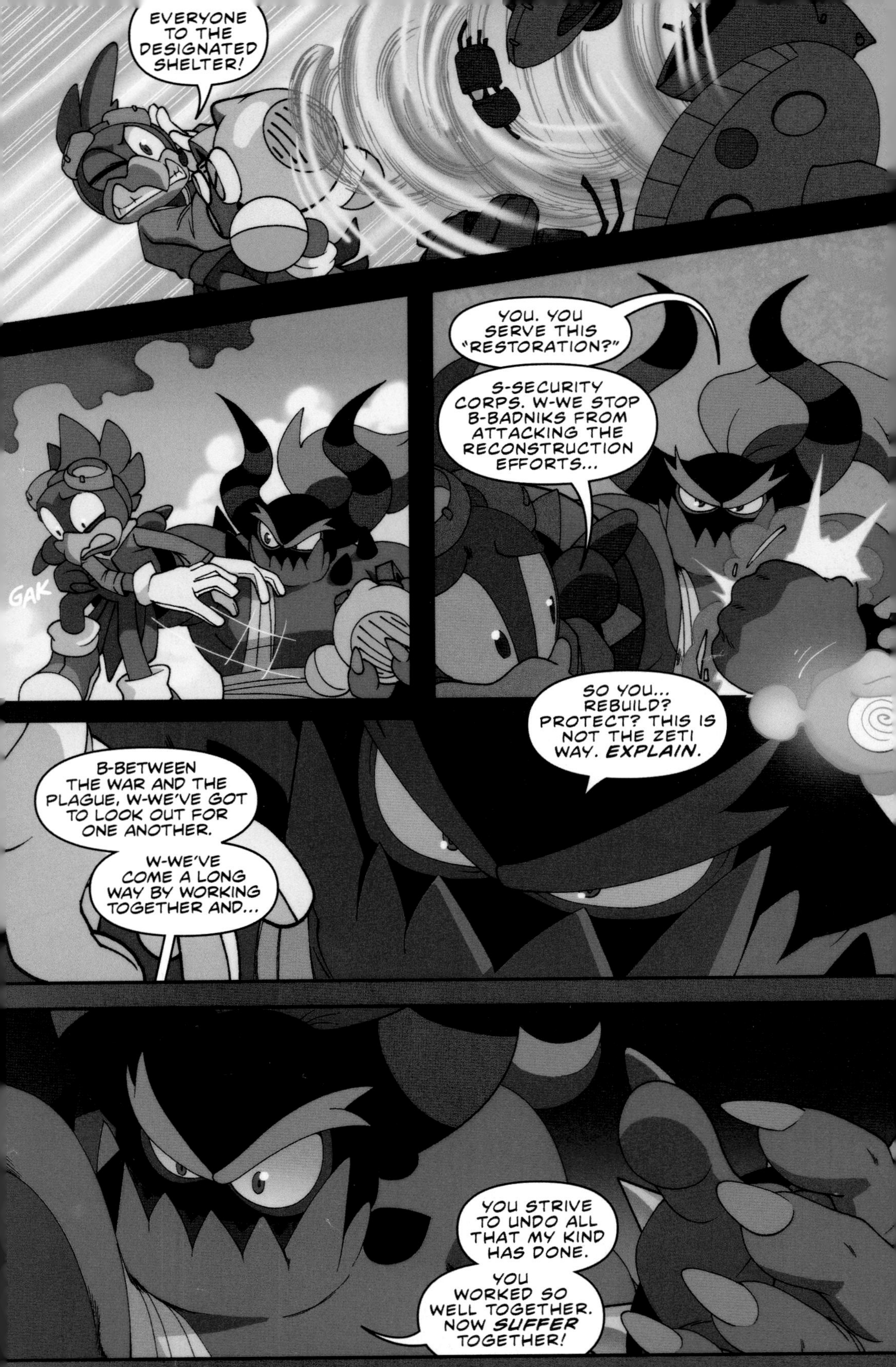
EVERYONE TO THE DESIGNATED SHELTER!
GAK
YOU. YOU SERVE THIS "RESTORATION?"
S-SECURITY CORPS. W-WE STOP B-BADNIKS FROM ATTACKING THE RECONSTRUCTION EFFORTS...
SO YOU... REBUILD? PROTECT? THIS IS NOT THE ZETI WAY. *EXPLAIN*.
B-BETWEEN THE WAR AND THE PLAGUE, W-WE'VE GOT TO LOOK OUT FOR ONE ANOTHER.
W-WE'VE COME A LONG WAY BY WORKING TOGETHER AND...
YOU STRIVE TO UNDO ALL THAT MY KIND HAS DONE.
YOU WORKED SO WELL TOGETHER. NOW *SUFFER* TOGETHER!

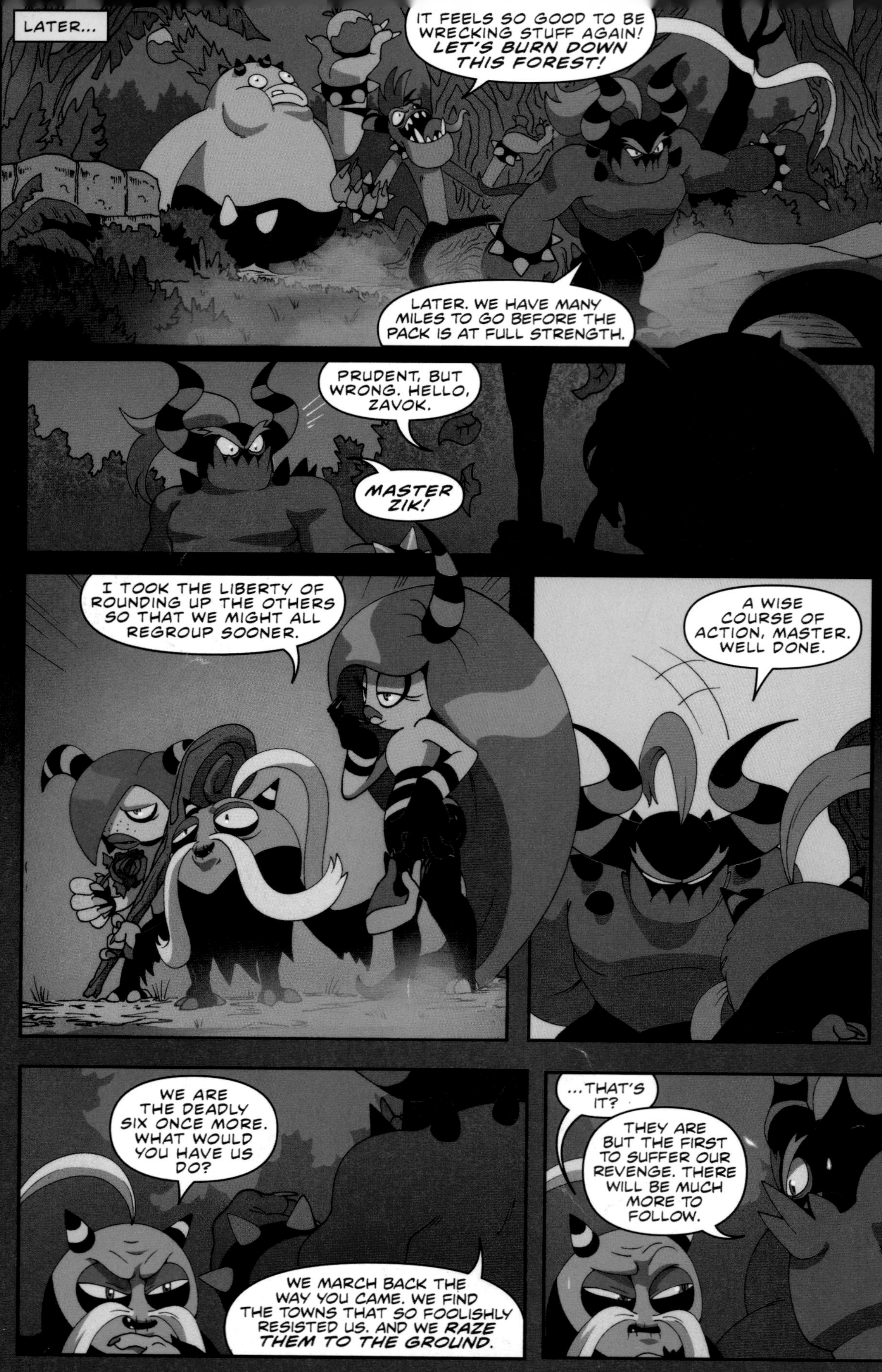
LATER...
IT FEELS SO GOOD TO BE WRECKING STUFF AGAIN! LET'S BURN DOWN THIS FOREST!
LATER. WE HAVE MANY MILES TO GO BEFORE THE PACK IS AT FULL STRENGTH.
PRUDENT, BUT WRONG. HELLO, ZAVOK.
MASTER ZIK!
I TOOK THE LIBERTY OF ROUNDING UP THE OTHERS SO THAT WE MIGHT ALL REGROUP SOONER.
A WISE COURSE OF ACTION, MASTER. WELL DONE.
WE ARE THE DEADLY SIX ONCE MORE. WHAT WOULD YOU HAVE US DO?
WE MARCH BACK THE WAY YOU CAME. WE FIND THE TOWNS THAT SO FOOLISHLY RESISTED US. AND WE RAZE THEM TO THE GROUND.
...THAT'S IT?
THEY ARE BUT THE FIRST TO SUFFER OUR REVENGE. THERE WILL BE MUCH MORE TO FOLLOW.

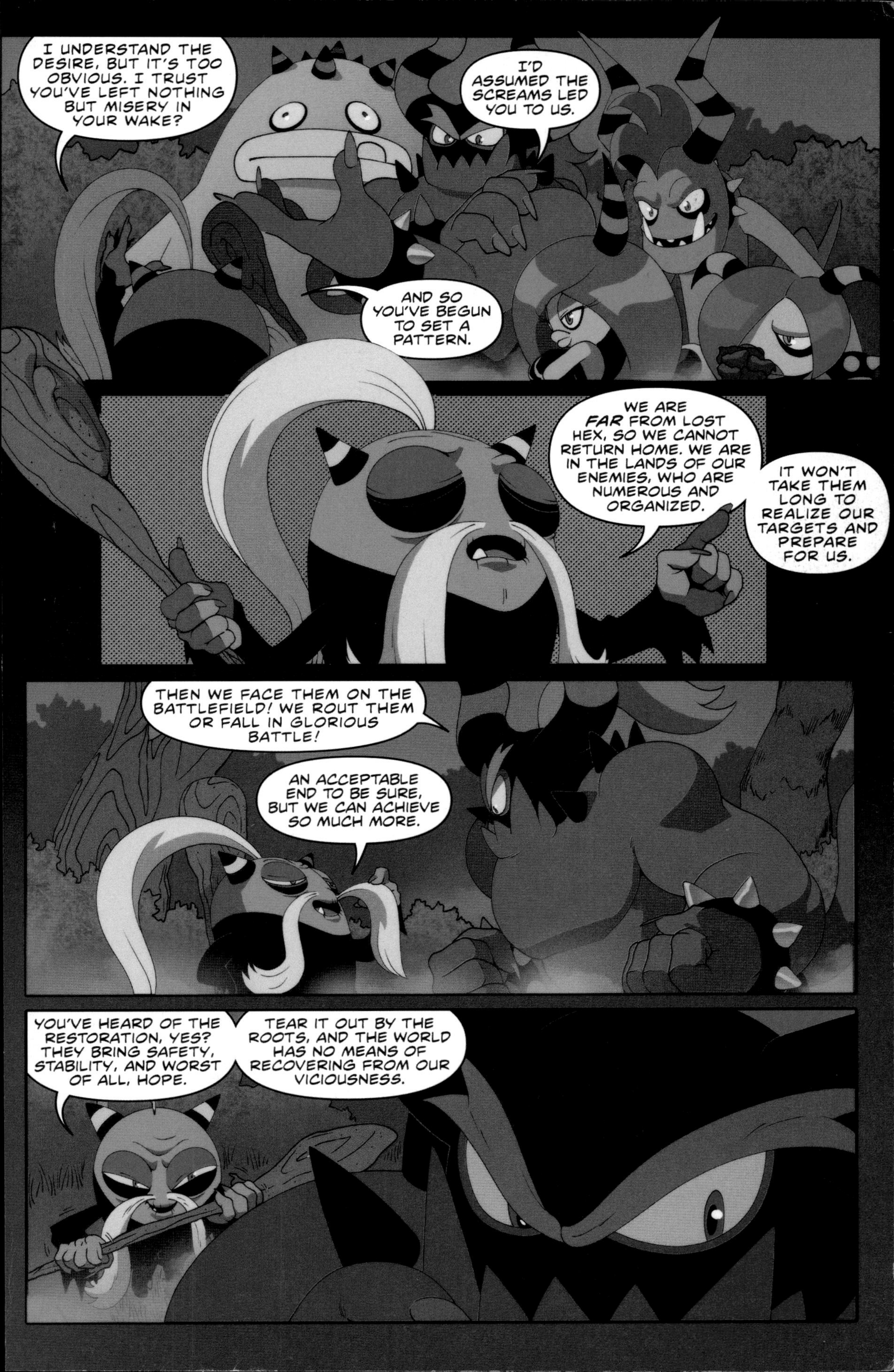
I UNDERSTAND THE DESIRE, BUT IT'S TOO OBVIOUS. I TRUST YOU'VE LEFT NOTHING BUT MISERY IN YOUR WAKE?
I'D ASSUMED THE SCREAMS LED YOU TO US.
AND SO YOU'VE BEGUN TO SET A PATTERN.
WE ARE *FAR* FROM LOST HEX, SO WE CANNOT RETURN HOME. WE ARE IN THE LANDS OF OUR ENEMIES, WHO ARE NUMEROUS AND ORGANIZED.
IT WON'T TAKE THEM LONG TO REALIZE OUR TARGETS AND PREPARE FOR US.
THEN WE FACE THEM ON THE BATTLEFIELD! WE ROUT THEM OR FALL IN GLORIOUS BATTLE!
AN ACCEPTABLE END TO BE SURE, BUT WE CAN ACHIEVE SO MUCH MORE.
YOU'VE HEARD OF THE RESTORATION, YES? THEY BRING SAFETY, STABILITY, AND WORST OF ALL, HOPE.
TEAR IT OUT BY THE ROOTS, AND THE WORLD HAS NO MEANS OF RECOVERING FROM OUR VICIOUSNESS.

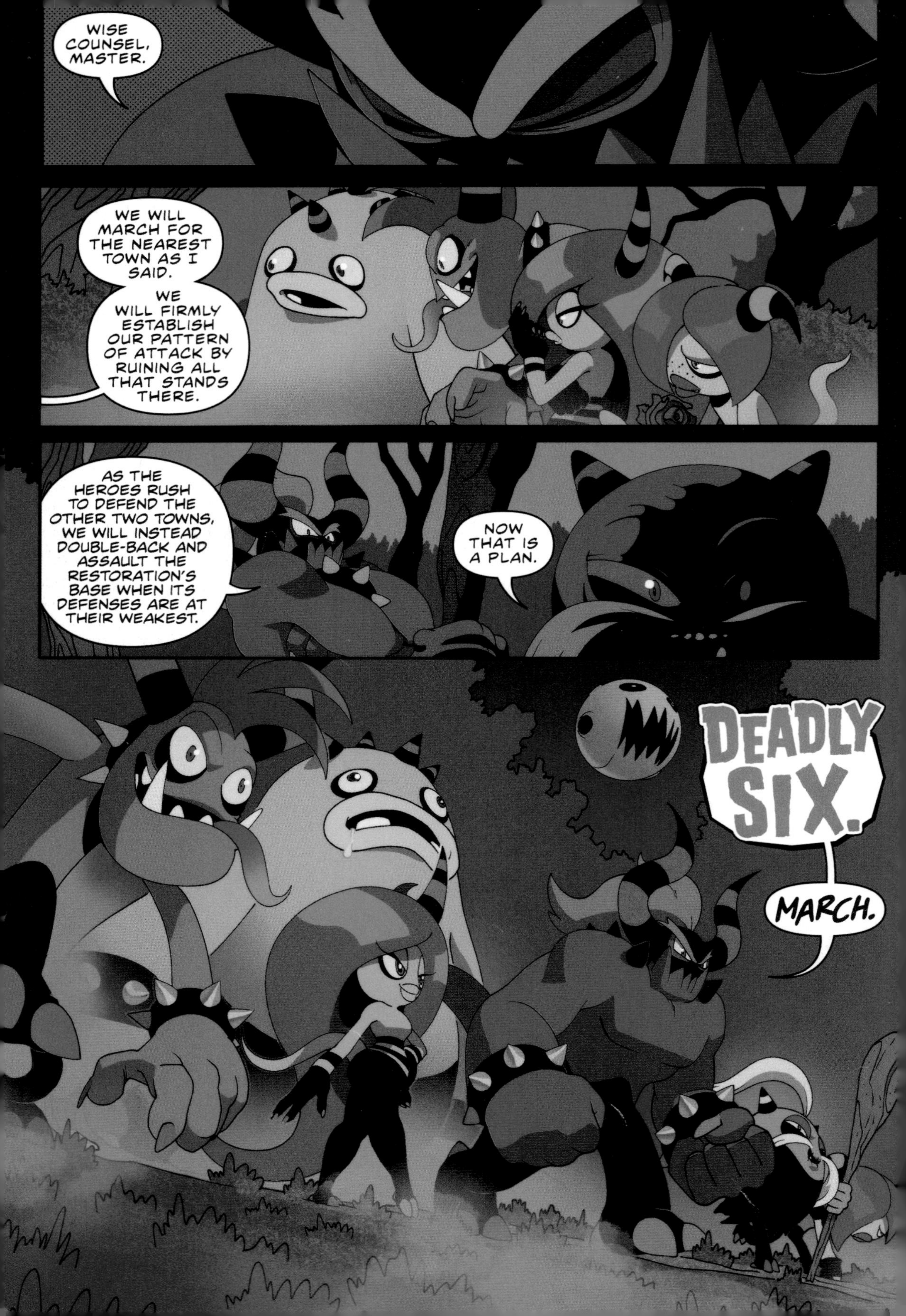
WISE COUNSEL, MASTER.
WE WILL MARCH FOR THE NEAREST TOWN AS I SAID.
WE WILL FIRMLY ESTABLISH OUR PATTERN OF ATTACK BY RUINING ALL THAT STANDS THERE.
AS THE HEROES RUSH TO DEFEND THE OTHER TWO TOWNS, WE WILL INSTEAD DOUBLE-BACK AND ASSAULT THE RESTORATION'S BASE WHEN ITS DEFENSES ARE AT THEIR WEAKEST.
NOW THAT IS A PLAN.
DEADLY SIX.
MARCH.

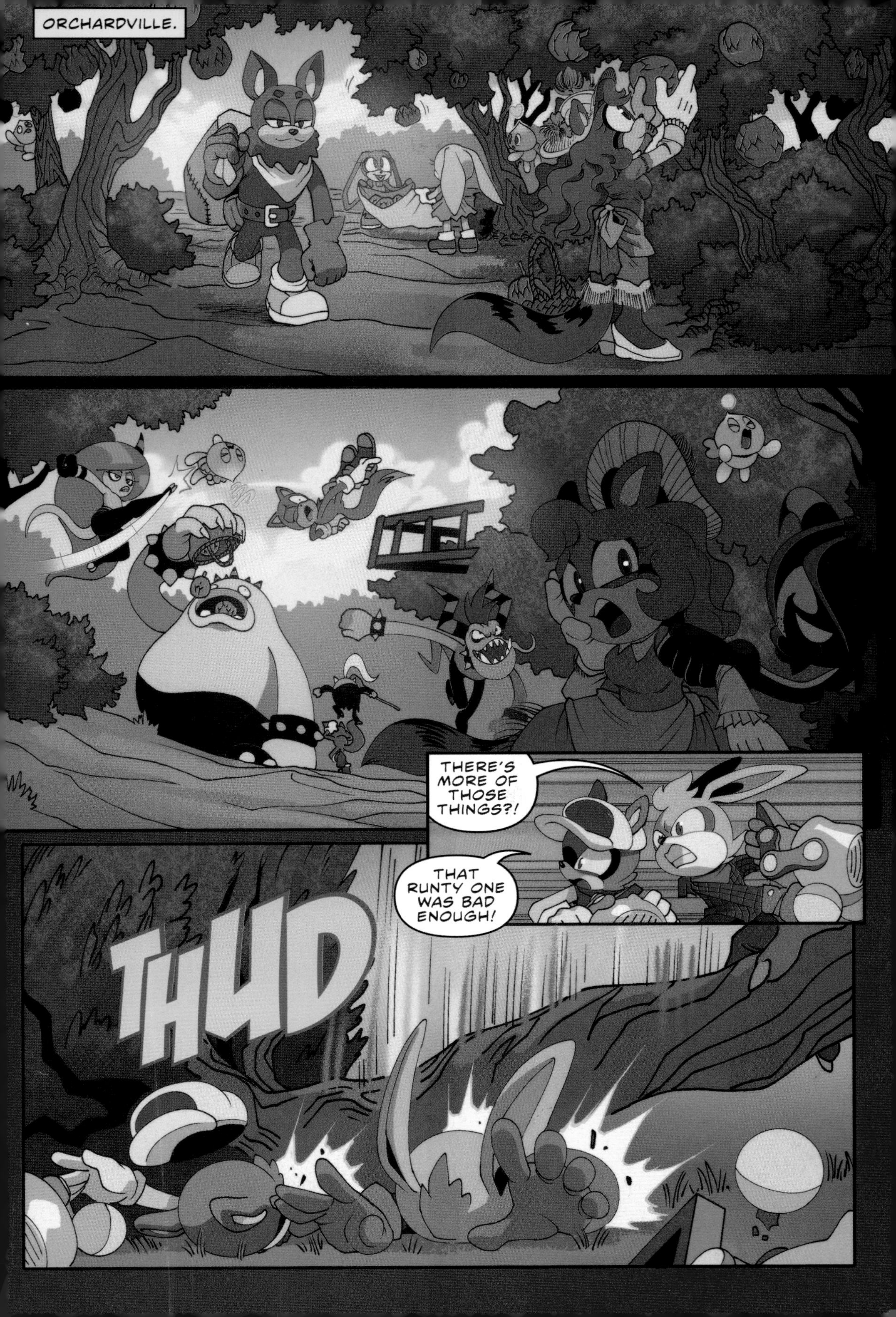
ORCHARDVILLE.
THERE'S MORE OF THOSE THINGS?!
THAT RUNTY ONE WAS BAD ENOUGH!
THUD

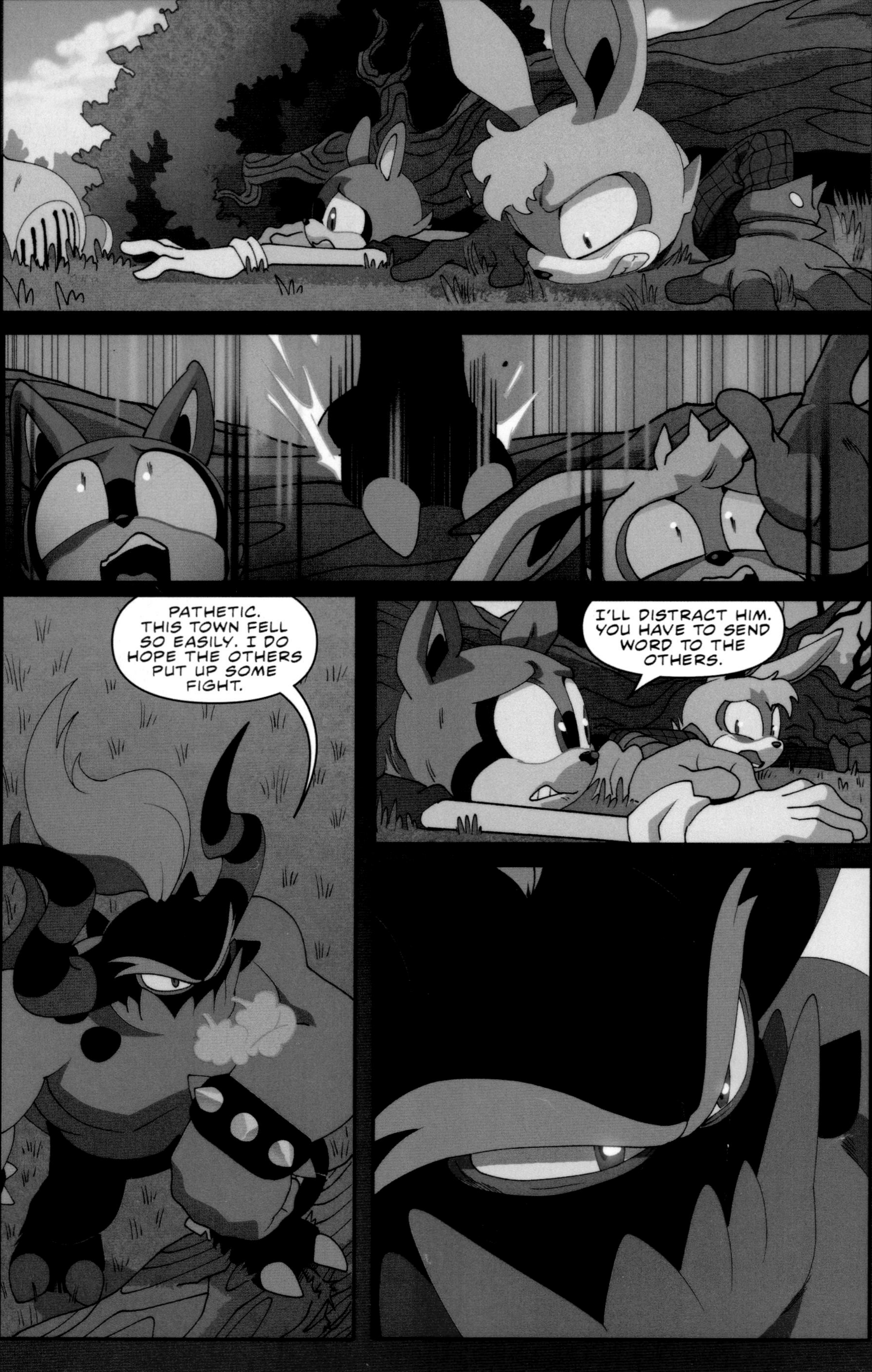

PATHETIC. THIS TOWN FELL SO EASILY. I DO HOPE THE OTHERS PUT UP SOME FIGHT.
I'LL DISTRACT HIM. YOU HAVE TO SEND WORD TO THE OTHERS.

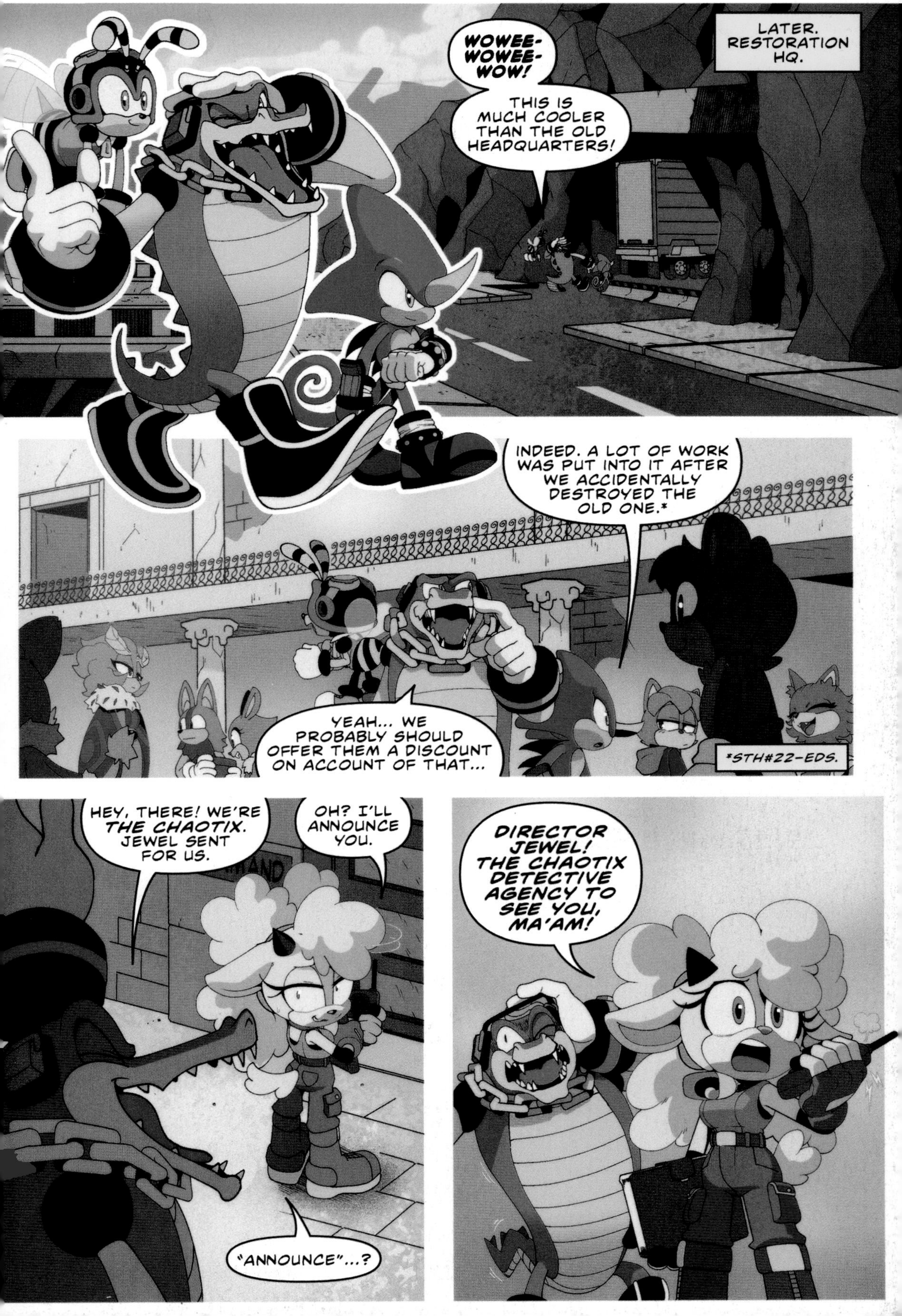
LATER. RESTORATION HQ.
WOWEE-WOWEE-WOW!
THIS IS MUCH COOLER THAN THE OLD HEADQUARTERS!
INDEED. A LOT OF WORK WAS PUT INTO IT AFTER WE ACCIDENTALLY DESTROYED THE OLD ONE.*
YEAH... WE PROBABLY SHOULD OFFER THEM A DISCOUNT ON ACCOUNT OF THAT...
*STH#22–EDS.
HEY, THERE! WE'RE THE CHAOTIX. JEWEL SENT FOR US.
OH? I'LL ANNOUNCE YOU.
"ANNOUNCE"...?
DIRECTOR JEWEL! THE CHAOTIX DETECTIVE AGENCY TO SEE YOU, MA'AM!

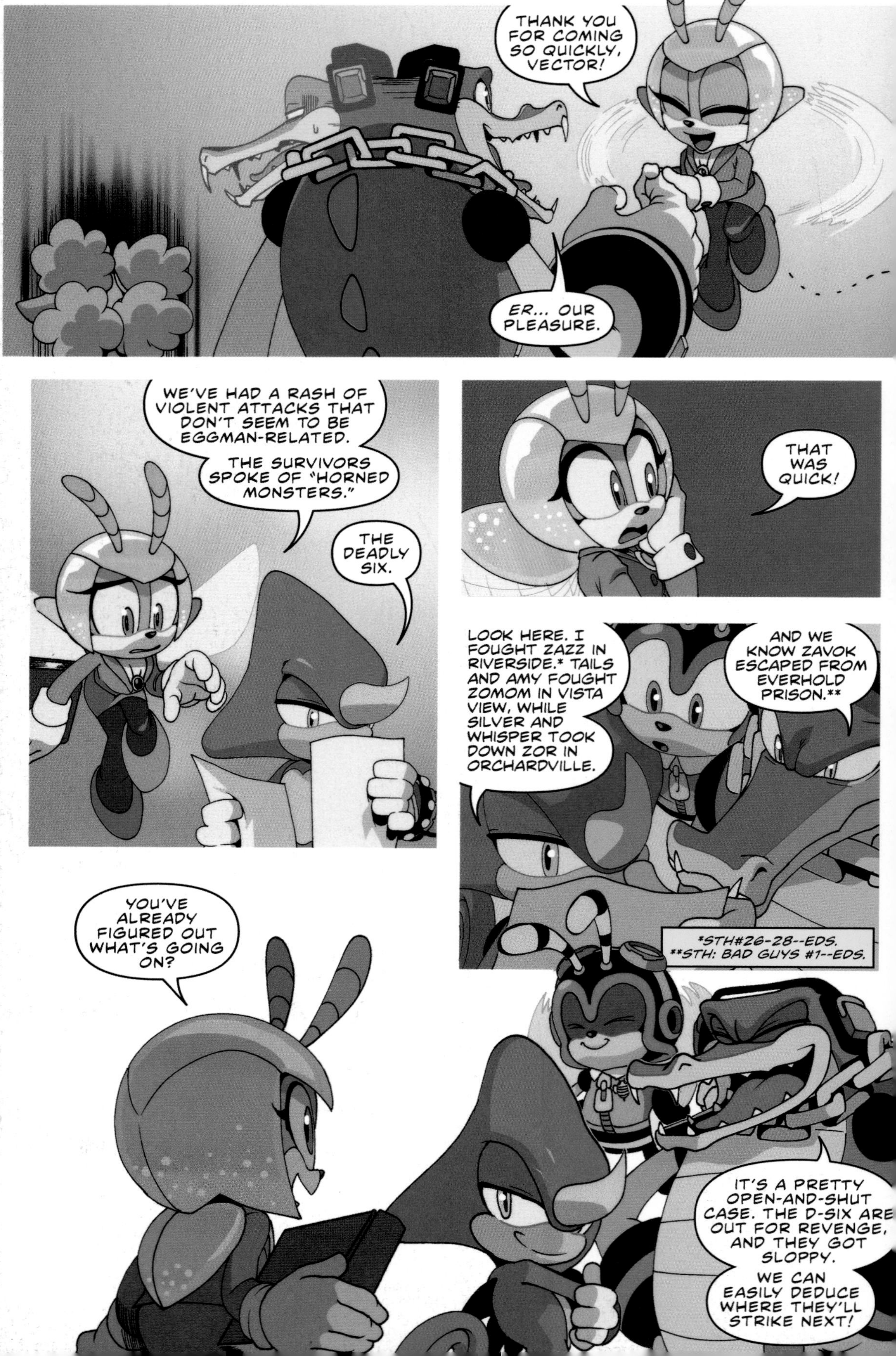
THANK YOU FOR COMING SO QUICKLY, VECTOR!
ER... OUR PLEASURE.
WE'VE HAD A RASH OF VIOLENT ATTACKS THAT DON'T SEEM TO BE EGGMAN-RELATED.
THE SURVIVORS SPOKE OF "HORNED MONSTERS."
THE DEADLY SIX.
THAT WAS QUICK!
LOOK HERE. I FOUGHT ZAZZ IN RIVERSIDE.* TAILS AND AMY FOUGHT ZOMOM IN VISTA VIEW, WHILE SILVER AND WHISPER TOOK DOWN ZOR IN ORCHARDVILLE.
AND WE KNOW ZAVOK ESCAPED FROM EVERHOLD PRISON.**
*STH#26-28--EDS.
**STH: BAD GUYS #1--EDS.
YOU'VE ALREADY FIGURED OUT WHAT'S GOING ON?
IT'S A PRETTY OPEN-AND-SHUT CASE. THE D-SIX ARE OUT FOR REVENGE, AND THEY GOT SLOPPY.
WE CAN EASILY DEDUCE WHERE THEY'LL STRIKE NEXT!

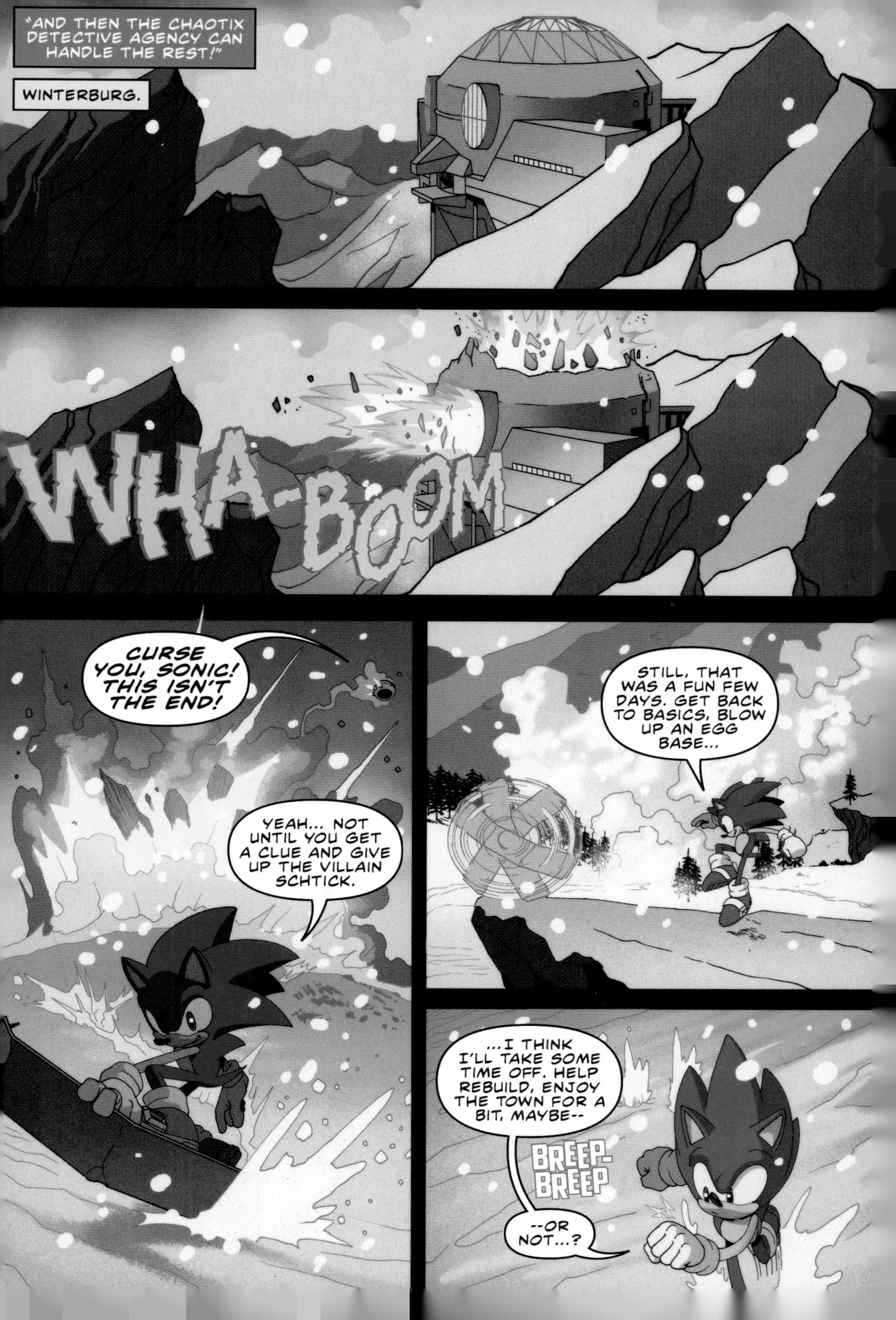
"AND THEN THE CHAOTIX DETECTIVE AGENCY CAN HANDLE THE REST!"
WINTERBURG.
WHA-BOOM
CURSE YOU, SONIC! THIS ISN'T THE END!
YEAH... NOT UNTIL YOU GET A CLUE AND GIVE UP THE VILLAIN SCHTICK.
STILL, THAT WAS A FUN FEW DAYS. GET BACK TO BASICS, BLOW UP AN EGG BASE...
...I THINK I'LL TAKE SOME TIME OFF. HELP REBUILD, ENJOY THE TOWN FOR A BIT, MAYBE--
BREEP-BREEP
--OR NOT...?

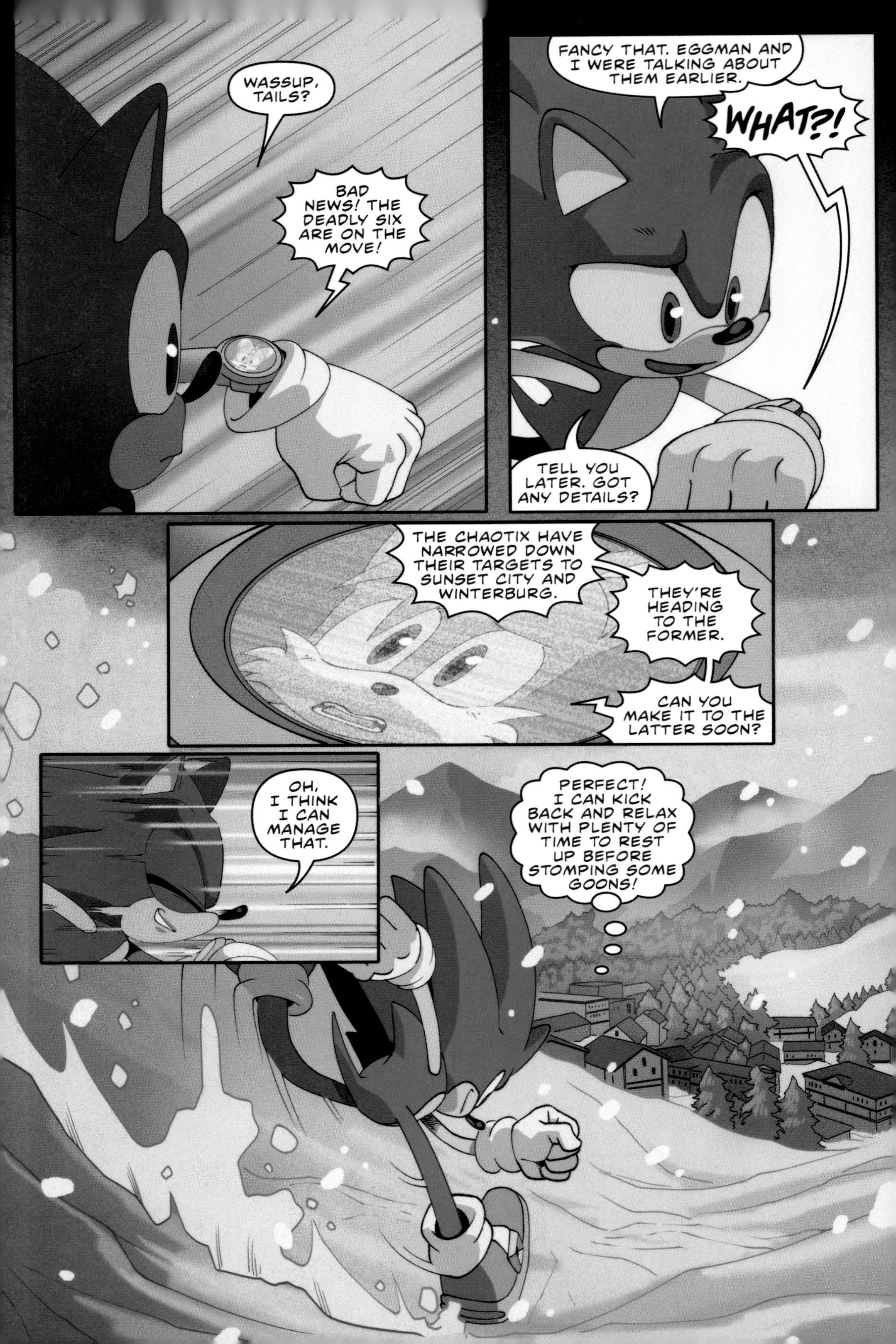
WASSUP, TAILS?
BAD NEWS! THE DEADLY SIX ARE ON THE MOVE!
FANCY THAT. EGGMAN AND I WERE TALKING ABOUT THEM EARLIER.
WHAT?!
TELL YOU LATER. GOT ANY DETAILS?
THE CHAOTIX HAVE NARROWED DOWN THEIR TARGETS TO SUNSET CITY AND WINTERBURG.
THEY'RE HEADING TO THE FORMER.
CAN YOU MAKE IT TO THE LATTER SOON?
OH, I THINK I CAN MANAGE THAT.
PERFECT! I CAN KICK BACK AND RELAX WITH PLENTY OF TIME TO REST UP BEFORE STOMPING SOME GOONS!

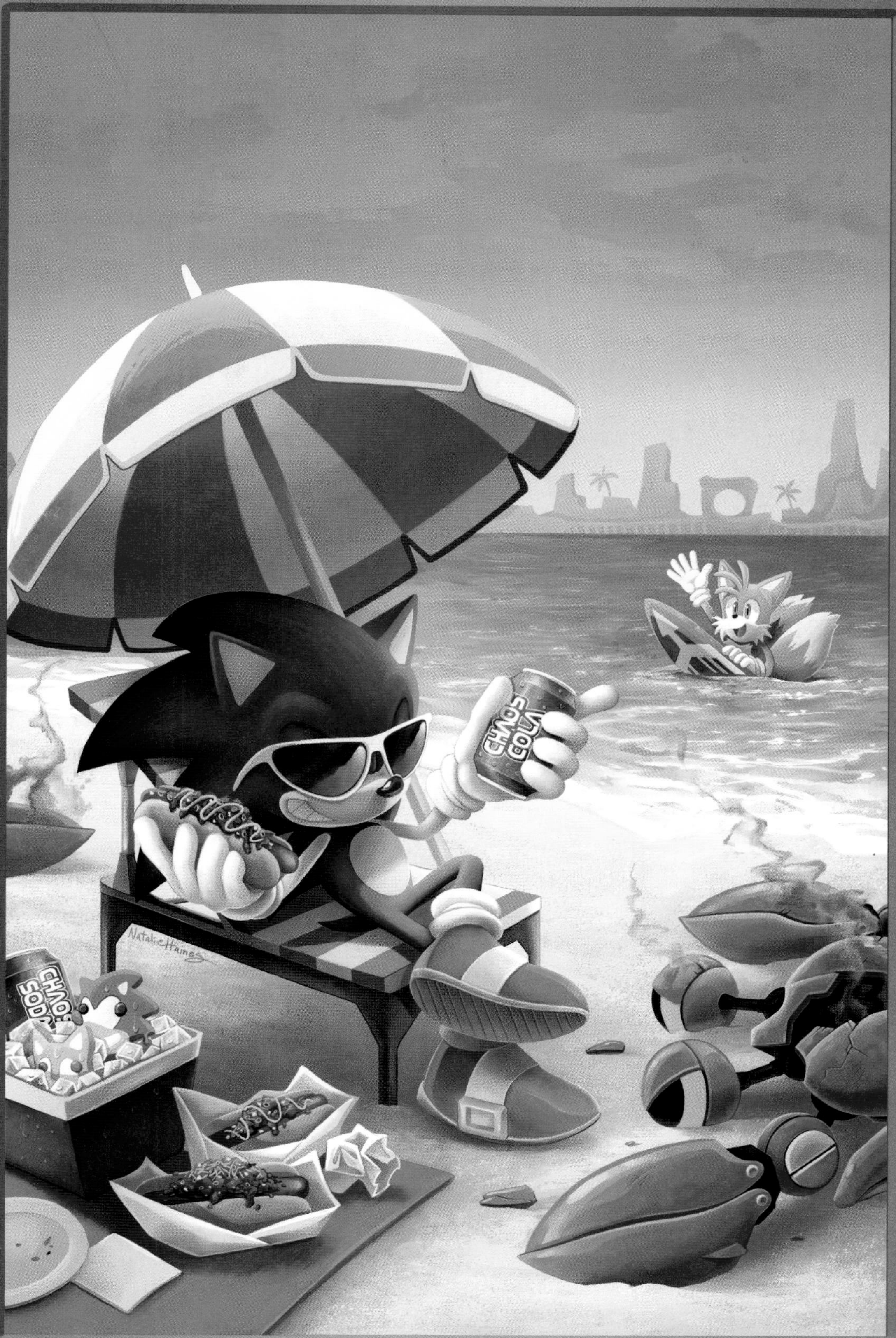
CHAOS SODA
NatalieHaines

ART BY **NATALIE HAINES**

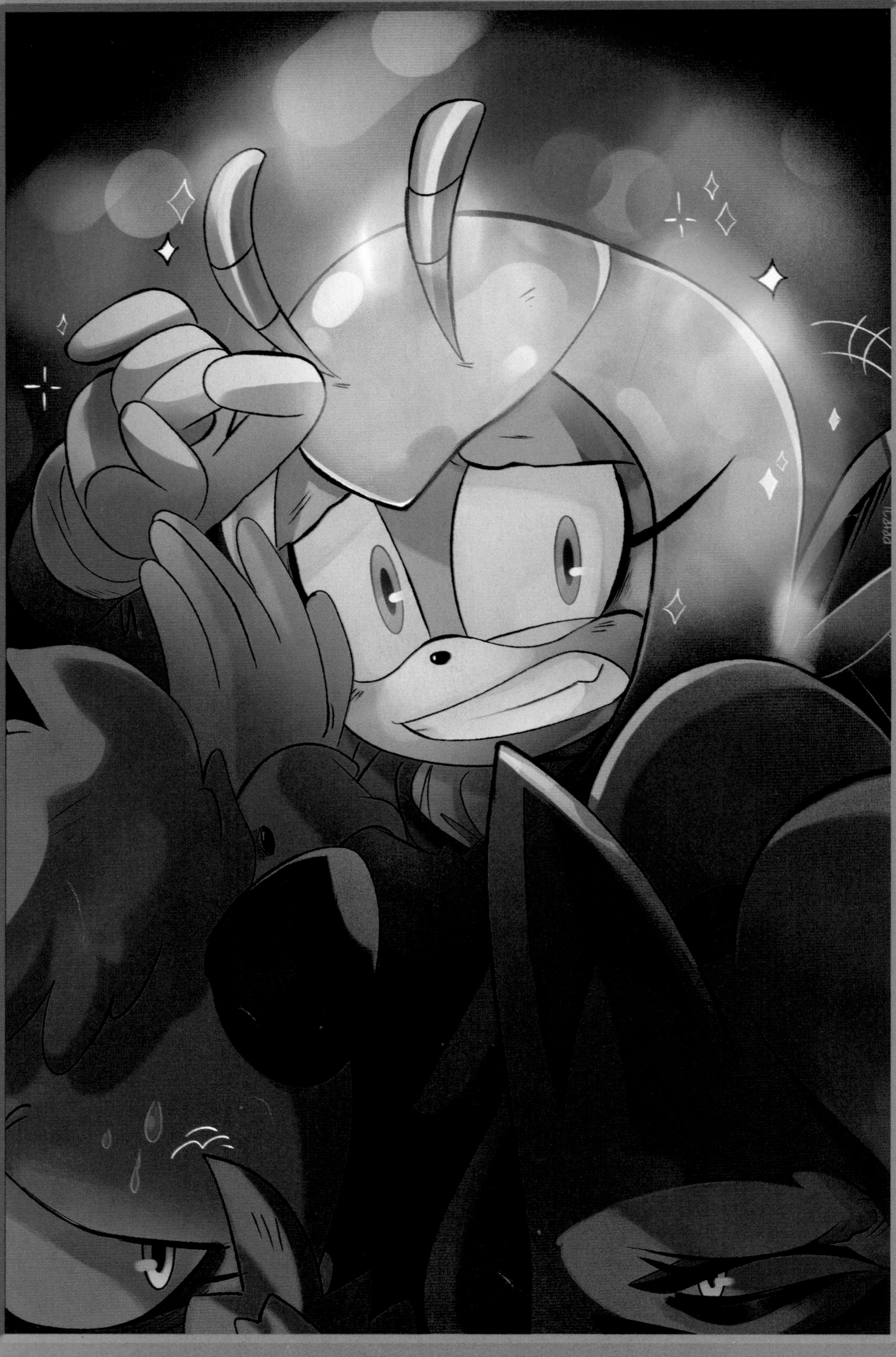

ART BY **PRISCILLA TRAMONTANO**

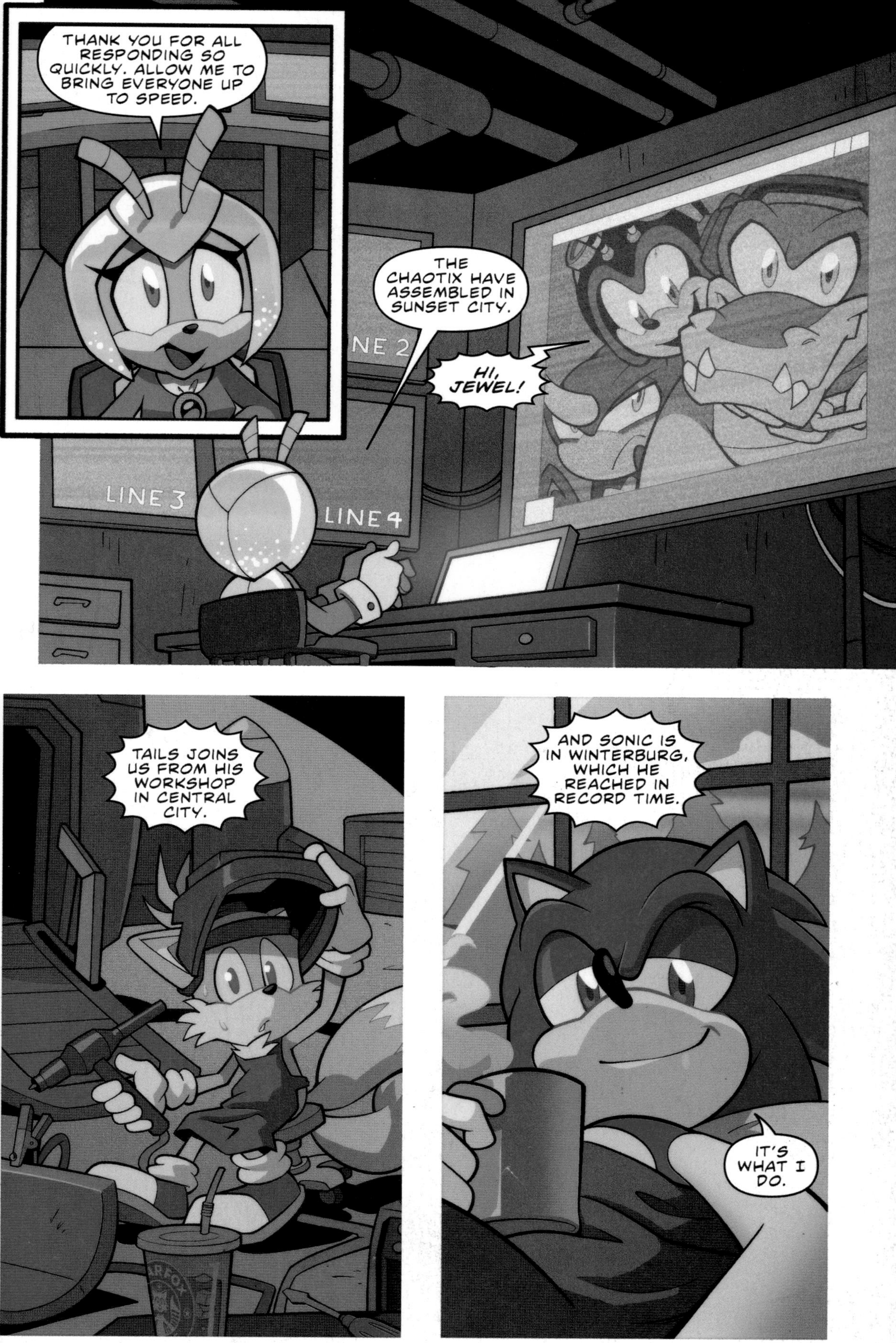
THANK YOU FOR ALL RESPONDING SO QUICKLY. ALLOW ME TO BRING EVERYONE UP TO SPEED.
LINE 2
LINE 3
LINE 4
THE CHAOTIX HAVE ASSEMBLED IN SUNSET CITY.
HI, JEWEL!
TAILS JOINS US FROM HIS WORKSHOP IN CENTRAL CITY.
AND SONIC IS IN WINTERBURG, WHICH HE REACHED IN RECORD TIME.
IT'S WHAT I DO.

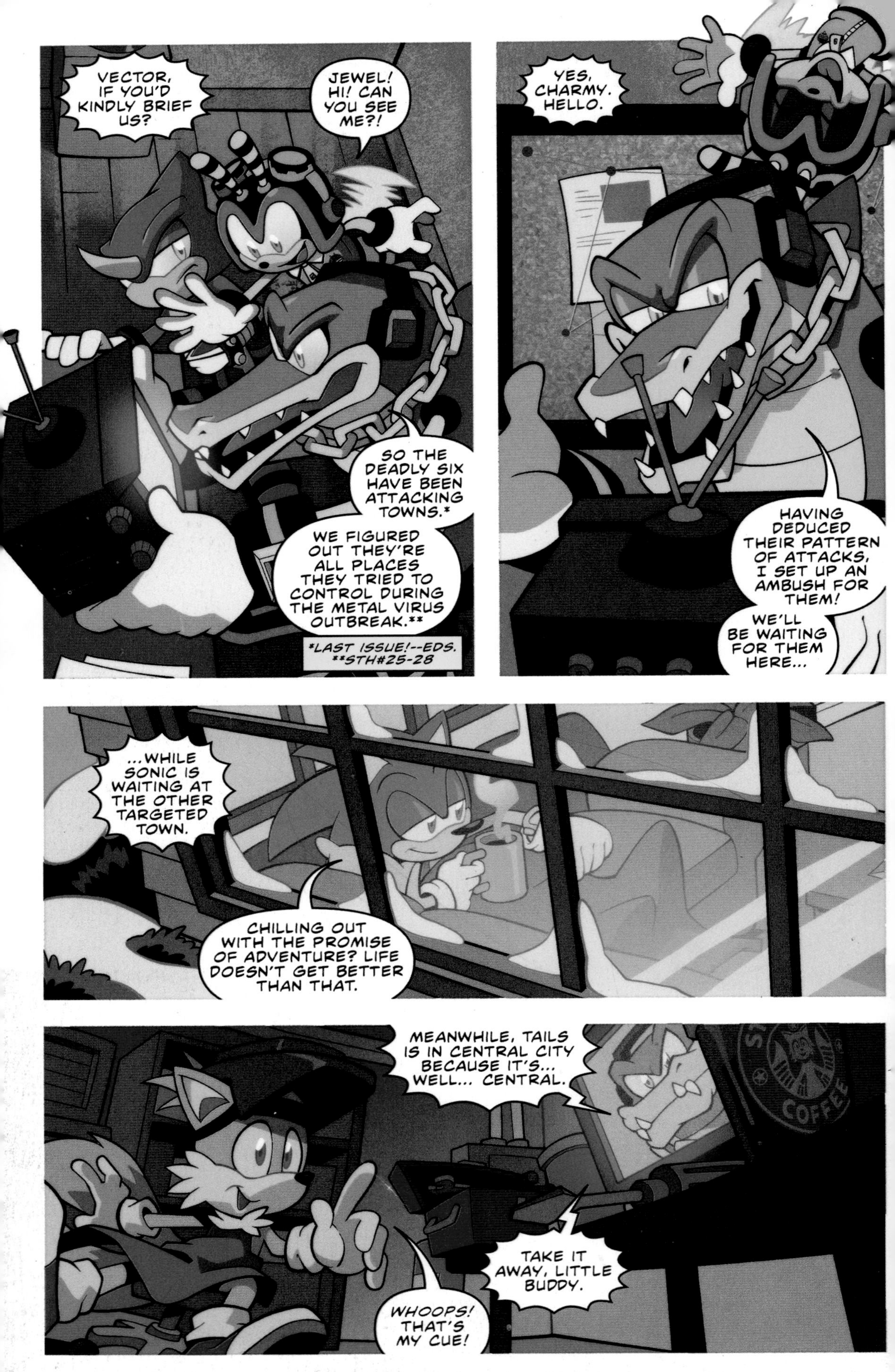
VECTOR, IF YOU'D KINDLY BRIEF US?
JEWEL! HI! CAN YOU SEE ME?!
SO THE DEADLY SIX HAVE BEEN ATTACKING TOWNS.*
WE FIGURED OUT THEY'RE ALL PLACES THEY TRIED TO CONTROL DURING THE METAL VIRUS OUTBREAK.**
*LAST ISSUE!--EDS.
**STH#25-28
YES, CHARMY. HELLO.
HAVING DEDUCED THEIR PATTERN OF ATTACKS, I SET UP AN AMBUSH FOR THEM!
WE'LL BE WAITING FOR THEM HERE...
...WHILE SONIC IS WAITING AT THE OTHER TARGETED TOWN.
CHILLING OUT WITH THE PROMISE OF ADVENTURE? LIFE DOESN'T GET BETTER THAN THAT.
MEANWHILE, TAILS IS IN CENTRAL CITY BECAUSE IT'S... WELL... CENTRAL.
COFFEE
TAKE IT AWAY, LITTLE BUDDY.
WHOOPS! THAT'S MY CUE!

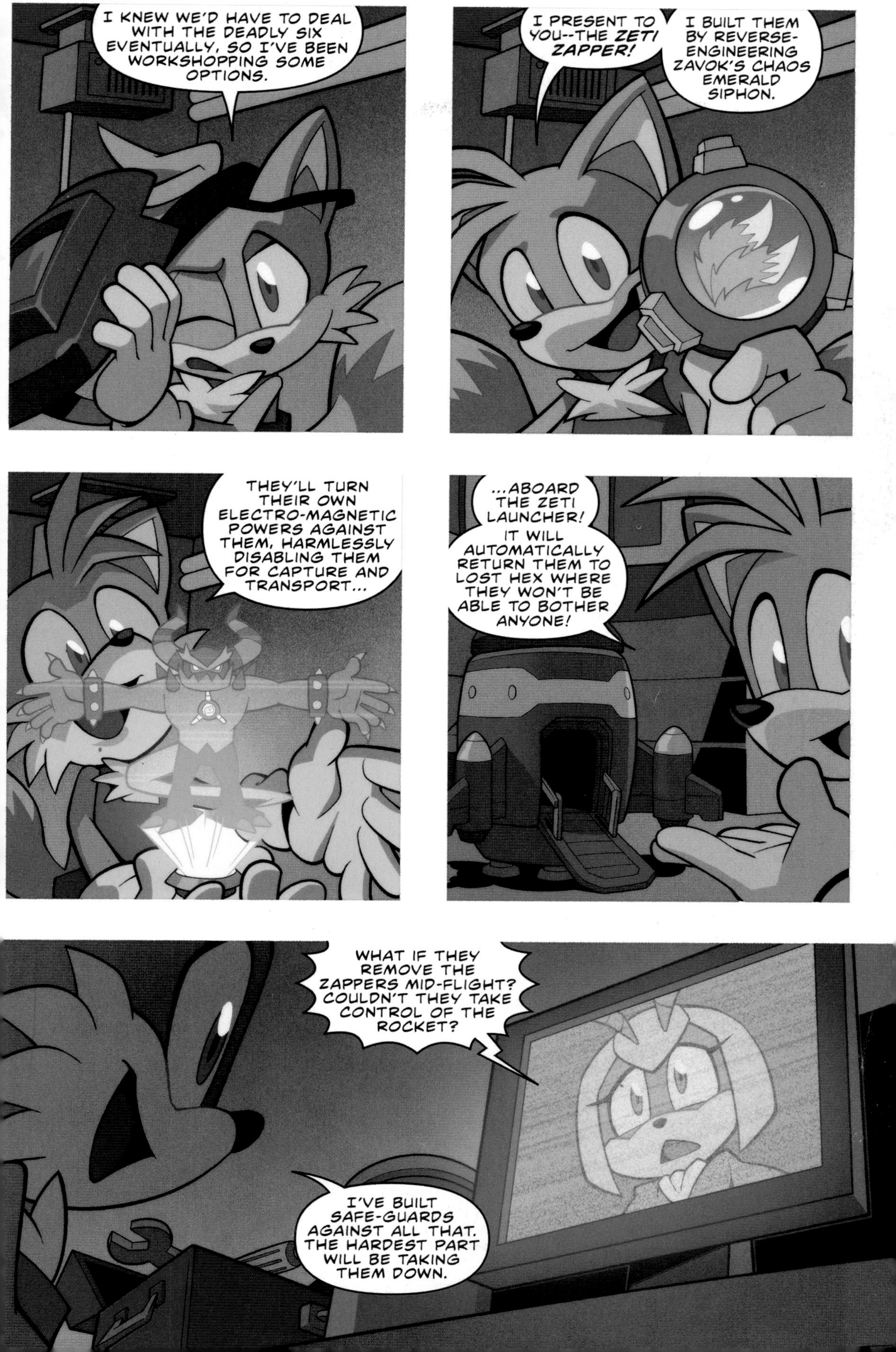
I KNEW WE'D HAVE TO DEAL WITH THE DEADLY SIX EVENTUALLY, SO I'VE BEEN WORKSHOPPING SOME OPTIONS.
I PRESENT TO YOU--THE *ZETI ZAPPER!*
I BUILT THEM BY REVERSE-ENGINEERING ZAVOK'S CHAOS EMERALD SIPHON.
THEY'LL TURN THEIR OWN ELECTRO-MAGNETIC POWERS AGAINST THEM, HARMLESSLY DISABLING THEM FOR CAPTURE AND TRANSPORT...
...ABOARD THE ZETI LAUNCHER!
IT WILL AUTOMATICALLY RETURN THEM TO LOST HEX WHERE THEY WON'T BE ABLE TO BOTHER ANYONE!
WHAT IF THEY REMOVE THE ZAPPERS MID-FLIGHT? COULDN'T THEY TAKE CONTROL OF THE ROCKET?
I'VE BUILT SAFE-GUARDS AGAINST ALL THAT. THE HARDEST PART WILL BE TAKING THEM DOWN.

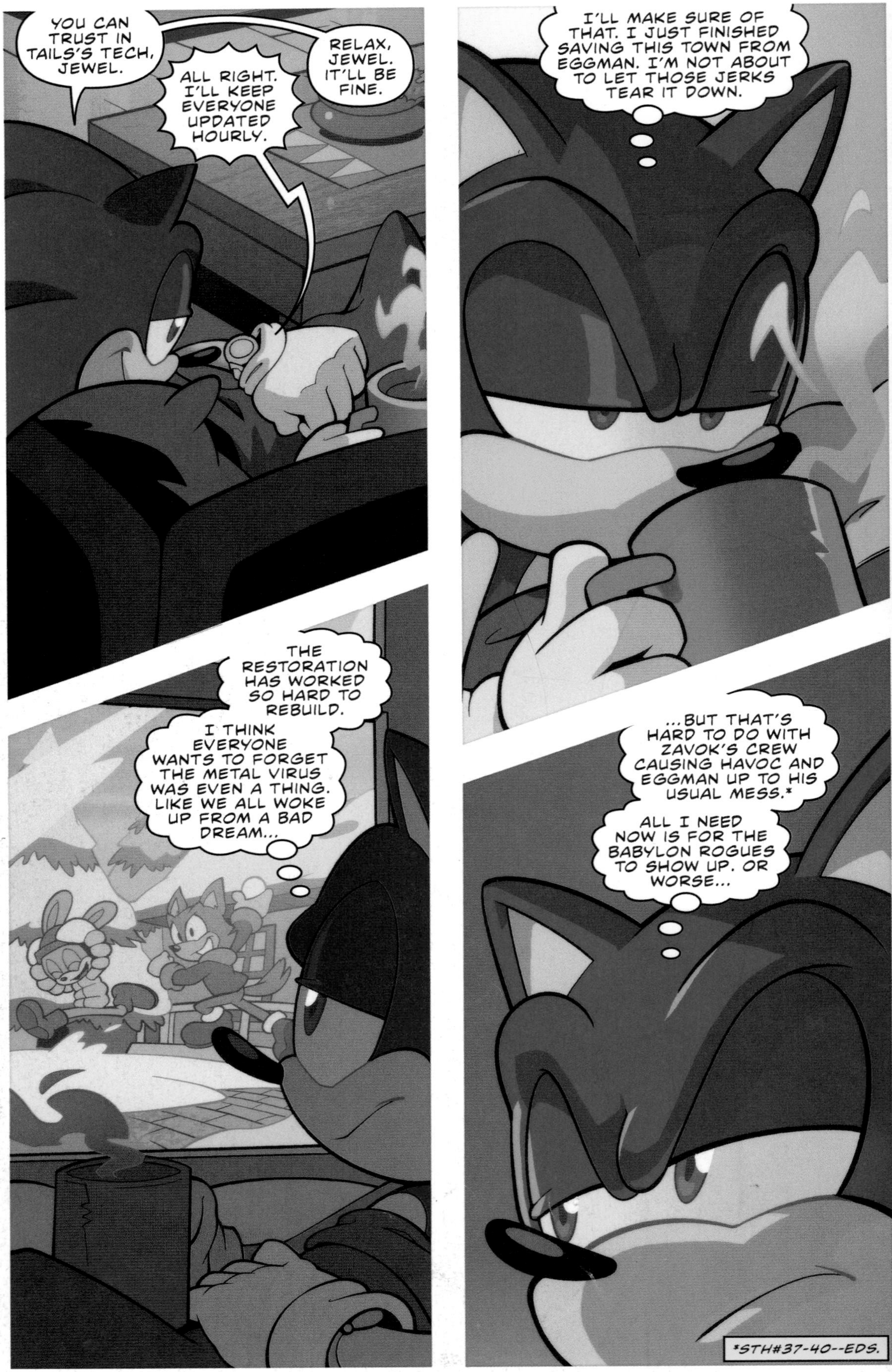
YOU CAN TRUST IN TAILS'S TECH, JEWEL.
RELAX, JEWEL. IT'LL BE FINE.
ALL RIGHT. I'LL KEEP EVERYONE UPDATED HOURLY.
I'LL MAKE SURE OF THAT. I JUST FINISHED SAVING THIS TOWN FROM EGGMAN. I'M NOT ABOUT TO LET THOSE JERKS TEAR IT DOWN.
THE RESTORATION HAS WORKED SO HARD TO REBUILD.
I THINK EVERYONE WANTS TO FORGET THE METAL VIRUS WAS EVEN A THING. LIKE WE ALL WOKE UP FROM A BAD DREAM...
...BUT THAT'S HARD TO DO WITH ZAVOK'S CREW CAUSING HAVOC AND EGGMAN UP TO HIS USUAL MESS.*
ALL I NEED NOW IS FOR THE BABYLON ROGUES TO SHOW UP. OR WORSE...
*STH#37-40--EDS.

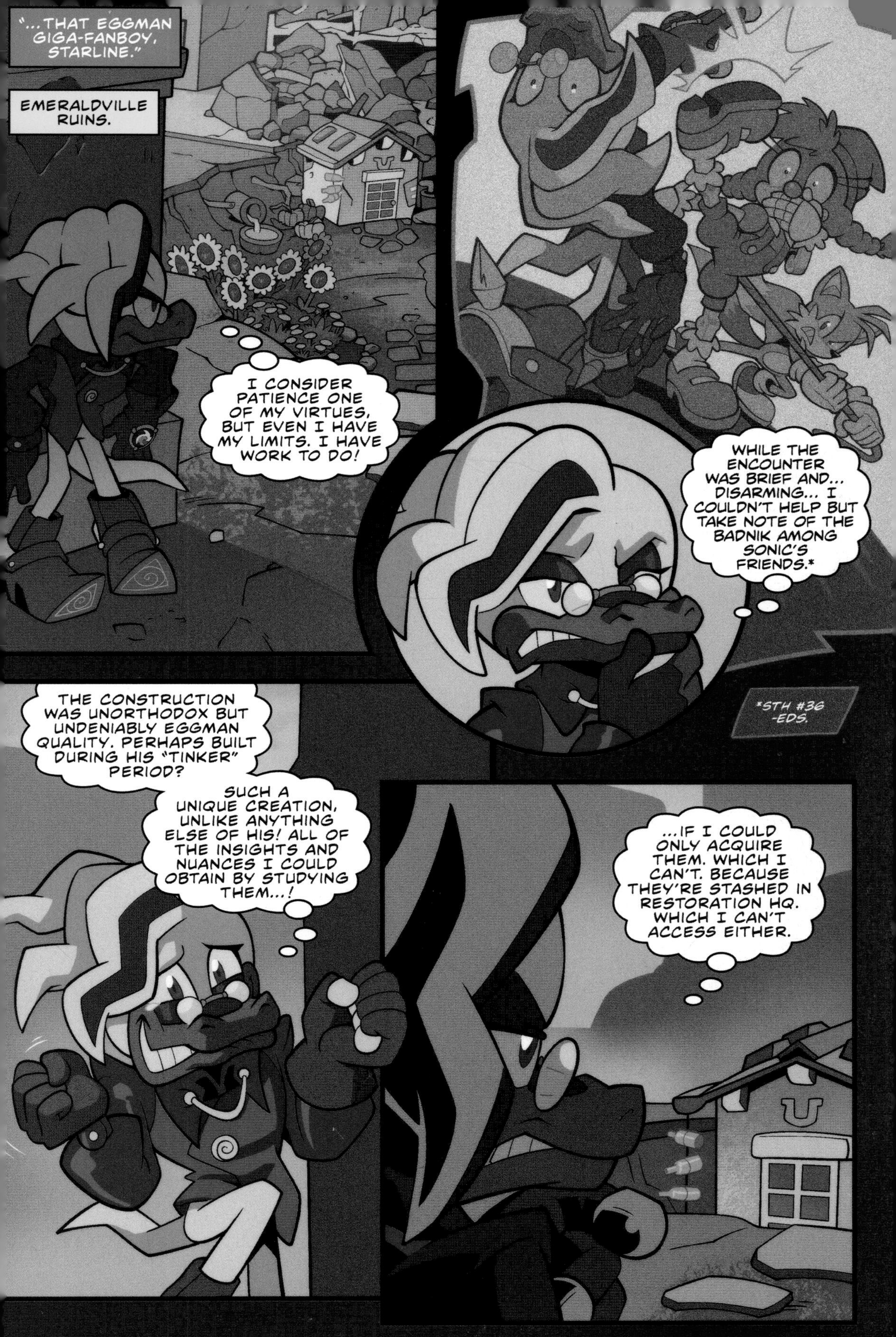
"...THAT EGGMAN GIGA-FANBOY, STARLINE."
EMERALDVILLE RUINS.
I CONSIDER PATIENCE ONE OF MY VIRTUES, BUT EVEN I HAVE MY LIMITS. I HAVE WORK TO DO!
WHILE THE ENCOUNTER WAS BRIEF AND... DISARMING... I COULDN'T HELP BUT TAKE NOTE OF THE BADNIK AMONG SONIC'S FRIENDS.*
*STH #36 -EDS.
THE CONSTRUCTION WAS UNORTHODOX BUT UNDENIABLY EGGMAN QUALITY. PERHAPS BUILT DURING HIS "TINKER" PERIOD?
SUCH A UNIQUE CREATION, UNLIKE ANYTHING ELSE OF HIS! ALL OF THE INSIGHTS AND NUANCES I COULD OBTAIN BY STUDYING THEM...!
...IF I COULD ONLY ACQUIRE THEM. WHICH I CAN'T. BECAUSE THEY'RE STASHED IN RESTORATION HQ. WHICH I CAN'T ACCESS EITHER.

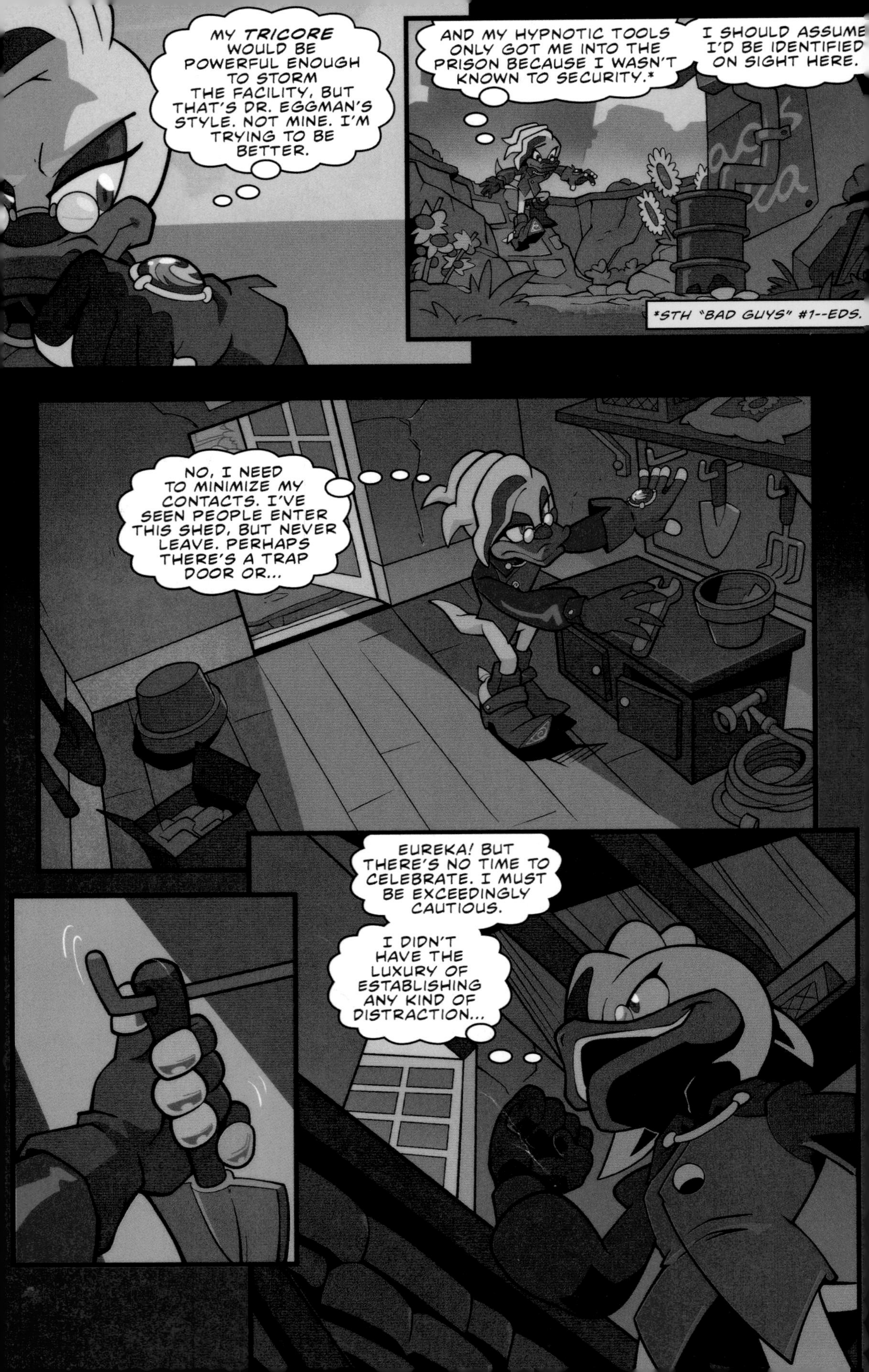
MY TRICORE WOULD BE POWERFUL ENOUGH TO STORM THE FACILITY, BUT THAT'S DR. EGGMAN'S STYLE. NOT MINE. I'M TRYING TO BE BETTER.
AND MY HYPNOTIC TOOLS ONLY GOT ME INTO THE PRISON BECAUSE I WASN'T KNOWN TO SECURITY.*
I SHOULD ASSUME I'D BE IDENTIFIED ON SIGHT HERE.
*STH "BAD GUYS" #1--EDS.
NO, I NEED TO MINIMIZE MY CONTACTS. I'VE SEEN PEOPLE ENTER THIS SHED, BUT NEVER LEAVE. PERHAPS THERE'S A TRAP DOOR OR...
EUREKA! BUT THERE'S NO TIME TO CELEBRATE. I MUST BE EXCEEDINGLY CAUTIOUS.
I DIDN'T HAVE THE LUXURY OF ESTABLISHING ANY KIND OF DISTRACTION...

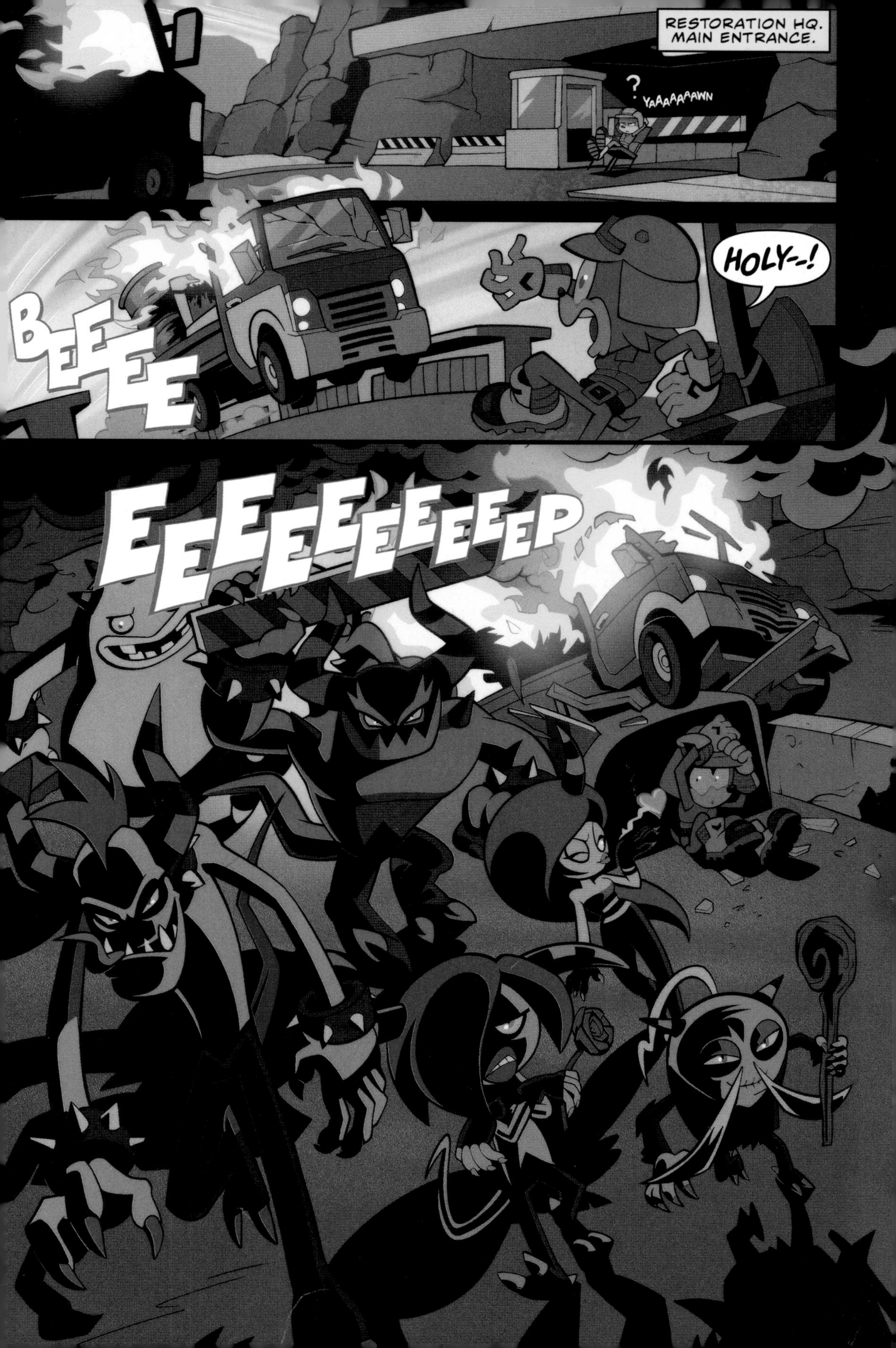
RESTORATION HQ.
MAIN ENTRANCE.
?
YAAAAAAAWN
HOLY--!
BEEEE
EEEEEEEEP

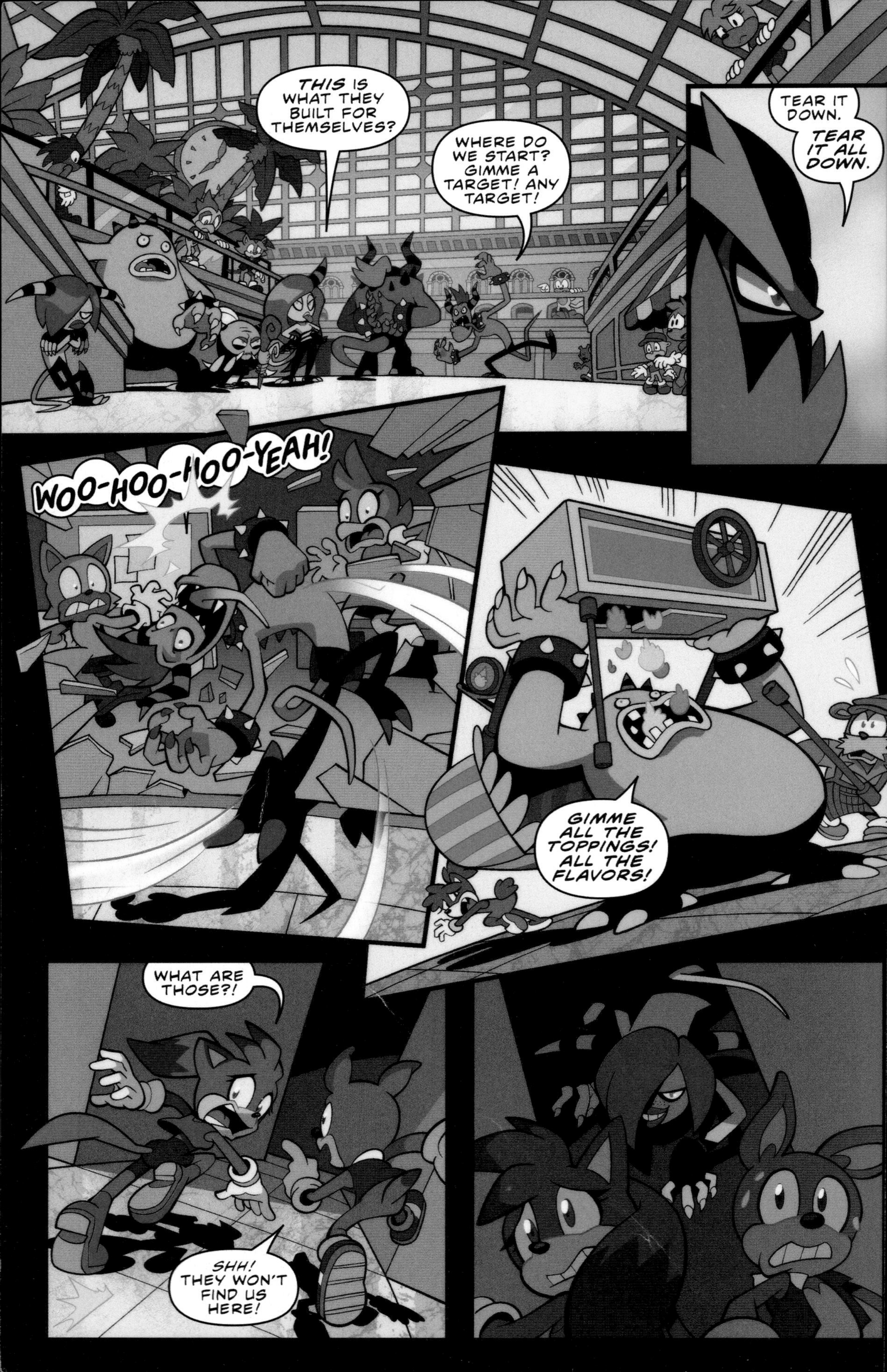

THIS is WHAT THEY BUILT FOR THEMSELVES?
WHERE DO WE START? GIMME A TARGET! ANY TARGET!
TEAR IT DOWN. TEAR IT ALL DOWN.
WOO-HOO-HOO-YEAH!
GIMME ALL THE TOPPINGS! ALL THE FLAVORS!
WHAT ARE THOSE?!
SHH! THEY WON'T FIND US HERE!

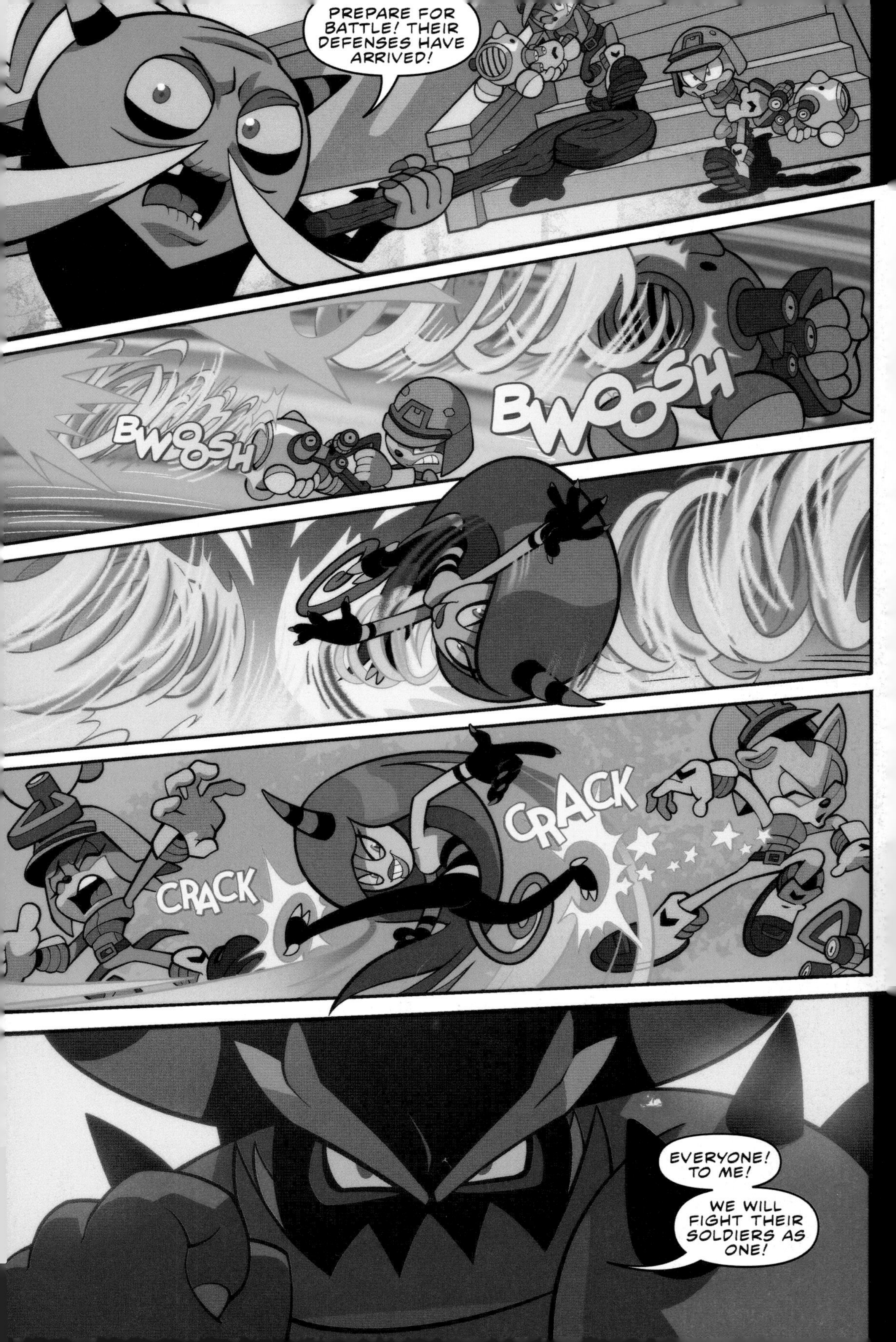
PREPARE FOR BATTLE! THEIR DEFENSES HAVE ARRIVED!
BWOOSH
BWOOSH
CRACK
CRACK
EVERYONE! TO ME!
WE WILL FIGHT THEIR SOLDIERS AS ONE!

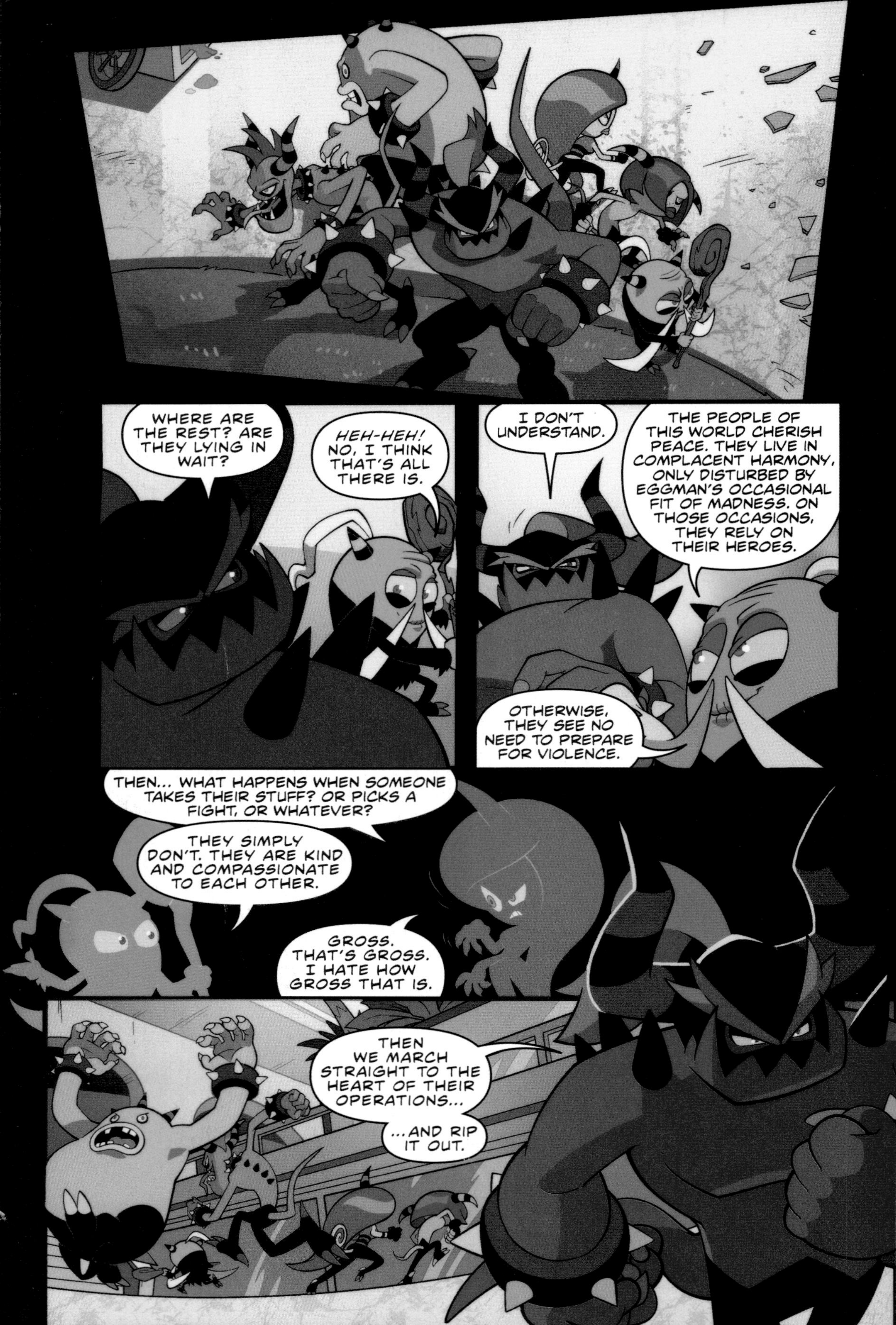
WHERE ARE THE REST? ARE THEY LYING IN WAIT?
HEH-HEH! NO, I THINK THAT'S ALL THERE IS.
I DON'T UNDERSTAND.
THE PEOPLE OF THIS WORLD CHERISH PEACE. THEY LIVE IN COMPLACENT HARMONY, ONLY DISTURBED BY EGGMAN'S OCCASIONAL FIT OF MADNESS. ON THOSE OCCASIONS, THEY RELY ON THEIR HEROES.
OTHERWISE, THEY SEE NO NEED TO PREPARE FOR VIOLENCE.
THEN... WHAT HAPPENS WHEN SOMEONE TAKES THEIR STUFF? OR PICKS A FIGHT, OR WHATEVER?
THEY SIMPLY DON'T. THEY ARE KIND AND COMPASSIONATE TO EACH OTHER.
GROSS. THAT'S GROSS. I HATE HOW GROSS THAT IS.
THEN WE MARCH STRAIGHT TO THE HEART OF THEIR OPERATIONS...
...AND RIP IT OUT.

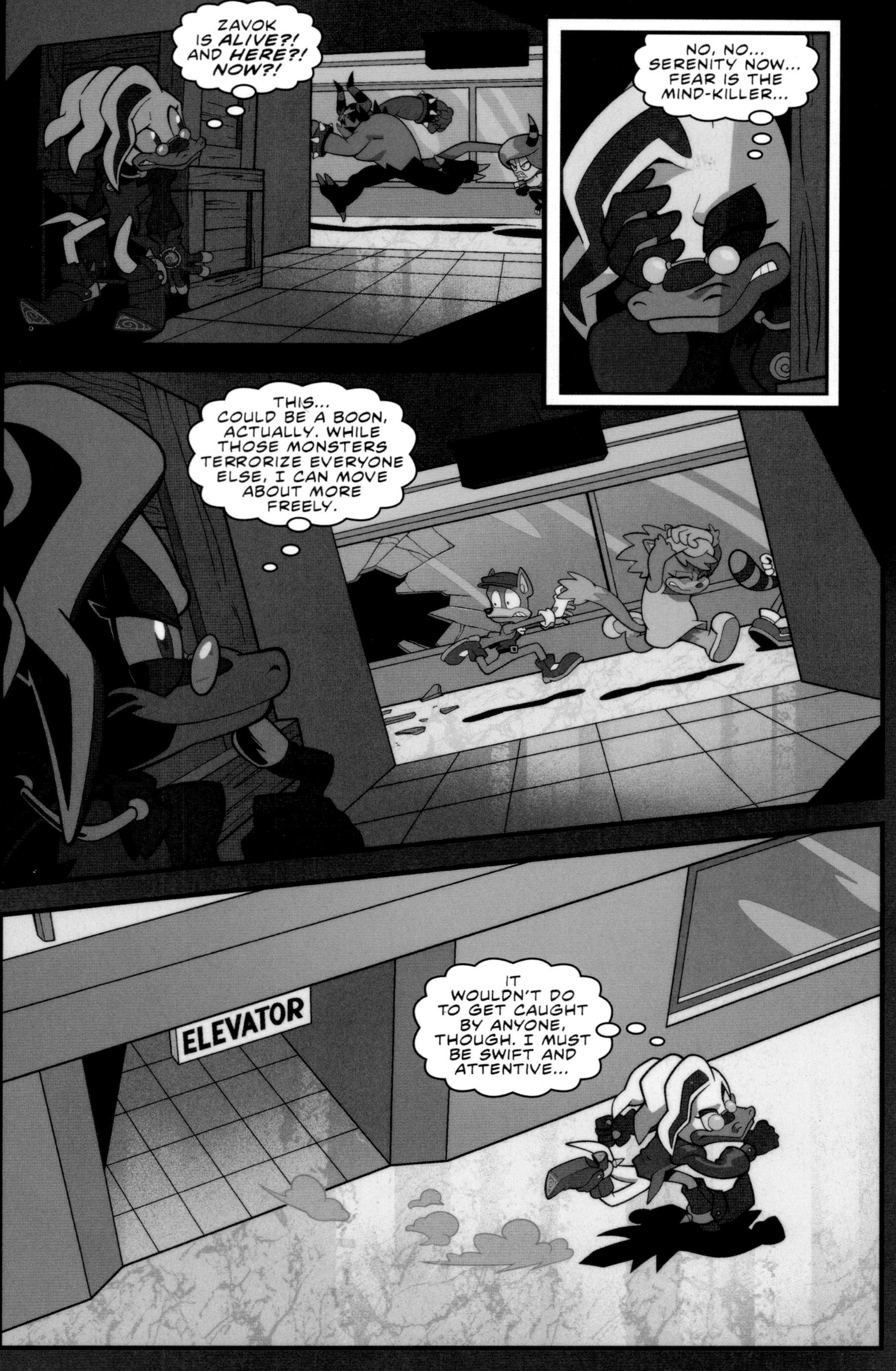

ZAVOK IS ALIVE?! AND HERE?! NOW?!
NO, NO... SERENITY NOW... FEAR IS THE MIND-KILLER...
THIS... COULD BE A BOON, ACTUALLY. WHILE THOSE MONSTERS TERRORIZE EVERYONE ELSE, I CAN MOVE ABOUT MORE FREELY.
ELEVATOR
IT WOULDN'T DO TO GET CAUGHT BY ANYONE, THOUGH. I MUST BE SWIFT AND ATTENTIVE...

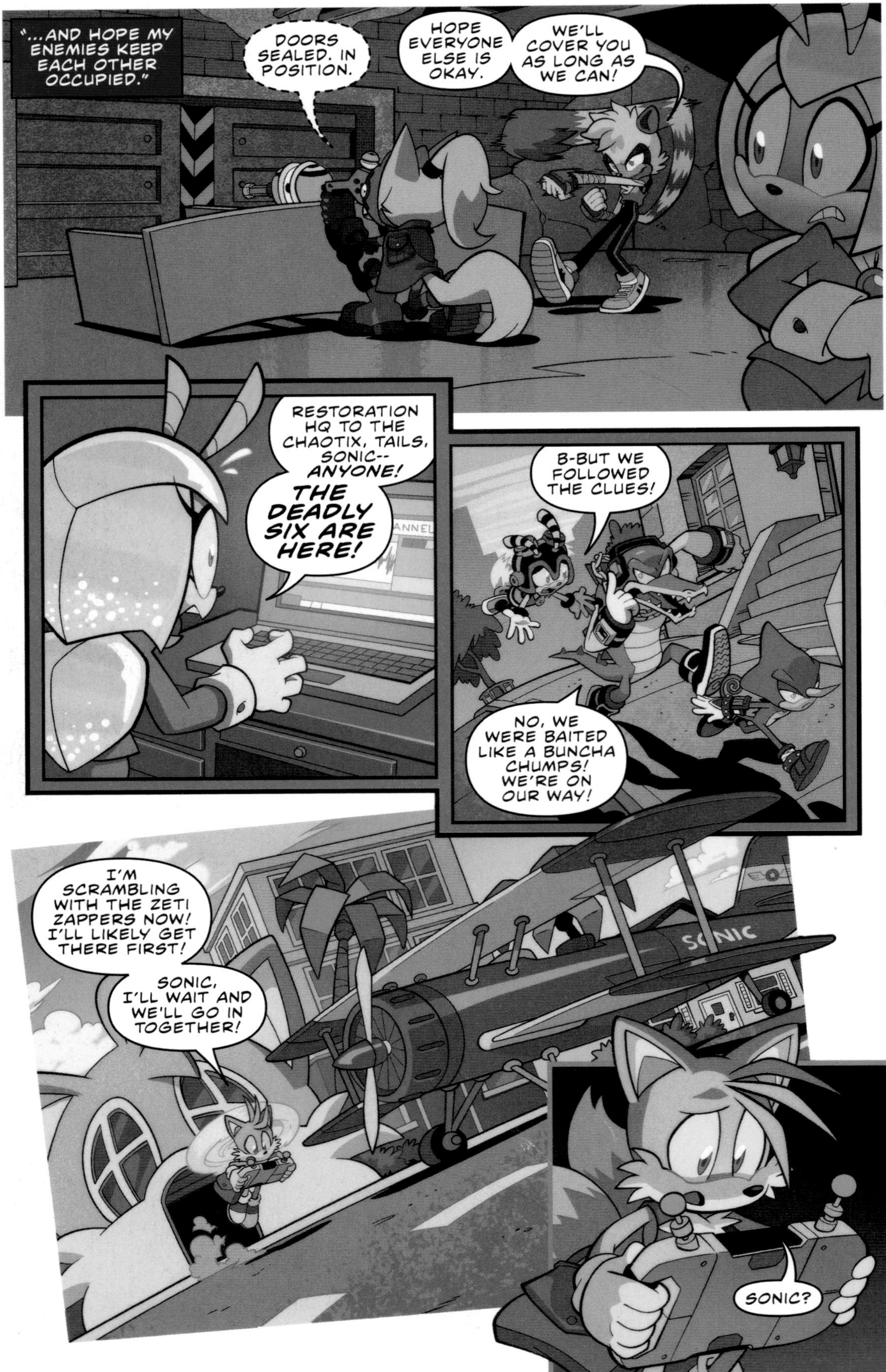
"...AND HOPE MY ENEMIES KEEP EACH OTHER OCCUPIED."
DOORS SEALED. IN POSITION.
HOPE EVERYONE ELSE IS OKAY.
WE'LL COVER YOU AS LONG AS WE CAN!
RESTORATION HQ TO THE CHAOTIX, TAILS, SONIC-- ANYONE!
THE DEADLY SIX ARE HERE!
B-BUT WE FOLLOWED THE CLUES!
NO, WE WERE BAITED LIKE A BUNCHA CHUMPS! WE'RE ON OUR WAY!
I'M SCRAMBLING WITH THE ZETI ZAPPERS NOW! I'LL LIKELY GET THERE FIRST!
SONIC, I'LL WAIT AND WE'LL GO IN TOGETHER!
SONIC
SONIC?

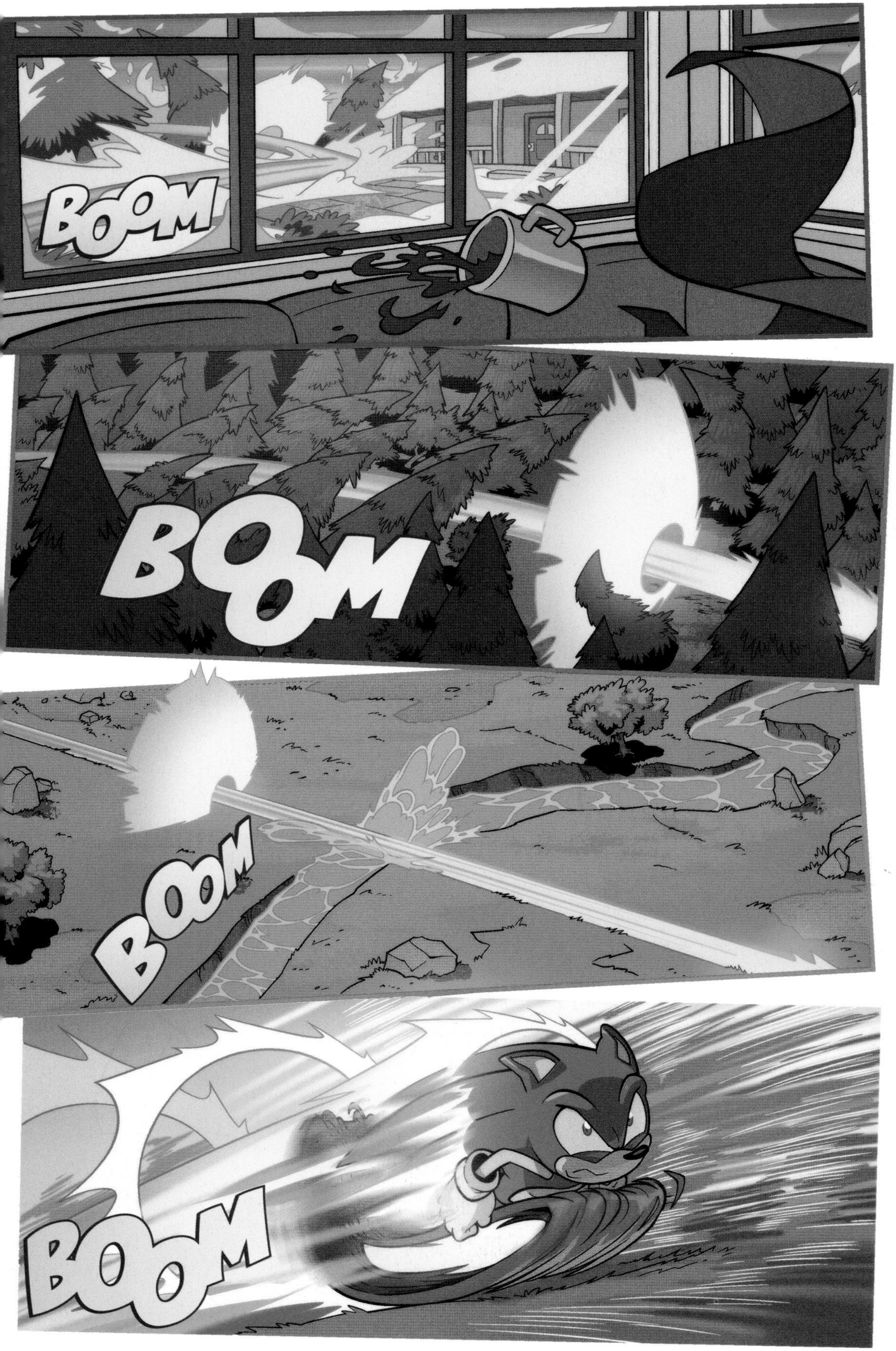
BOOM
BOOM
BOOM
BOOM

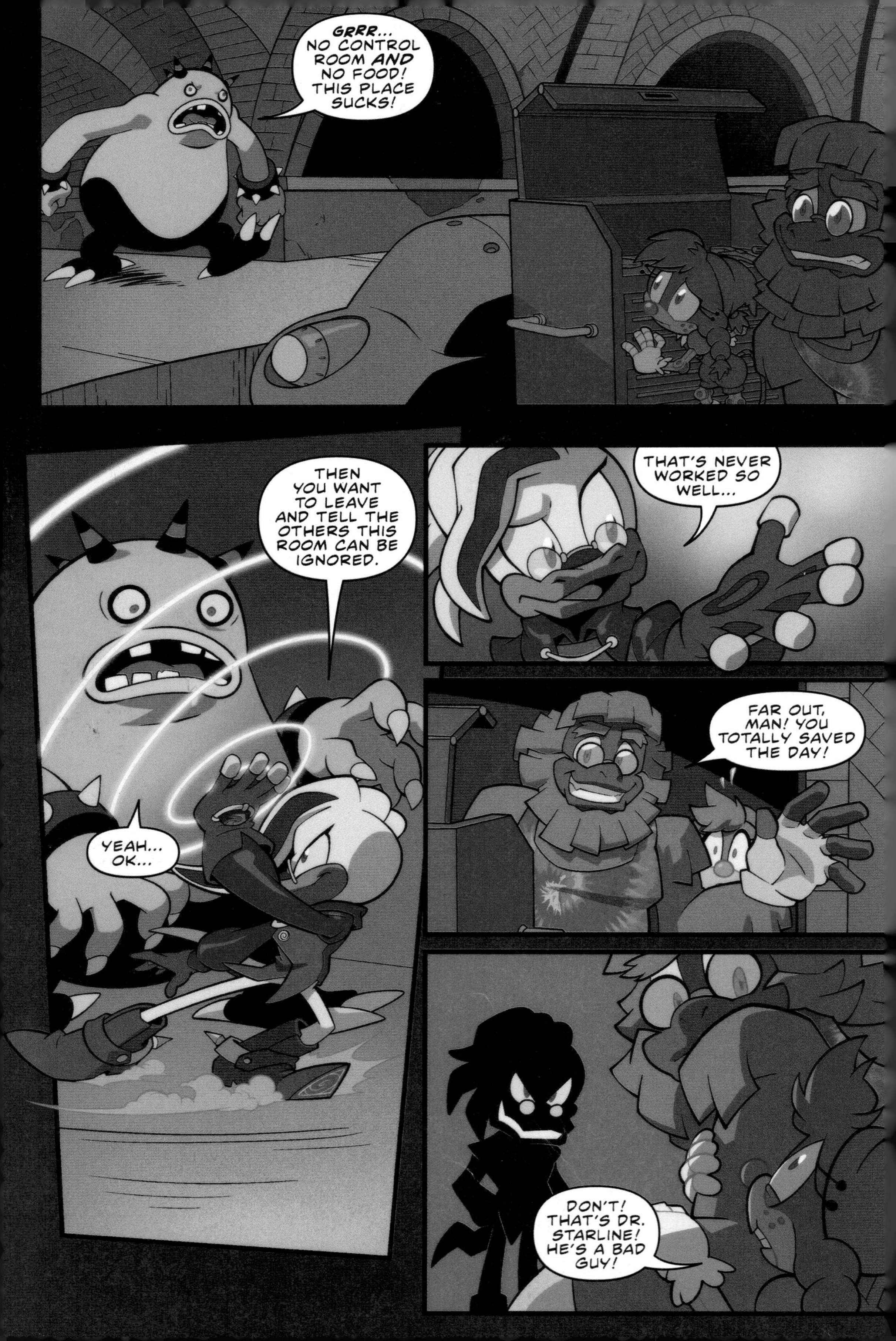
GRRR... NO CONTROL ROOM AND NO FOOD! THIS PLACE SUCKS!
THEN YOU WANT TO LEAVE AND TELL THE OTHERS THIS ROOM CAN BE IGNORED.
YEAH... OK...
THAT'S NEVER WORKED SO WELL...
FAR OUT, MAN! YOU TOTALLY SAVED THE DAY!
DON'T! THAT'S DR. STARLINE! HE'S A BAD GUY!

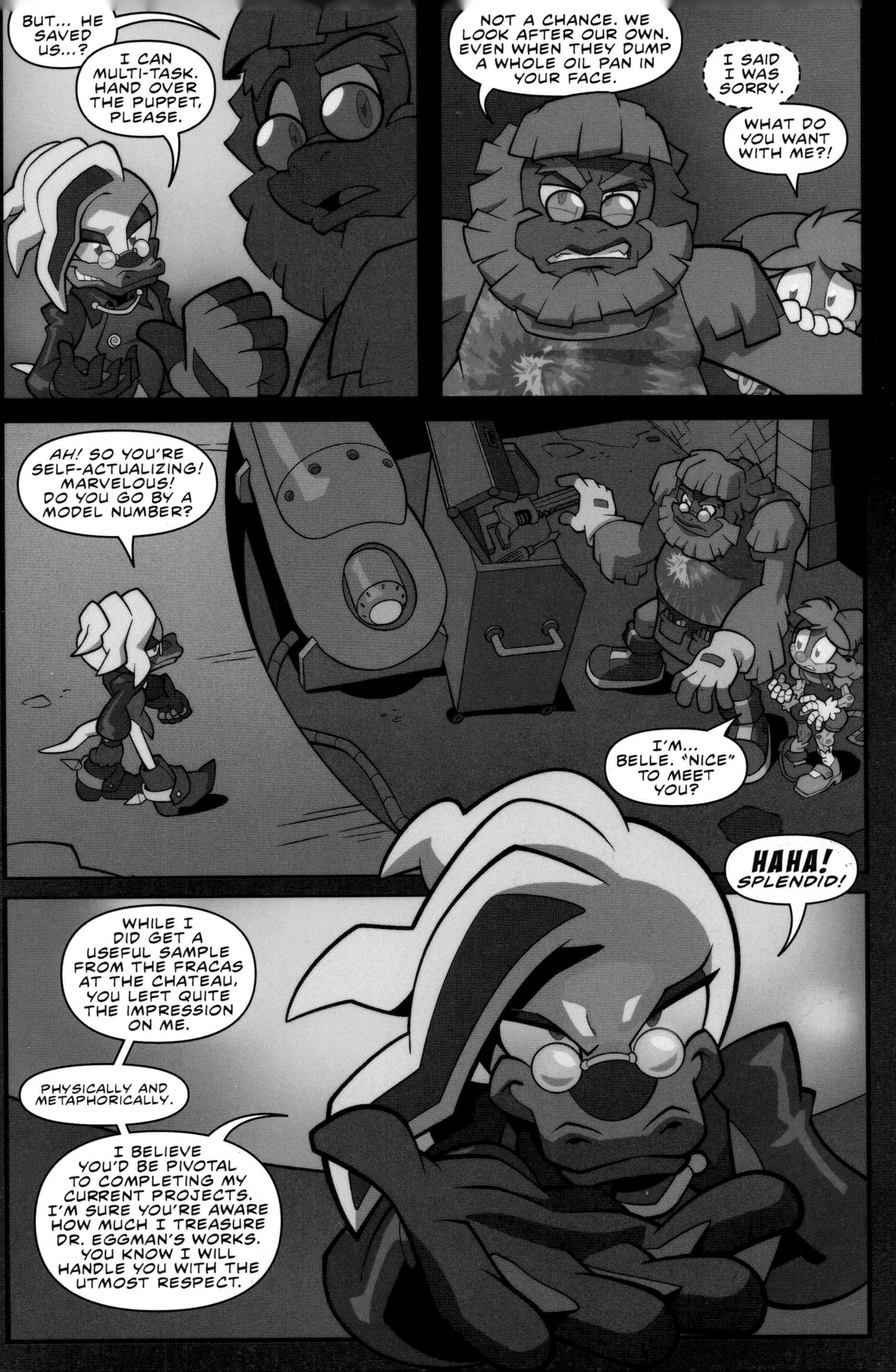
BUT... HE SAVED US...?
I CAN MULTI-TASK. HAND OVER THE PUPPET, PLEASE.
NOT A CHANCE. WE LOOK AFTER OUR OWN. EVEN WHEN THEY DUMP A WHOLE OIL PAN IN YOUR FACE.
I SAID I WAS SORRY.
WHAT DO YOU WANT WITH ME?!
AH! SO YOU'RE SELF-ACTUALIZING! MARVELOUS! DO YOU GO BY A MODEL NUMBER?
I'M... BELLE. "NICE" TO MEET YOU?
HAHA! SPLENDID!
WHILE I DID GET A USEFUL SAMPLE FROM THE FRACAS AT THE CHATEAU, YOU LEFT QUITE THE IMPRESSION ON ME.
PHYSICALLY AND METAPHORICALLY.
I BELIEVE YOU'D BE PIVOTAL TO COMPLETING MY CURRENT PROJECTS. I'M SURE YOU'RE AWARE HOW MUCH I TREASURE DR. EGGMAN'S WORKS. YOU KNOW I WILL HANDLE YOU WITH THE UTMOST RESPECT.

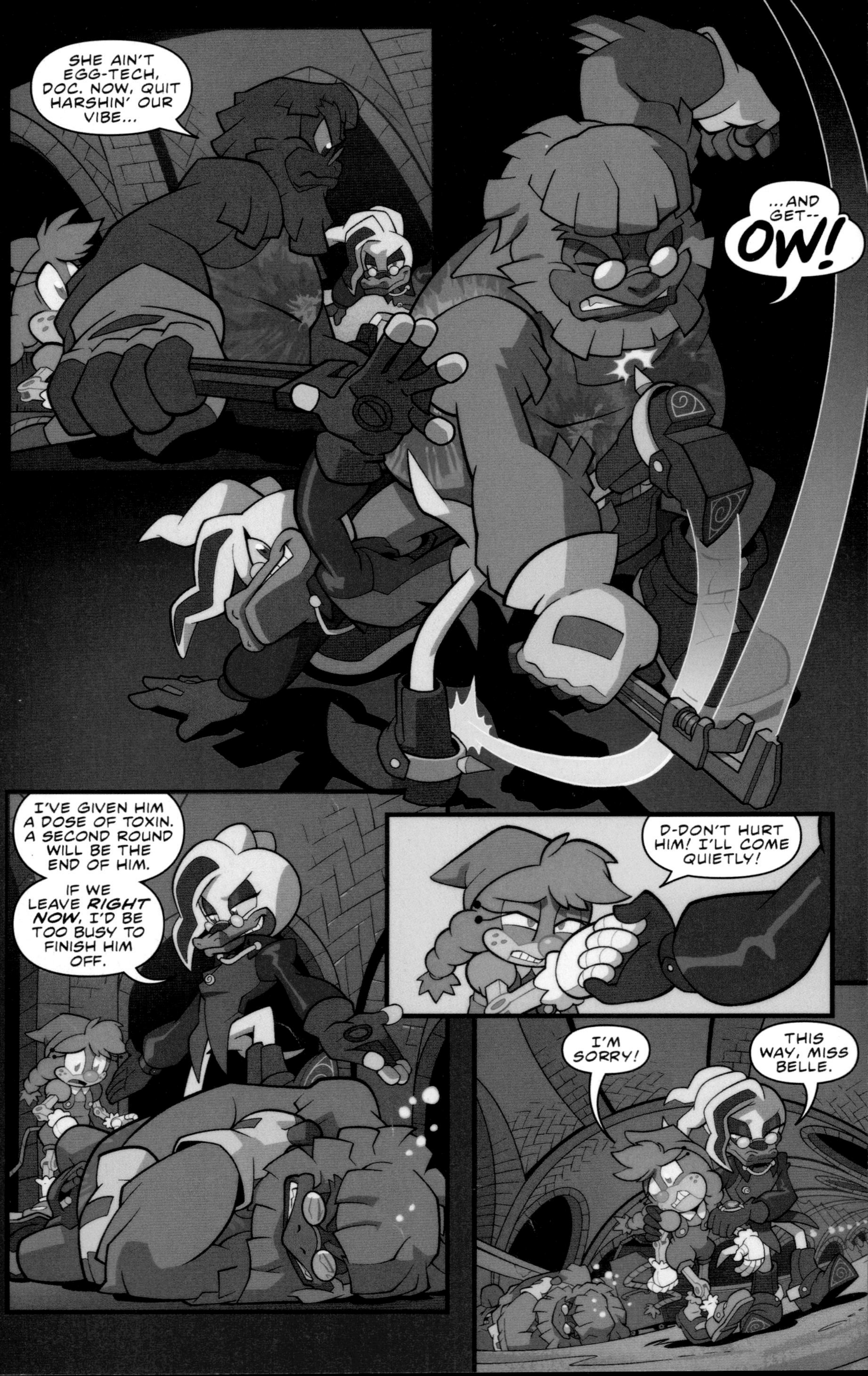
SHE AIN'T EGG-TECH, DOC. NOW, QUIT HARSHIN' OUR VIBE...
...AND GET--
OW!
I'VE GIVEN HIM A DOSE OF TOXIN. A SECOND ROUND WILL BE THE END OF HIM.
IF WE LEAVE RIGHT NOW, I'D BE TOO BUSY TO FINISH HIM OFF.
D-DON'T HURT HIM! I'LL COME QUIETLY!
I'M SORRY!
THIS WAY, MISS BELLE.

ELEVATOR
ELEVATOR

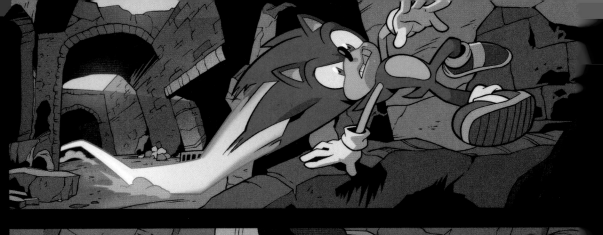

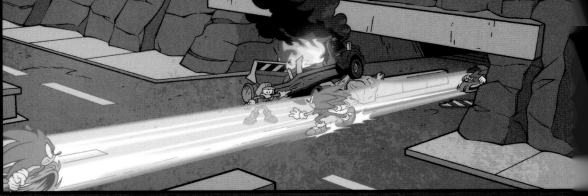

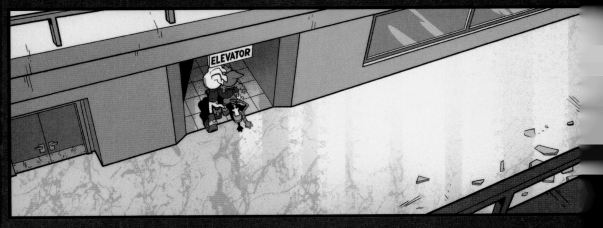

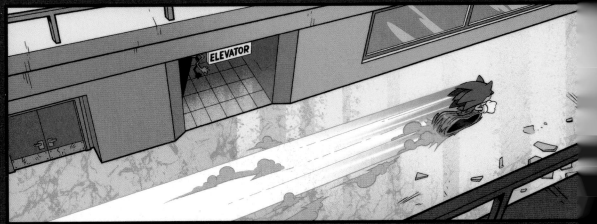

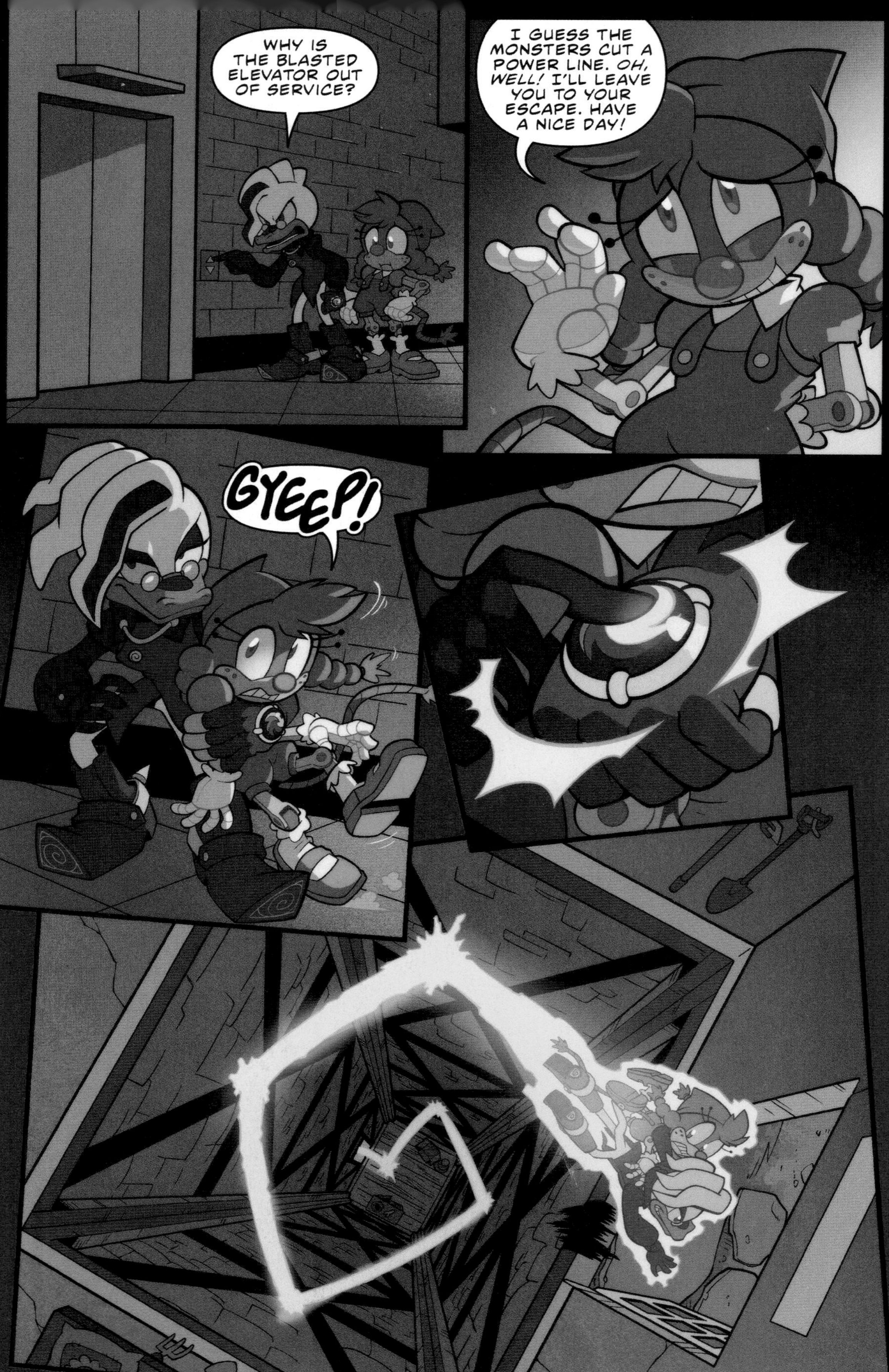
WHY IS THE BLASTED ELEVATOR OUT OF SERVICE?
I GUESS THE MONSTERS CUT A POWER LINE. *OH, WELL!* I'LL LEAVE YOU TO YOUR ESCAPE. HAVE A NICE DAY!
GYEEP!

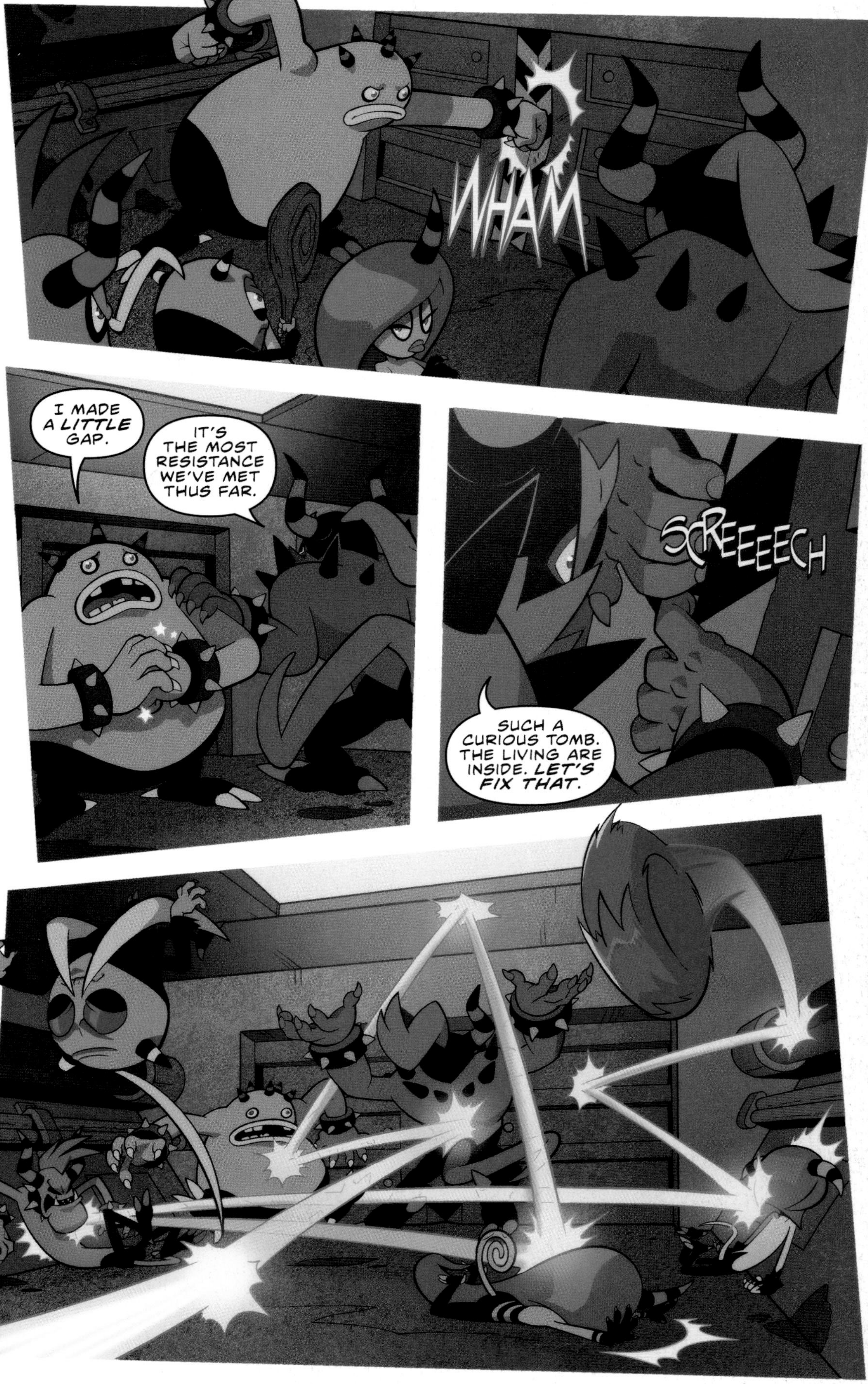
WHAM
I MADE A LITTLE GAP.
IT'S THE MOST RESISTANCE WE'VE MET THUS FAR.
SCREEEEECH
SUCH A CURIOUS TOMB. THE LIVING ARE INSIDE. LET'S FIX THAT.

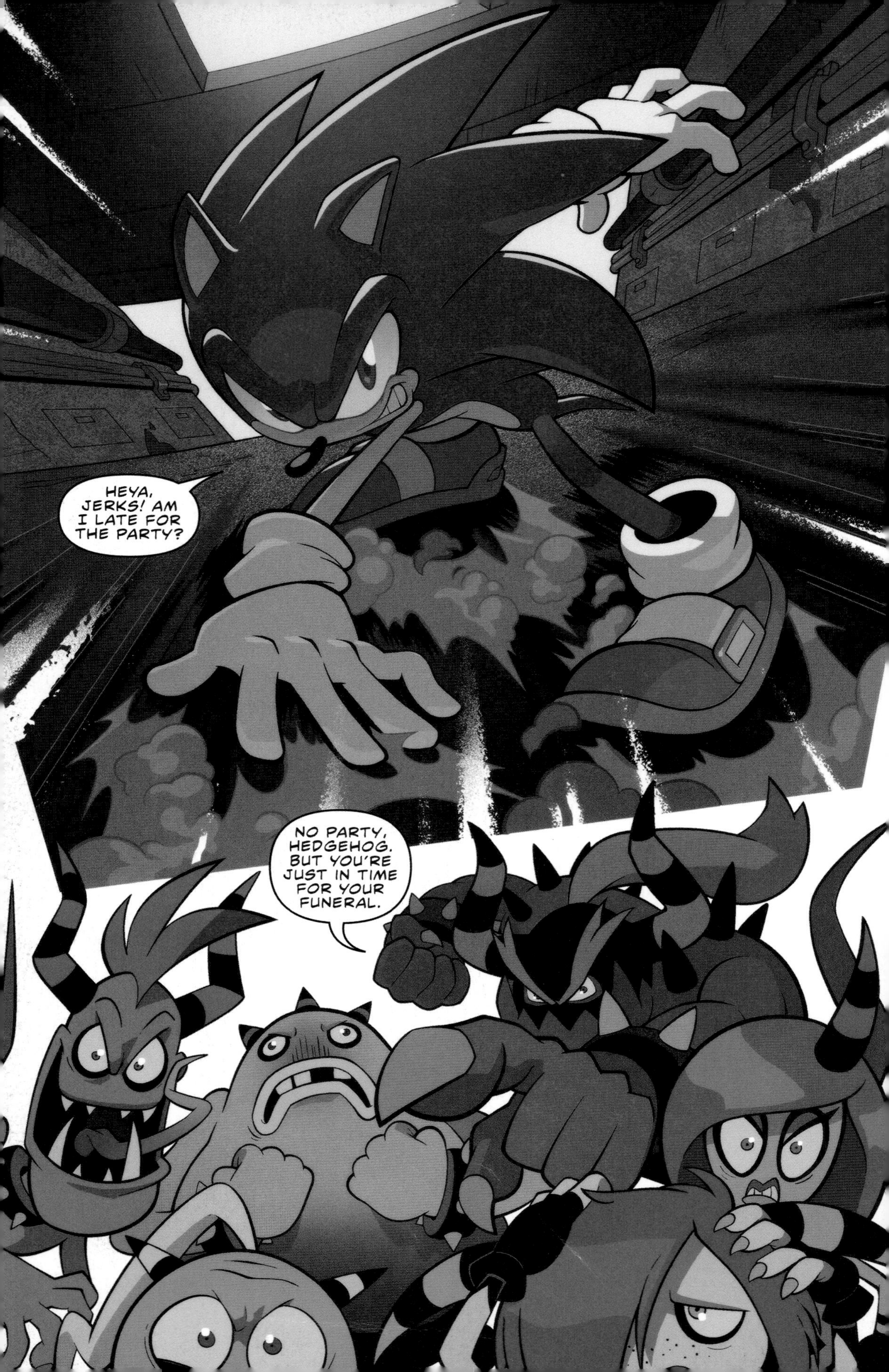
HEYA, JERKS! AM I LATE FOR THE PARTY?
NO PARTY, HEDGEHOG. BUT YOU'RE JUST IN TIME FOR YOUR FUNERAL.

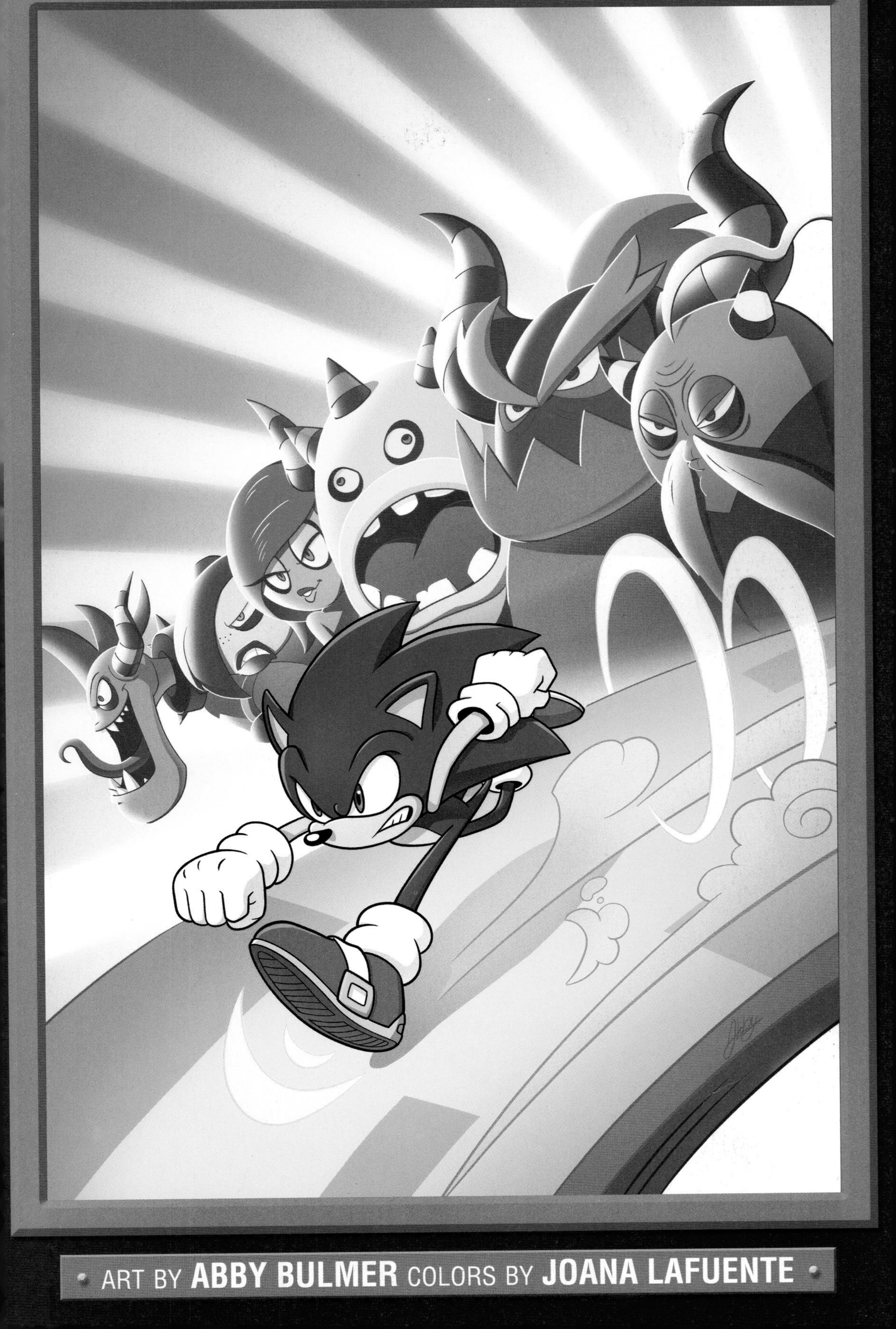

ART BY **ABBY BULMER** COLORS BY **JOANA LAFUENTE**

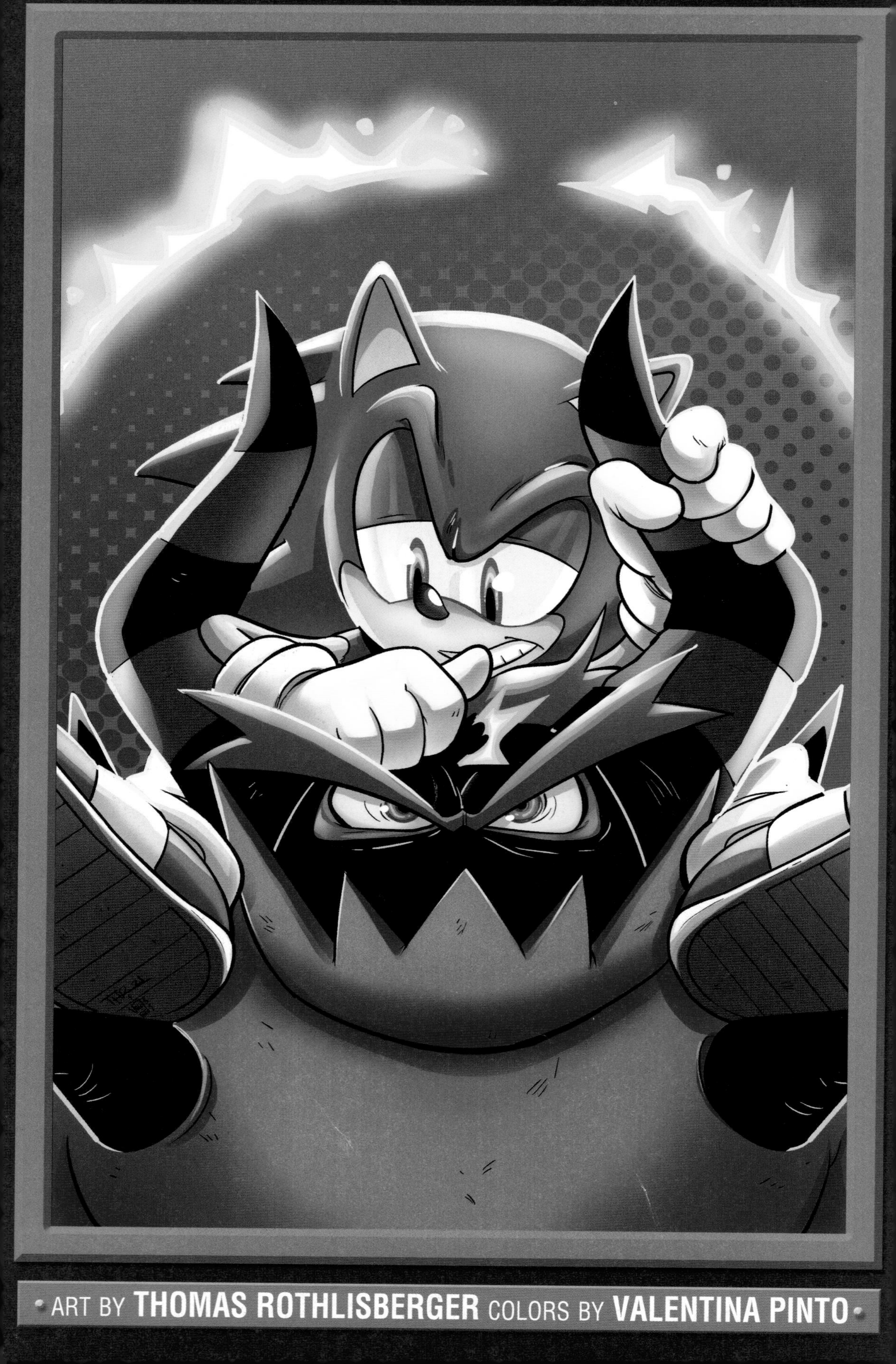

ART BY **THOMAS ROTHLISBERGER** COLORS BY **VALENTINA PINTO**

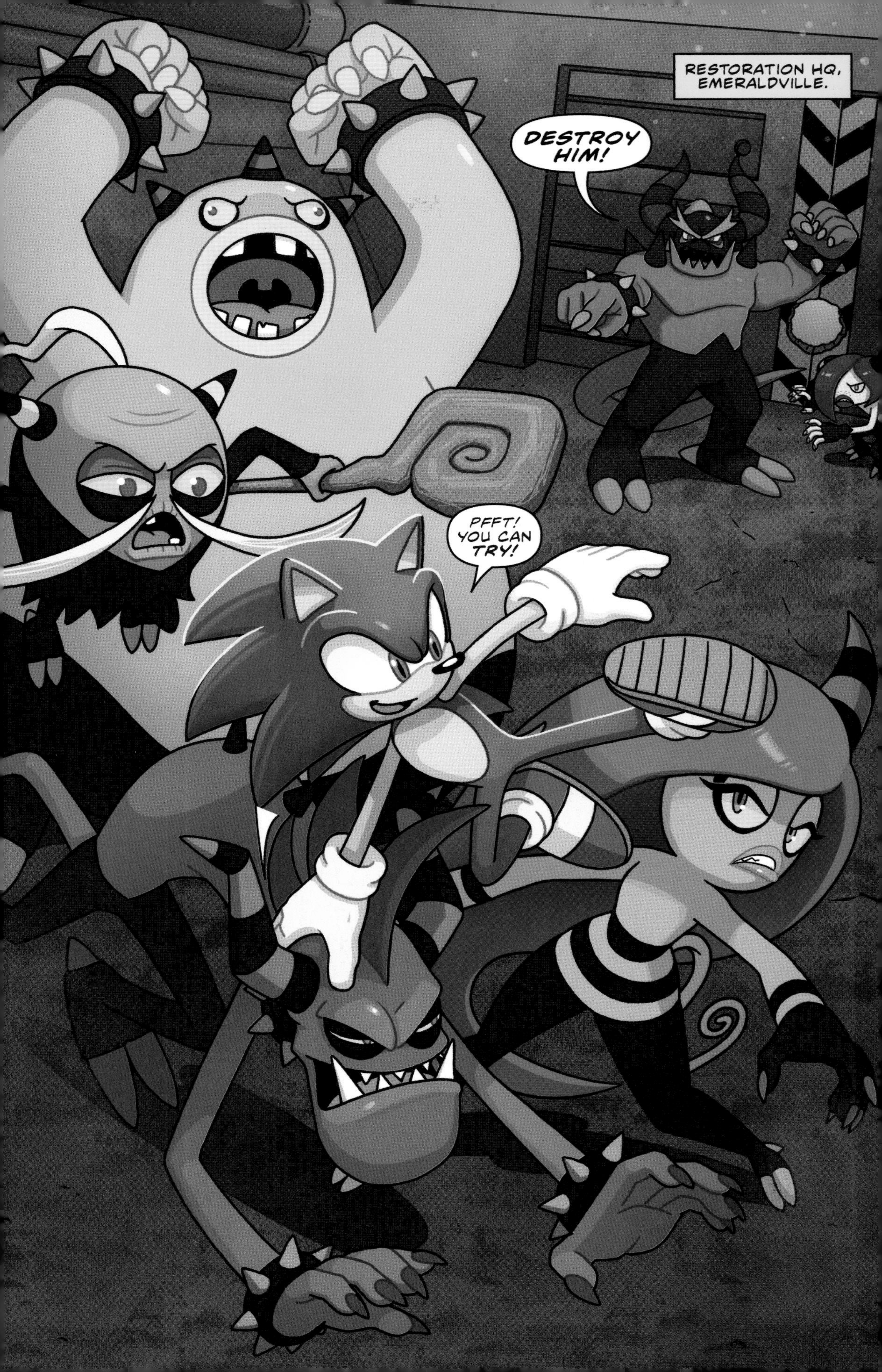
RESTORATION HQ, EMERALDVILLE.
DESTROY HIM!
PFFT! YOU CAN TRY!

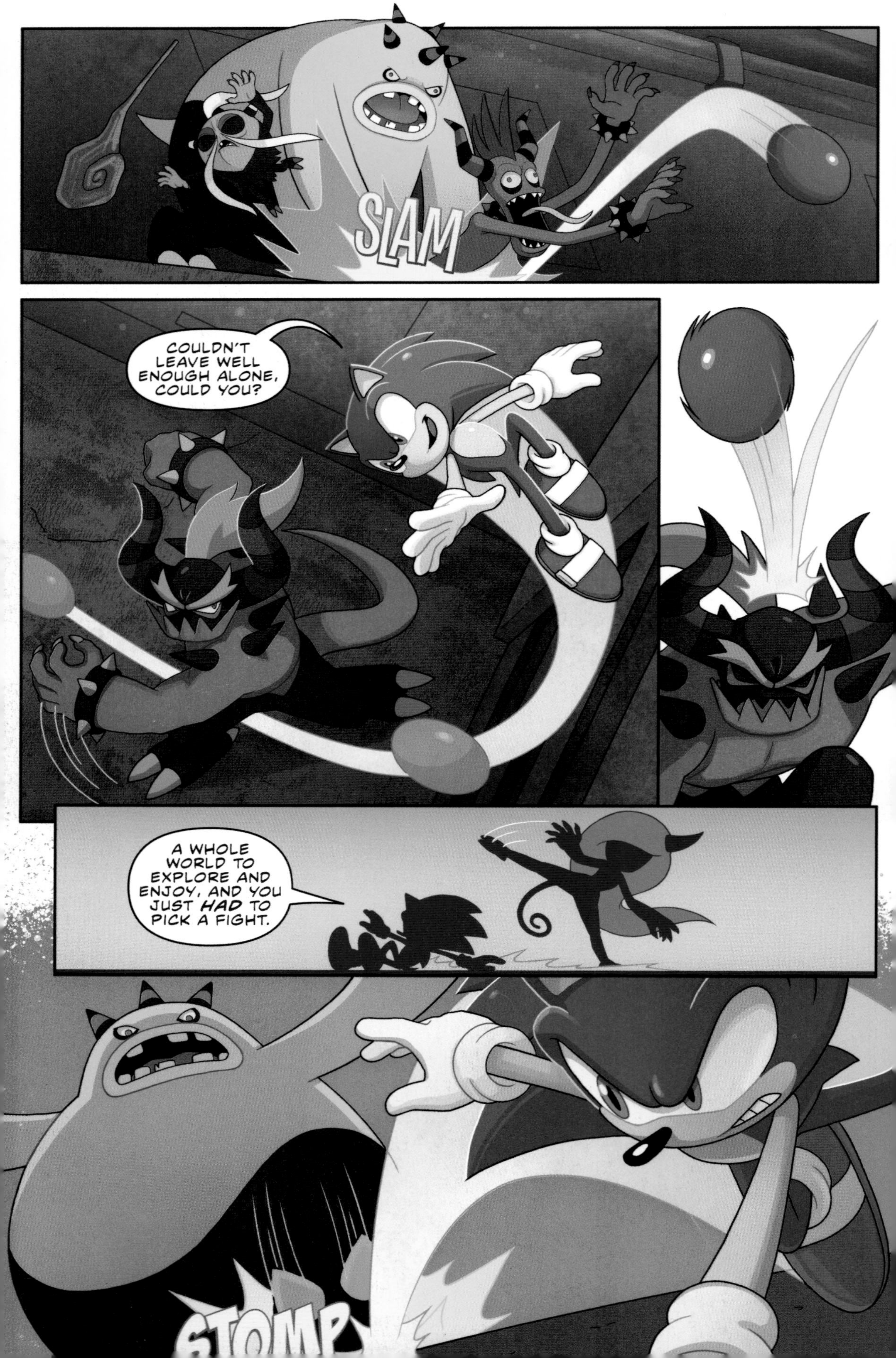
SLAM
COULDN'T LEAVE WELL ENOUGH ALONE, COULD YOU?
A WHOLE WORLD TO EXPLORE AND ENJOY, AND YOU JUST *HAD* TO PICK A FIGHT.
STOMP

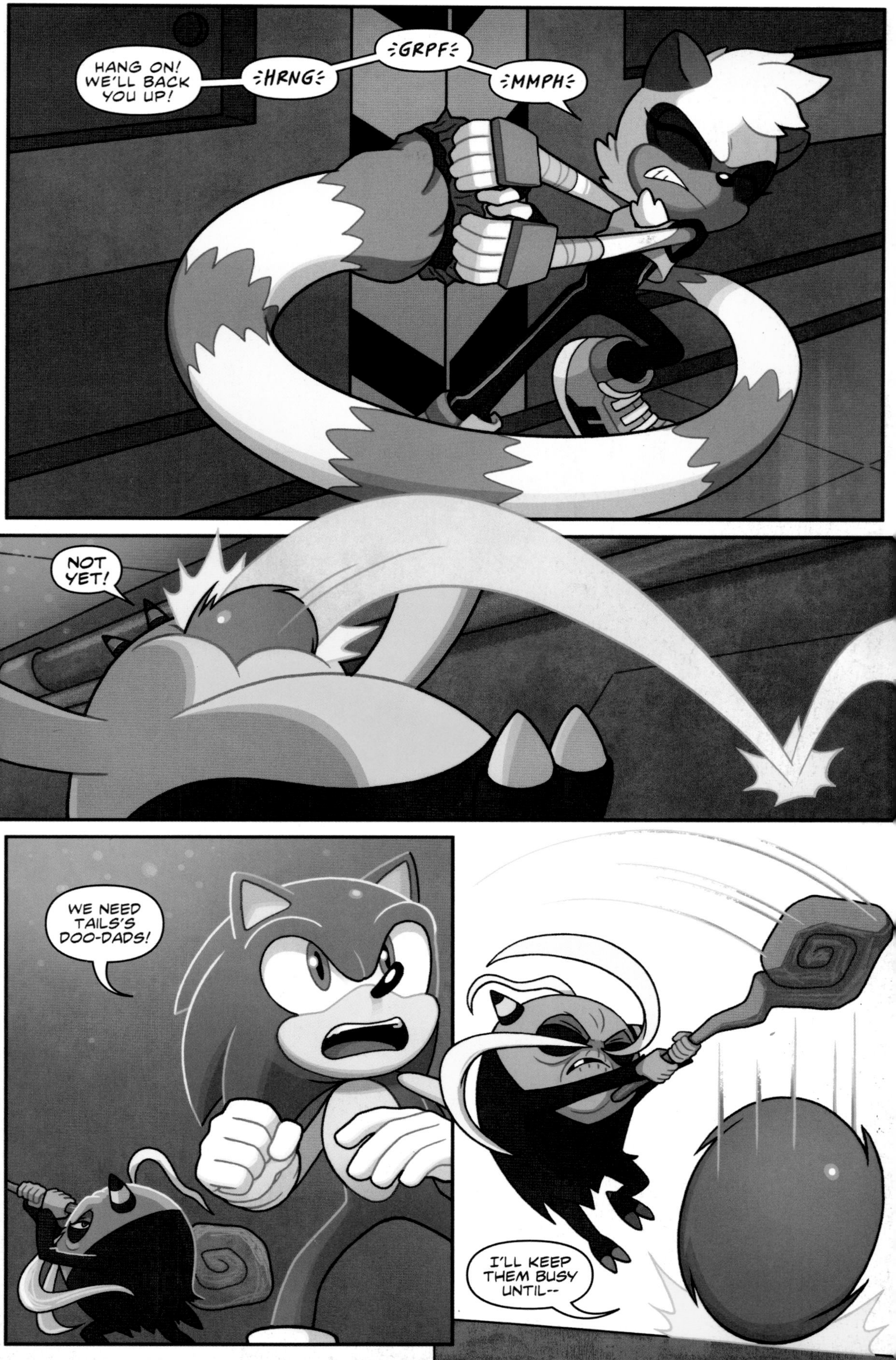
HANG ON! WE'LL BACK YOU UP!
HRNG
GRPF
MMPH
NOT YET!
WE NEED TAILS'S DOO-DADS!
I'LL KEEP THEM BUSY UNTIL--

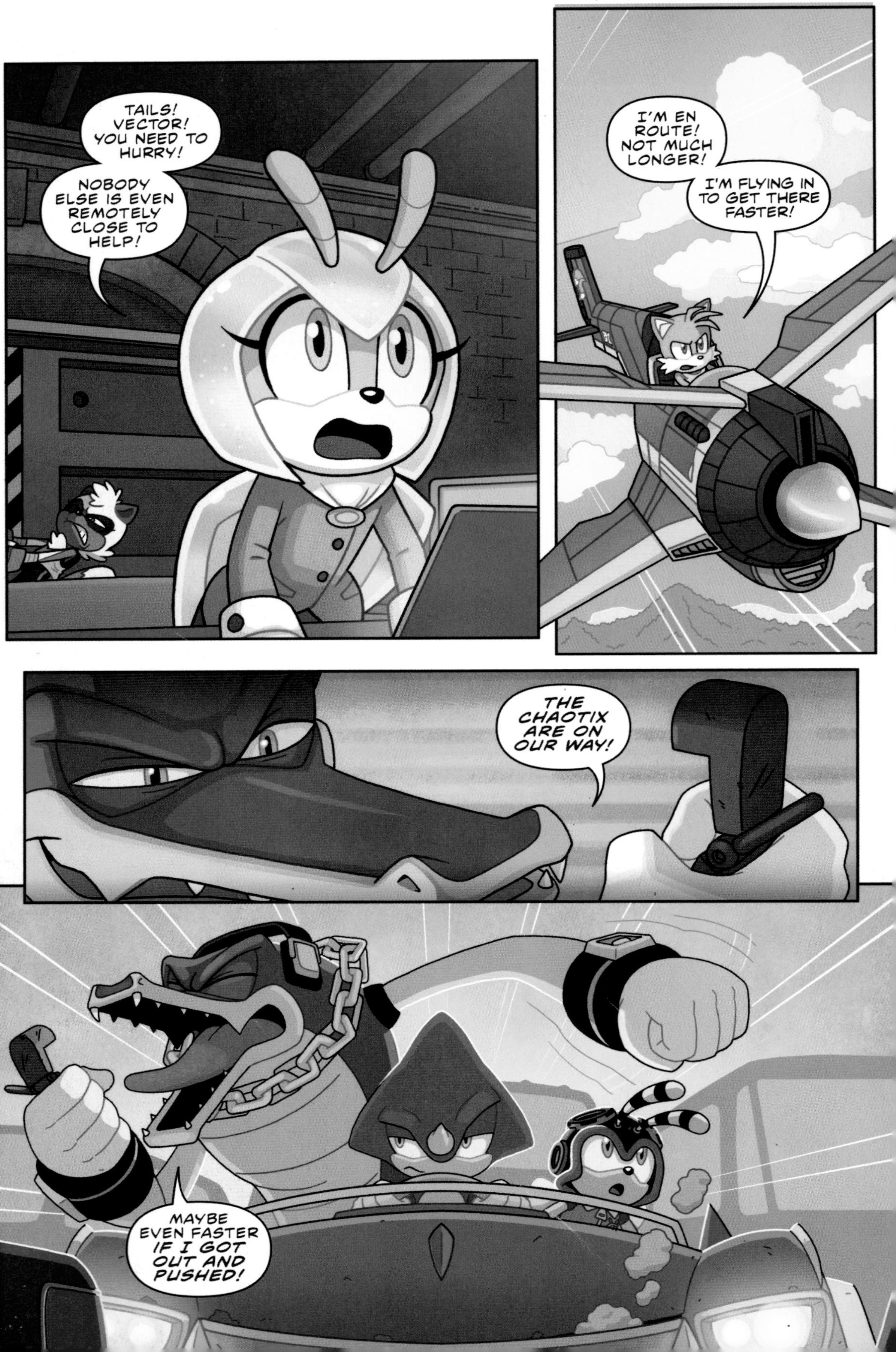
TAILS! VECTOR! YOU NEED TO HURRY!
NOBODY ELSE IS EVEN REMOTELY CLOSE TO HELP!
I'M EN ROUTE! NOT MUCH LONGER!
I'M FLYING IN TO GET THERE FASTER!
THE CHAOTIX ARE ON OUR WAY!
MAYBE EVEN FASTER IF I GOT OUT AND PUSHED!

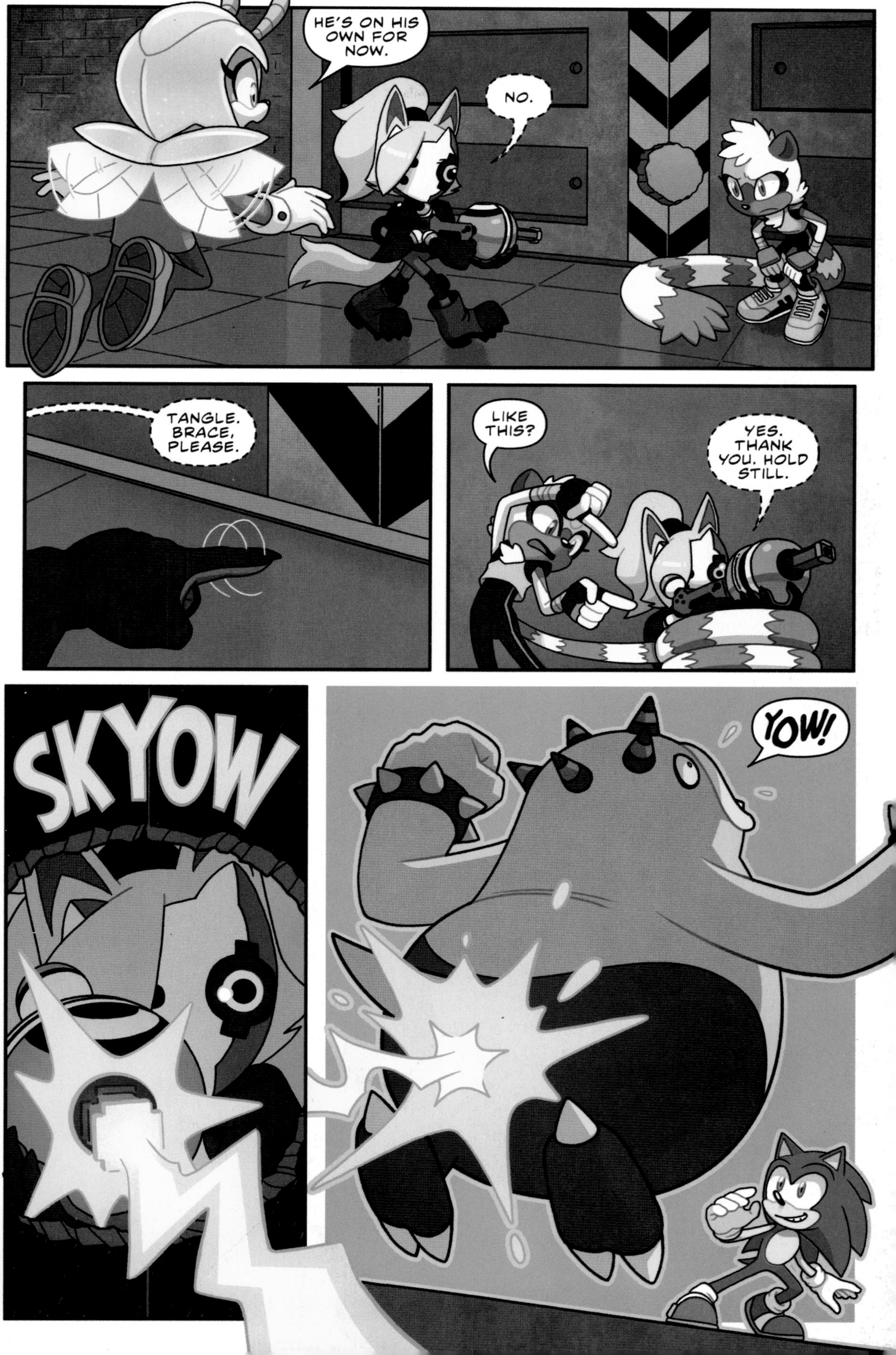

HE'S ON HIS OWN FOR NOW.
NO.
TANGLE. BRACE, PLEASE.
LIKE THIS?
YES. THANK YOU. HOLD STILL.
SKYOW
YOW!

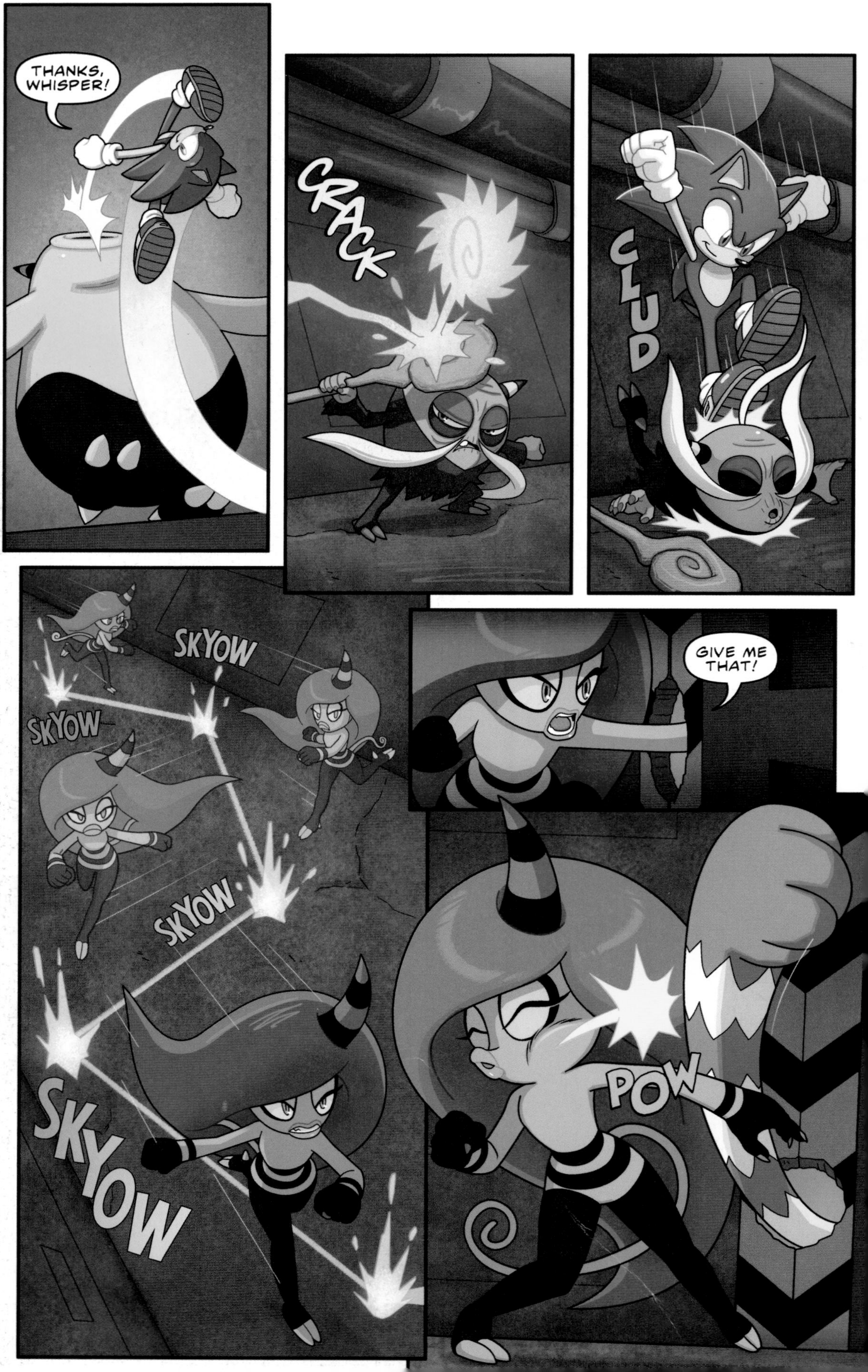
THANKS, WHISPER!
CRACK
CLUD
SKYOW
SKYOW
SKYOW
SKYOW
GIVE ME THAT!
POW

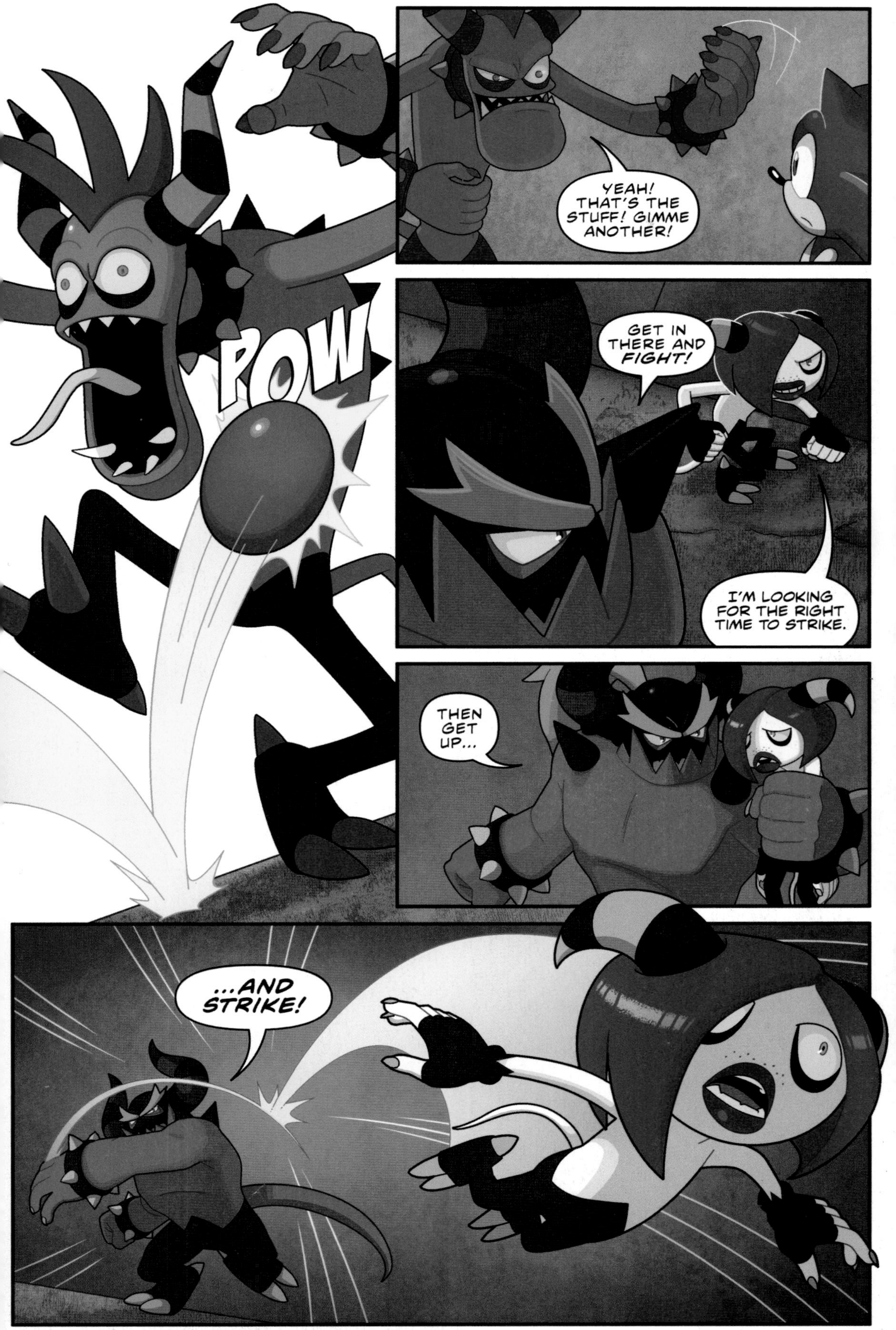
POW
YEAH! THAT'S THE STUFF! GIMME ANOTHER!
GET IN THERE AND FIGHT!
I'M LOOKING FOR THE RIGHT TIME TO STRIKE.
THEN GET UP...
...AND STRIKE!

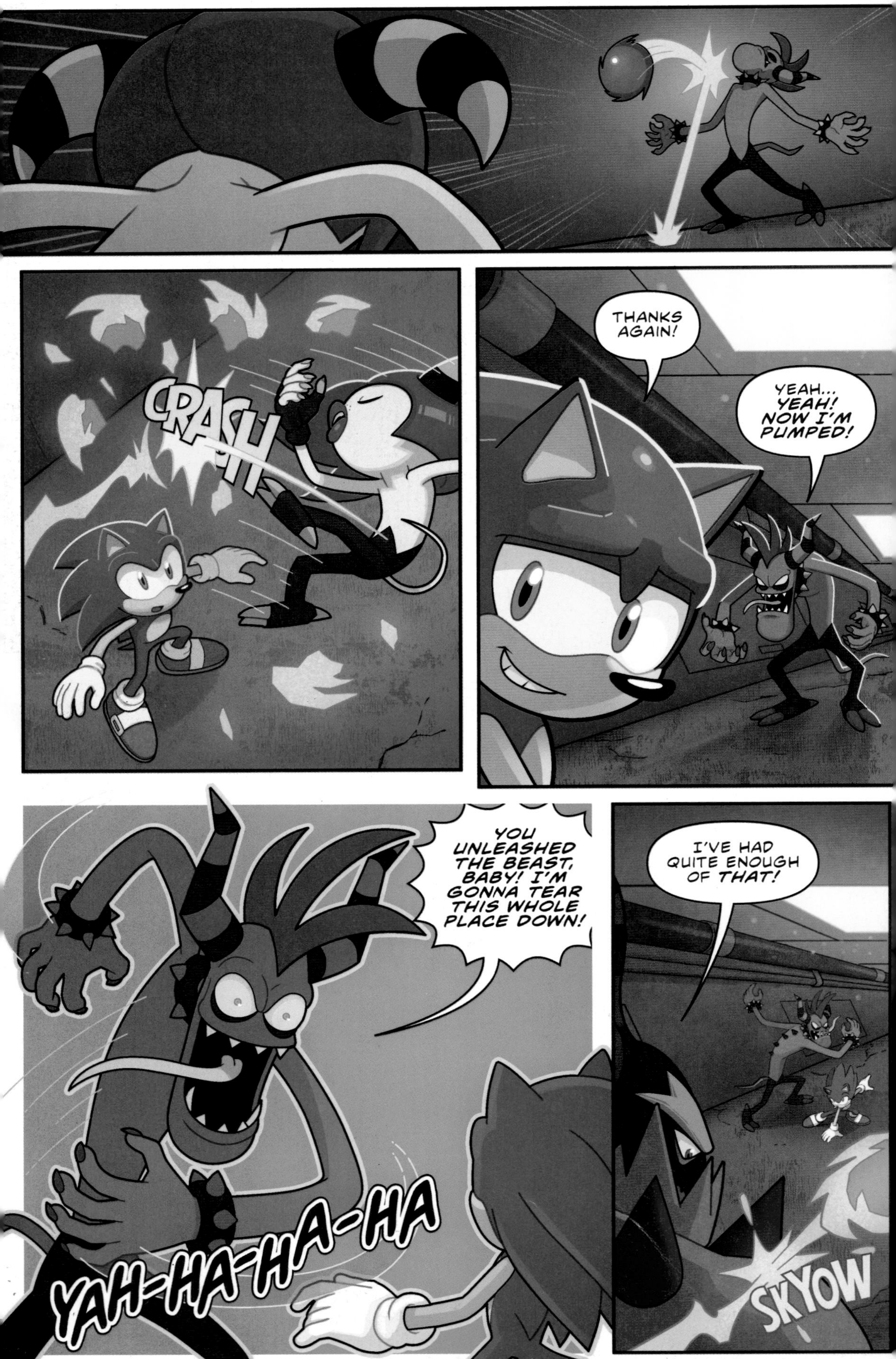
CRASH
THANKS AGAIN!
YEAH... YEAH! NOW I'M PUMPED!
YOU UNLEASHED THE BEAST, BABY! I'M GONNA TEAR THIS WHOLE PLACE DOWN!
YAH-HA-HA-HA
I'VE HAD QUITE ENOUGH OF THAT!
SKYOW

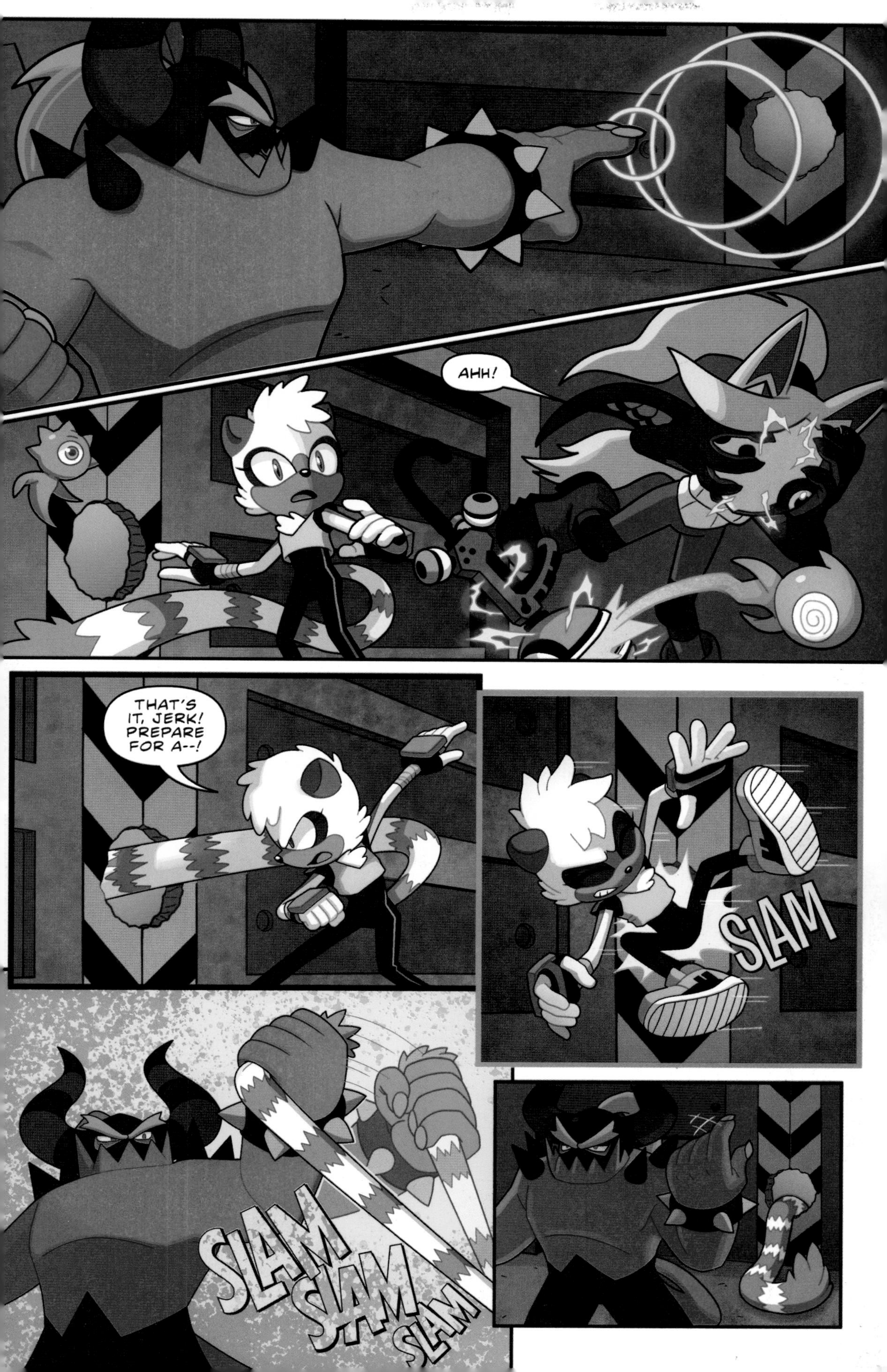

AHH!
THAT'S IT, JERK! PREPARE FOR A--!
SLAM
SLAM
SLAM
SLAM

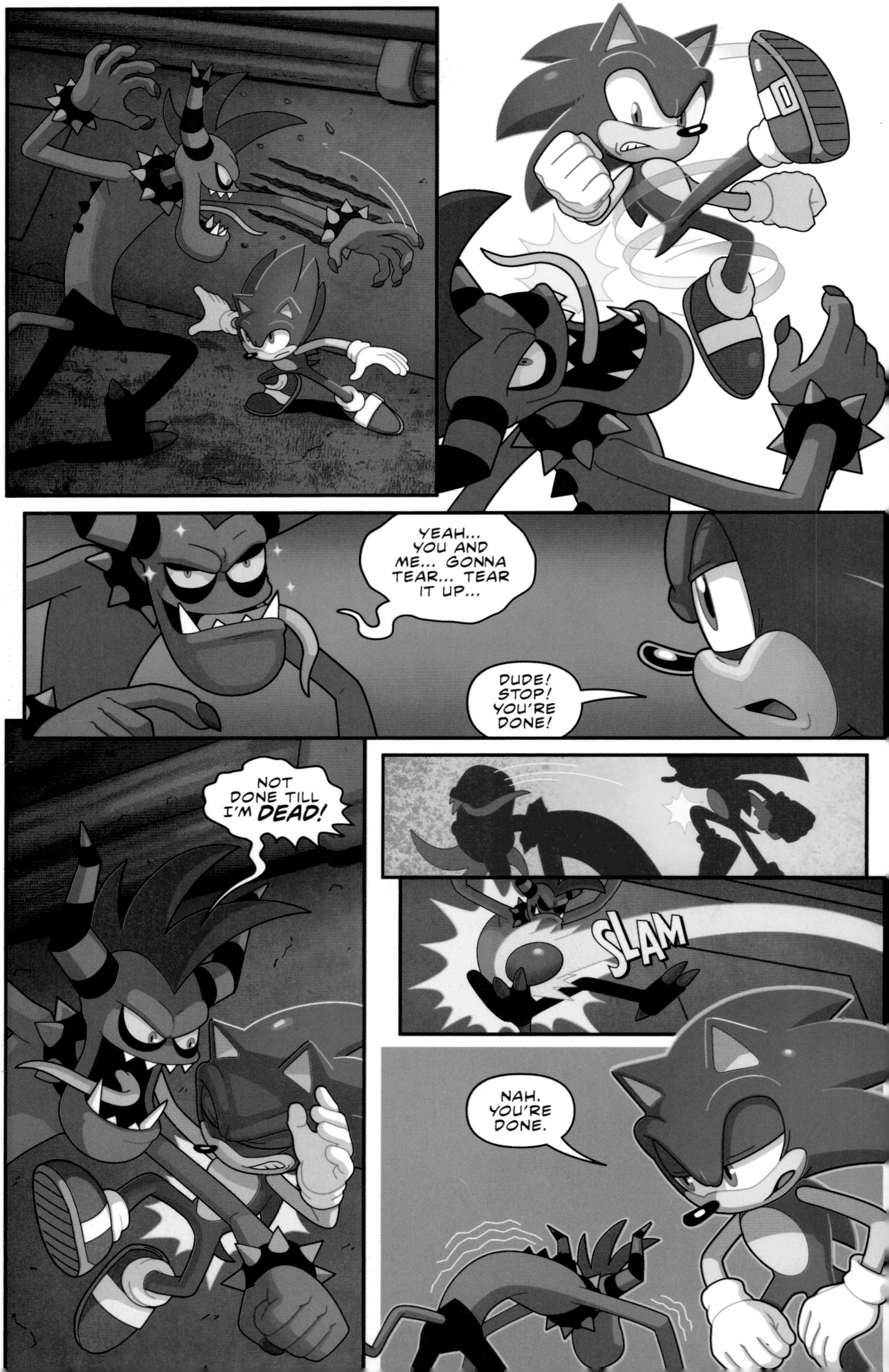
YEAH... YOU AND ME... GONNA TEAR... TEAR IT UP...
DUDE! STOP! YOU'RE DONE!
NOT DONE TILL I'M DEAD!
SLAM
NAH. YOU'RE DONE.

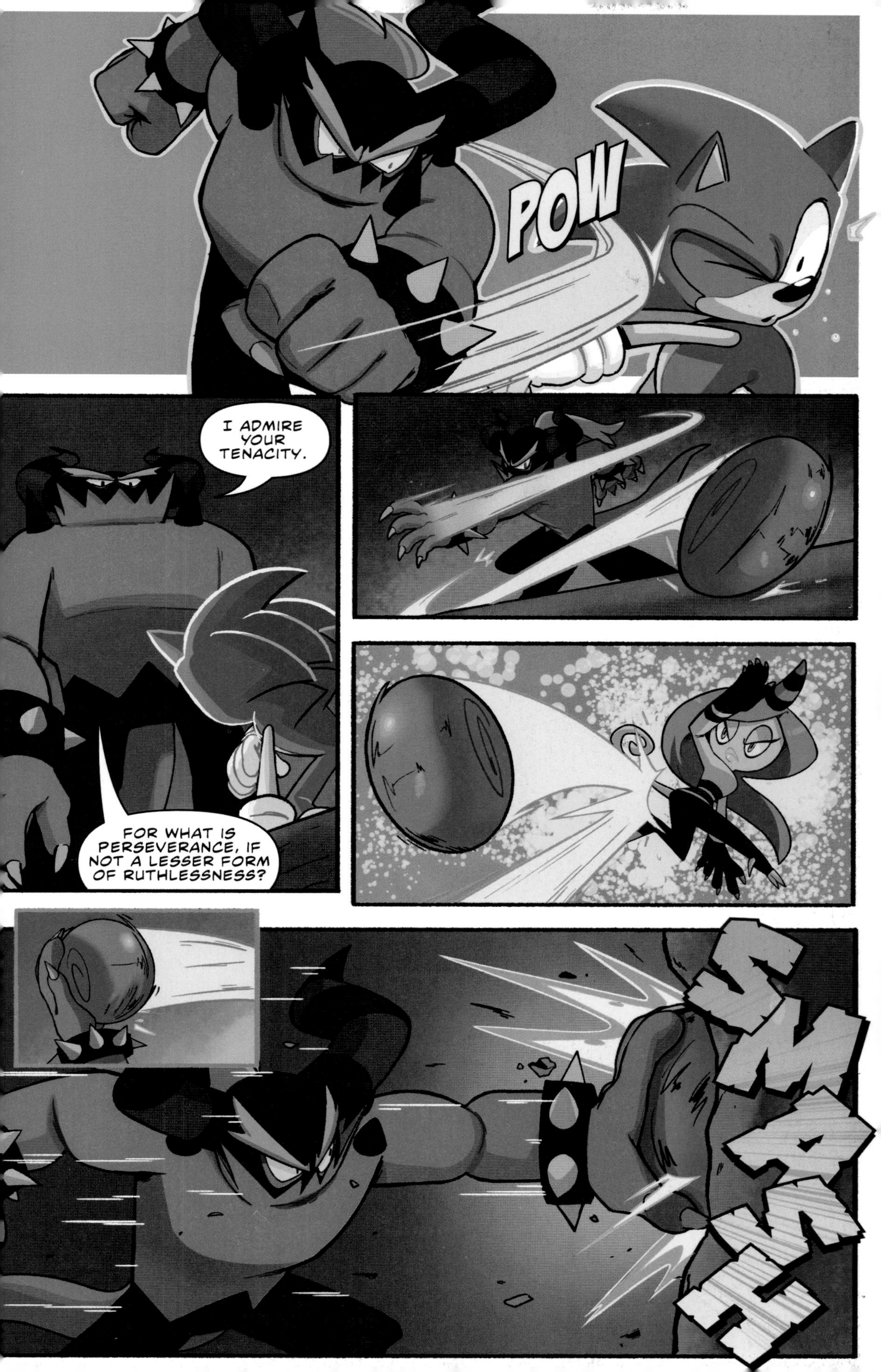
POW
I ADMIRE YOUR TENACITY.
FOR WHAT IS PERSEVERANCE, IF NOT A LESSER FORM OF RUTHLESSNESS?
SMASH

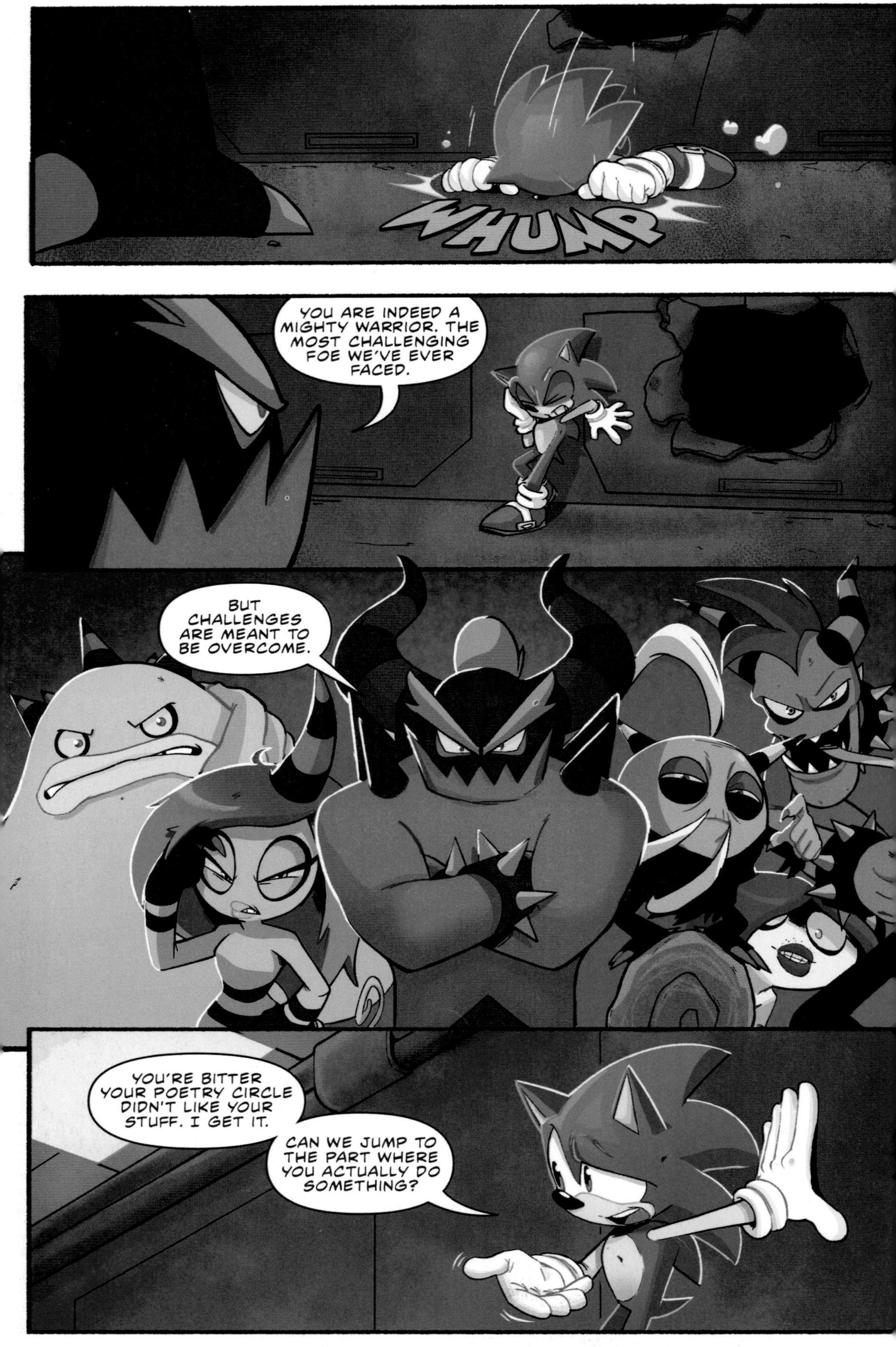

WHUMP
YOU ARE INDEED A MIGHTY WARRIOR. THE MOST CHALLENGING FOE WE'VE EVER FACED.
BUT CHALLENGES ARE MEANT TO BE OVERCOME.
YOU'RE BITTER YOUR POETRY CIRCLE DIDN'T LIKE YOUR STUFF. I GET IT.
CAN WE JUMP TO THE PART WHERE YOU ACTUALLY DO SOMETHING?

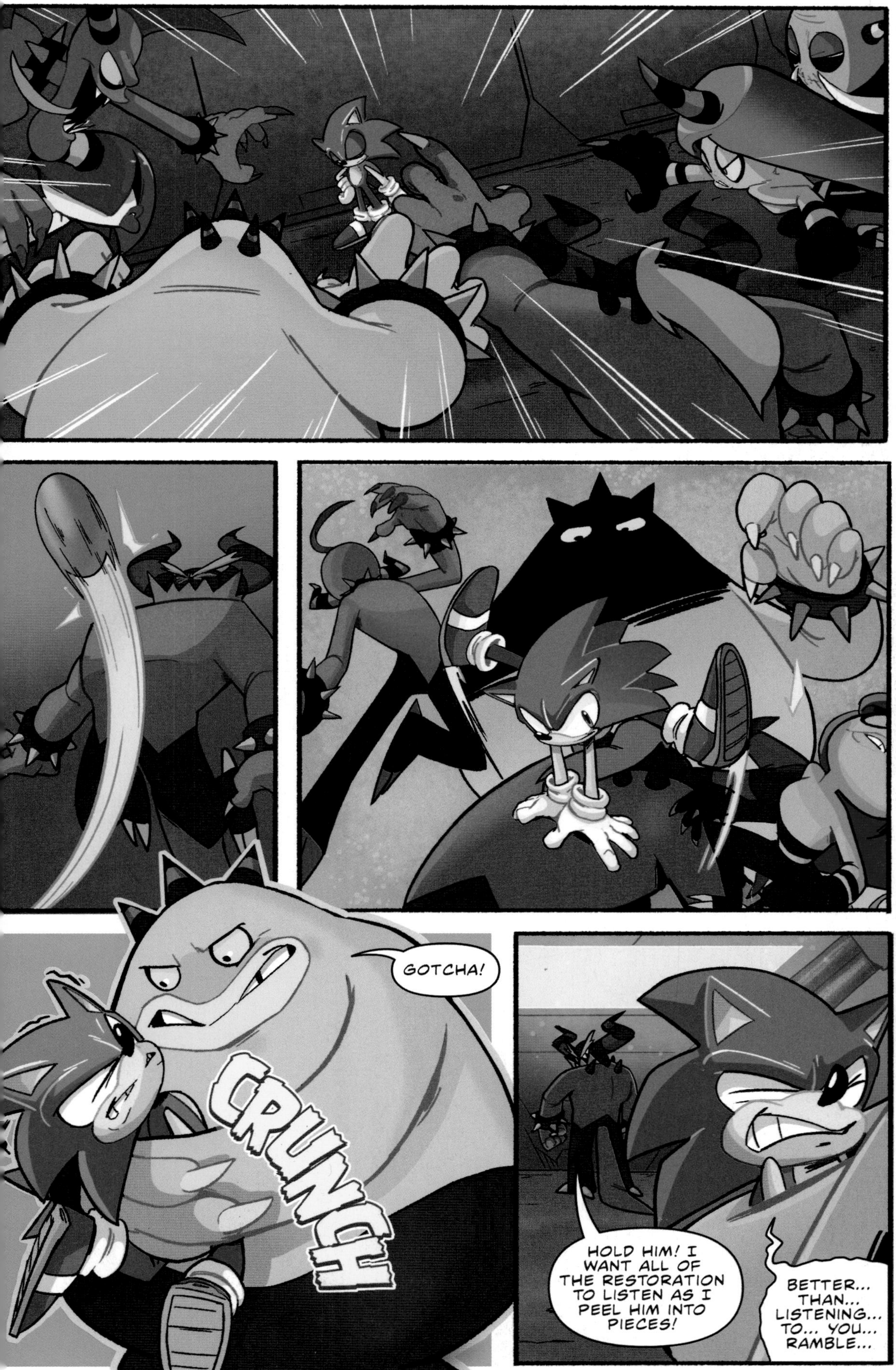
GOTCHA!
CRUNCH
HOLD HIM! I WANT ALL OF THE RESTORATION TO LISTEN AS I PEEL HIM INTO PIECES!
BETTER... THAN... LISTENING... TO... YOU... RAMBLE...

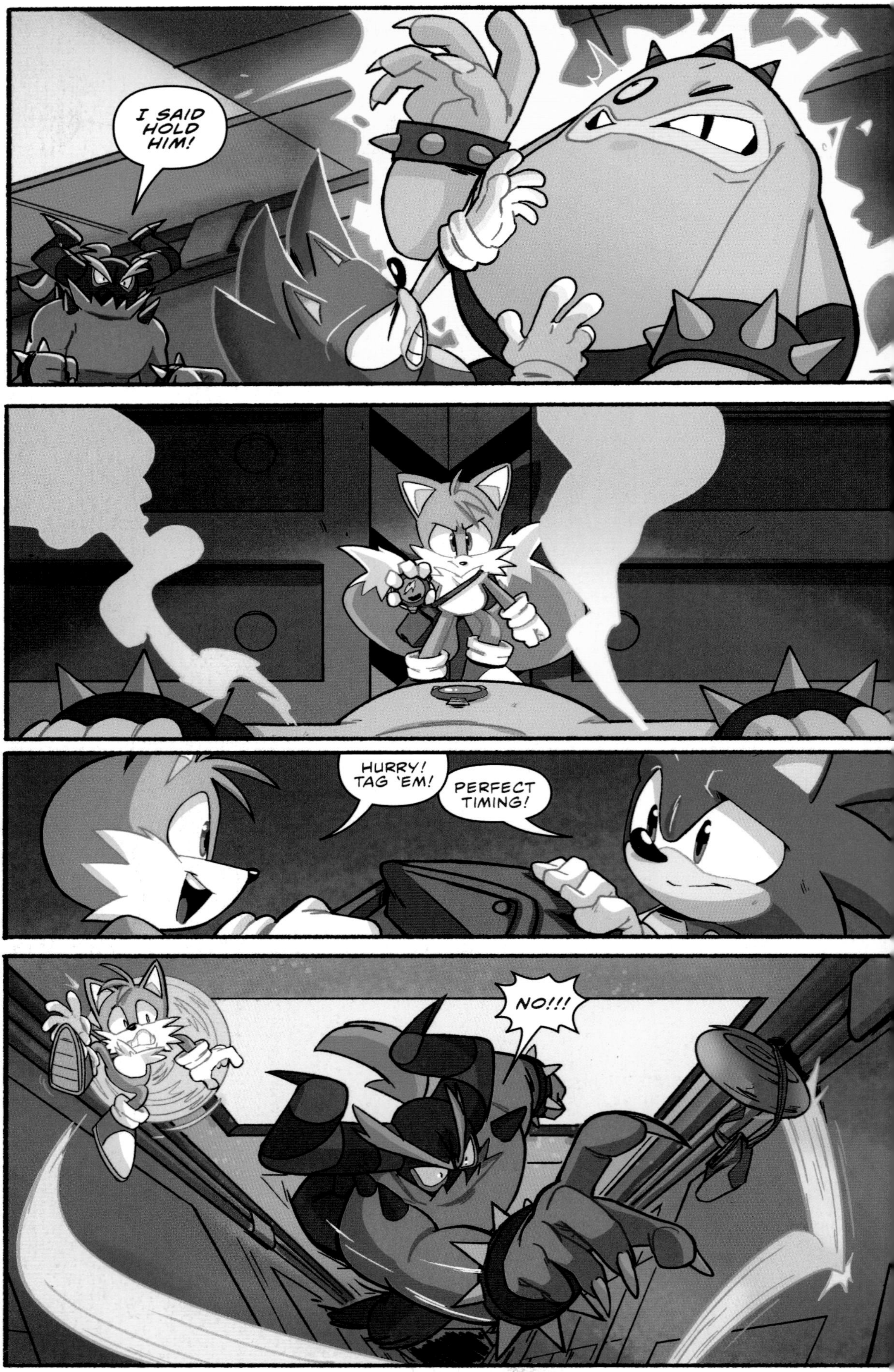
I SAID HOLD HIM!
HURRY! TAG 'EM!
PERFECT TIMING!
NO!!!

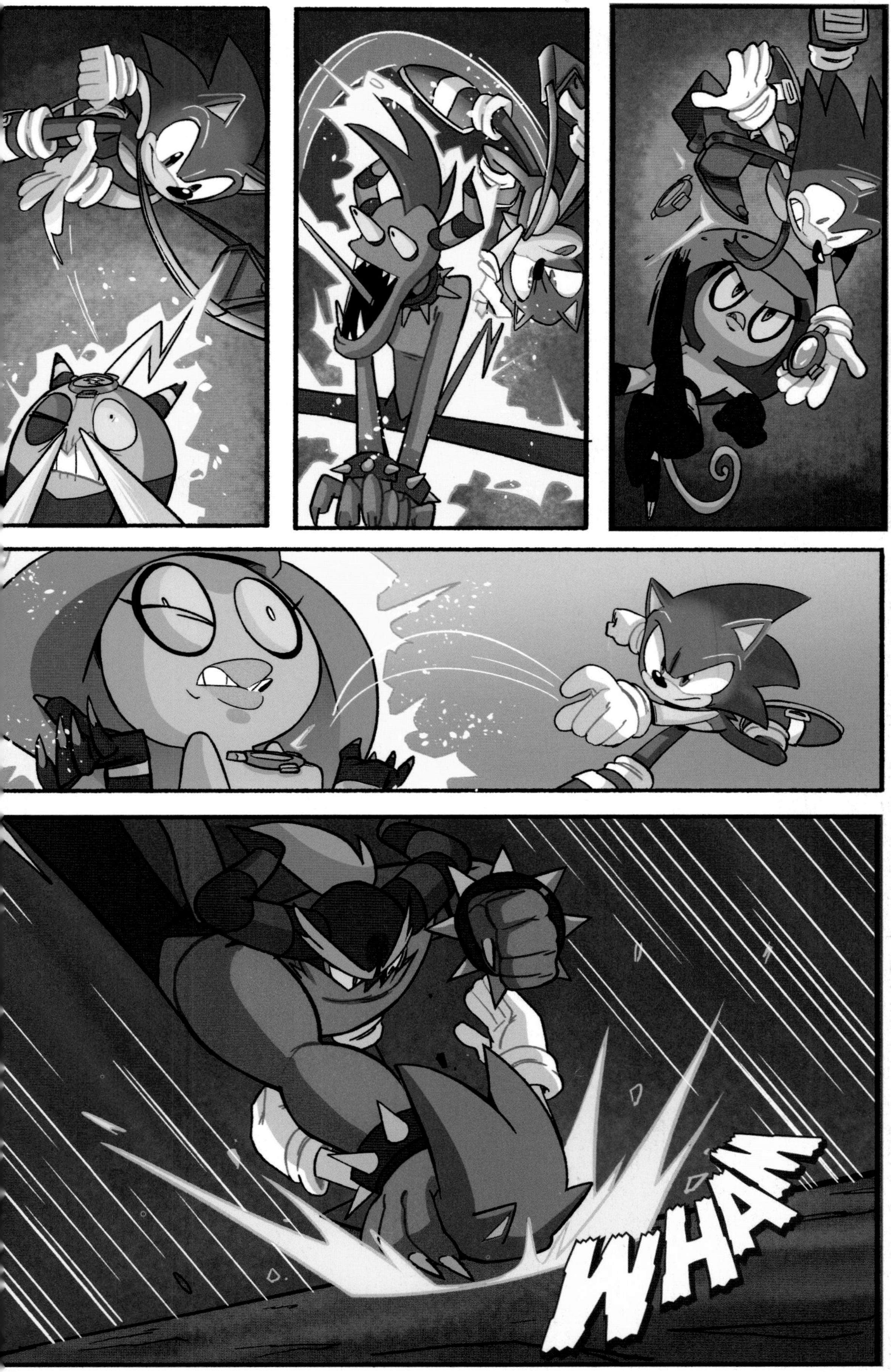
WHAM

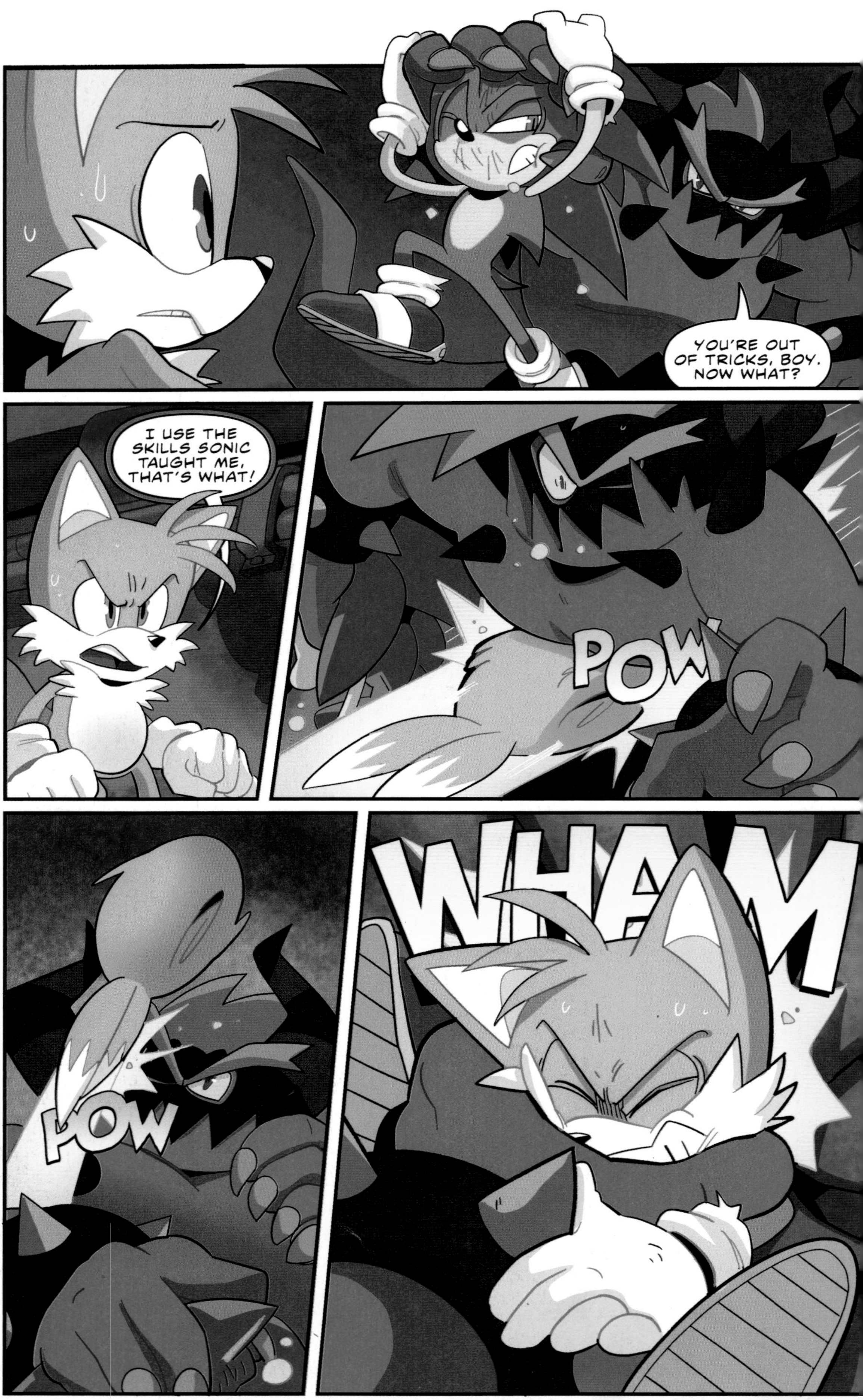
YOU'RE OUT OF TRICKS, BOY. NOW WHAT?
I USE THE SKILLS SONIC TAUGHT ME, THAT'S WHAT!
POW
POW
WHAM

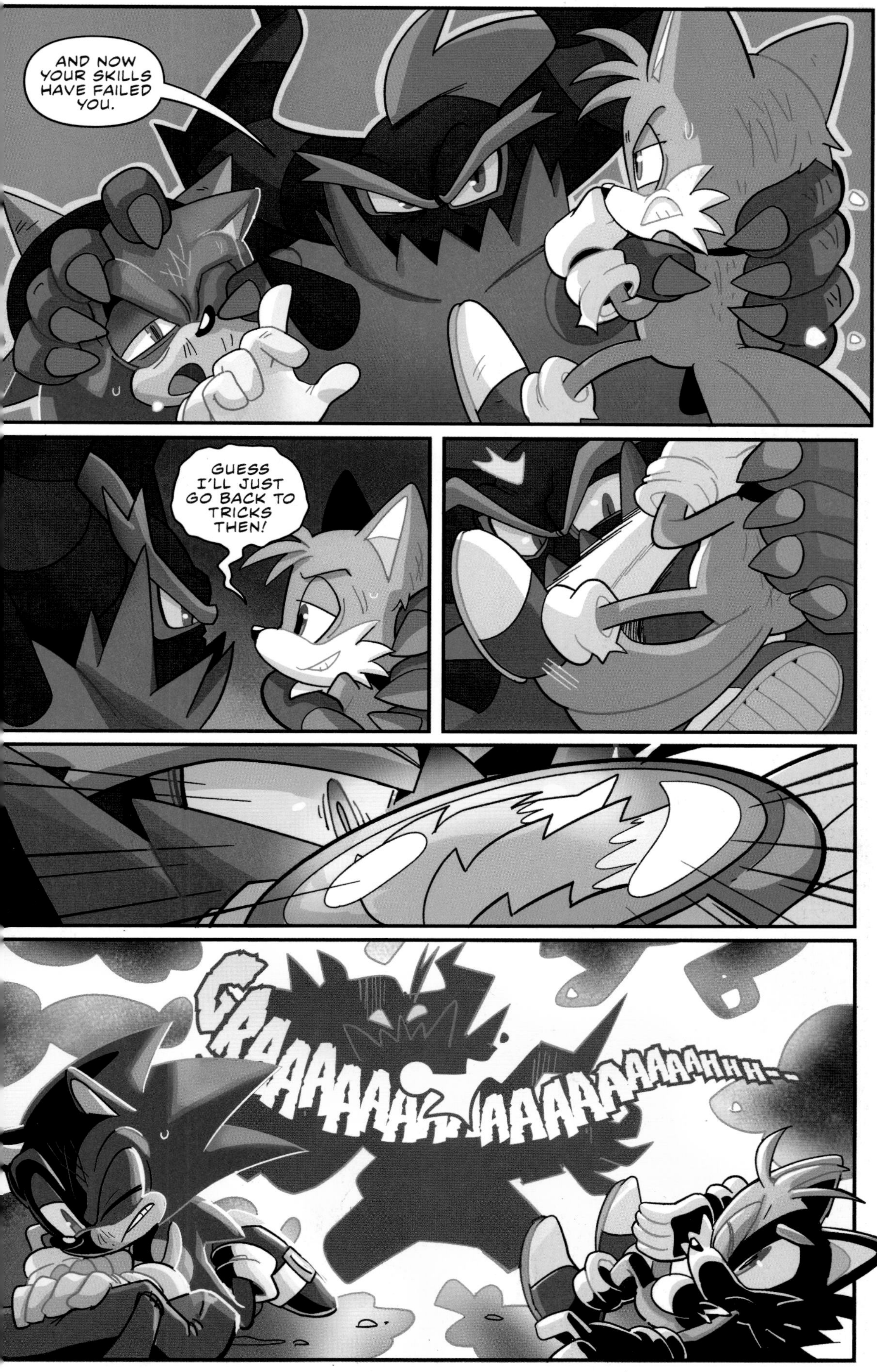
AND NOW YOUR SKILLS HAVE FAILED YOU.
GUESS I'LL JUST GO BACK TO TRICKS THEN!
GRAAAAAAAAAAAAAAAAAHHH--

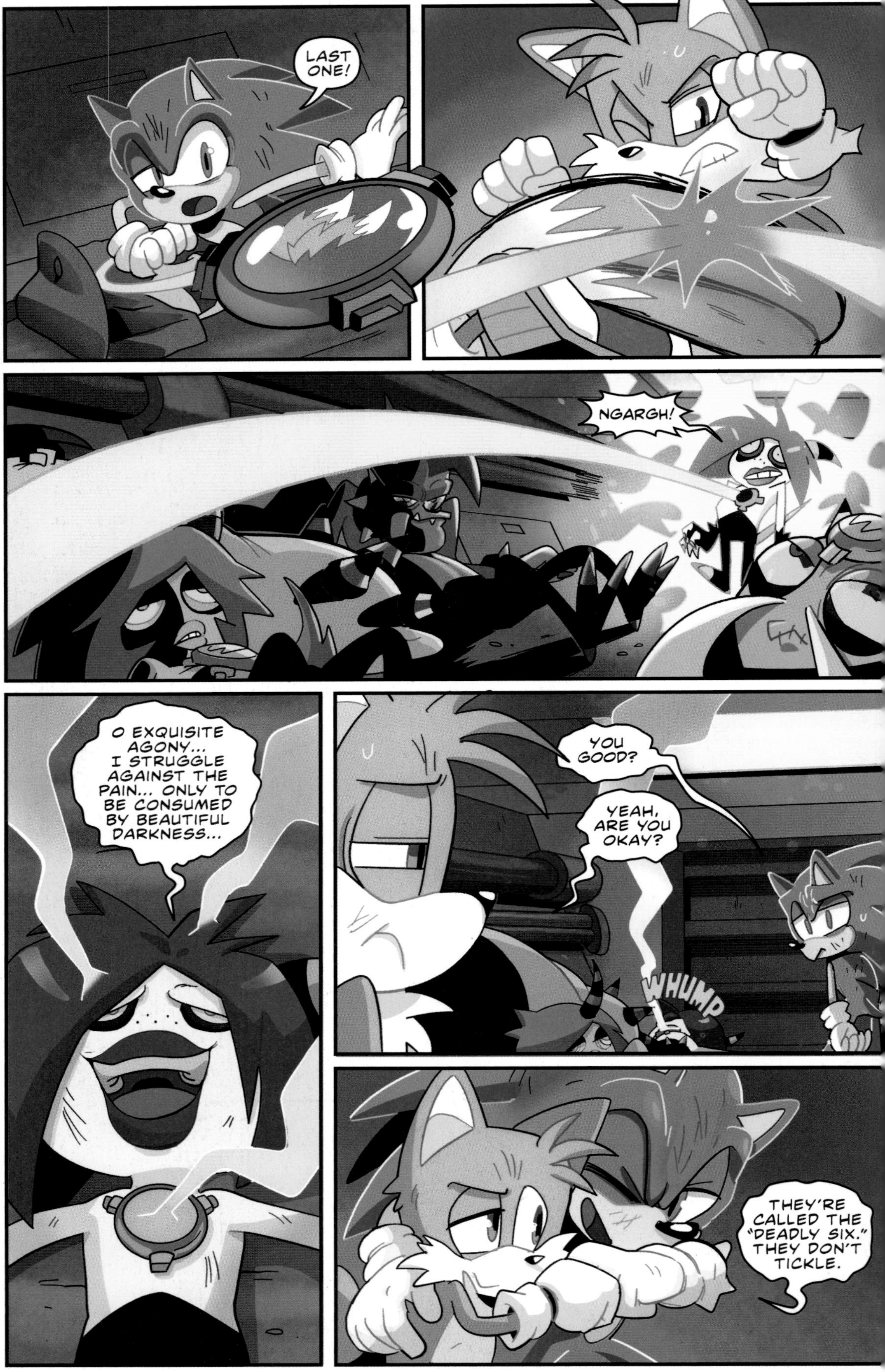
LAST ONE!
NGARGH!
O EXQUISITE AGONY... I STRUGGLE AGAINST THE PAIN... ONLY TO BE CONSUMED BY BEAUTIFUL DARKNESS...
YOU GOOD?
YEAH, ARE YOU OKAY?
WHUMP
THEY'RE CALLED THE "DEADLY SIX." THEY DON'T TICKLE.

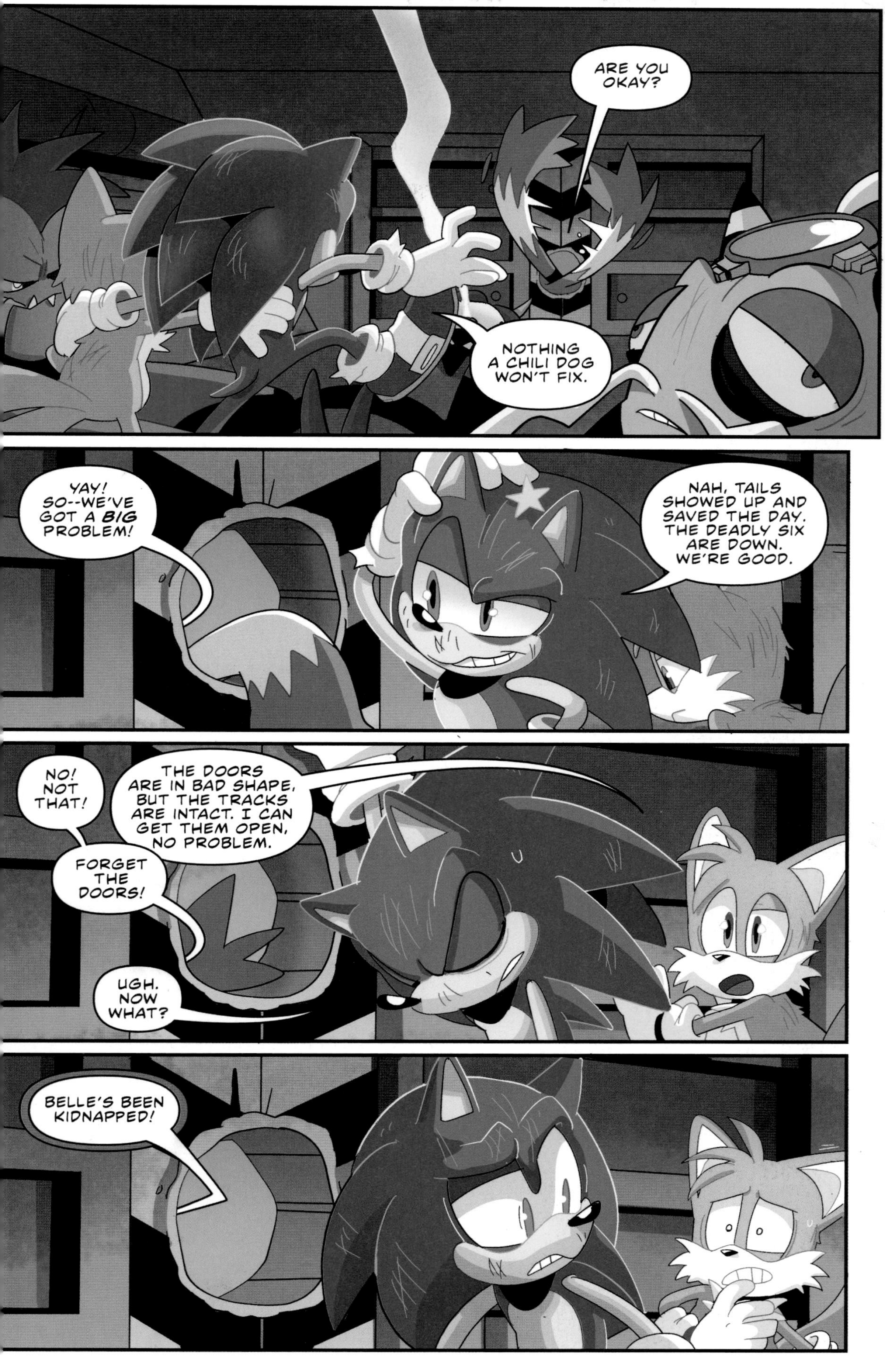
ARE YOU OKAY?
NOTHING A CHILI DOG WON'T FIX.
YAY! SO--WE'VE GOT A BIG PROBLEM!
NAH, TAILS SHOWED UP AND SAVED THE DAY. THE DEADLY SIX ARE DOWN. WE'RE GOOD.
NO! NOT THAT!
THE DOORS ARE IN BAD SHAPE, BUT THE TRACKS ARE INTACT. I CAN GET THEM OPEN, NO PROBLEM.
FORGET THE DOORS!
UGH. NOW WHAT?
BELLE'S BEEN KIDNAPPED!

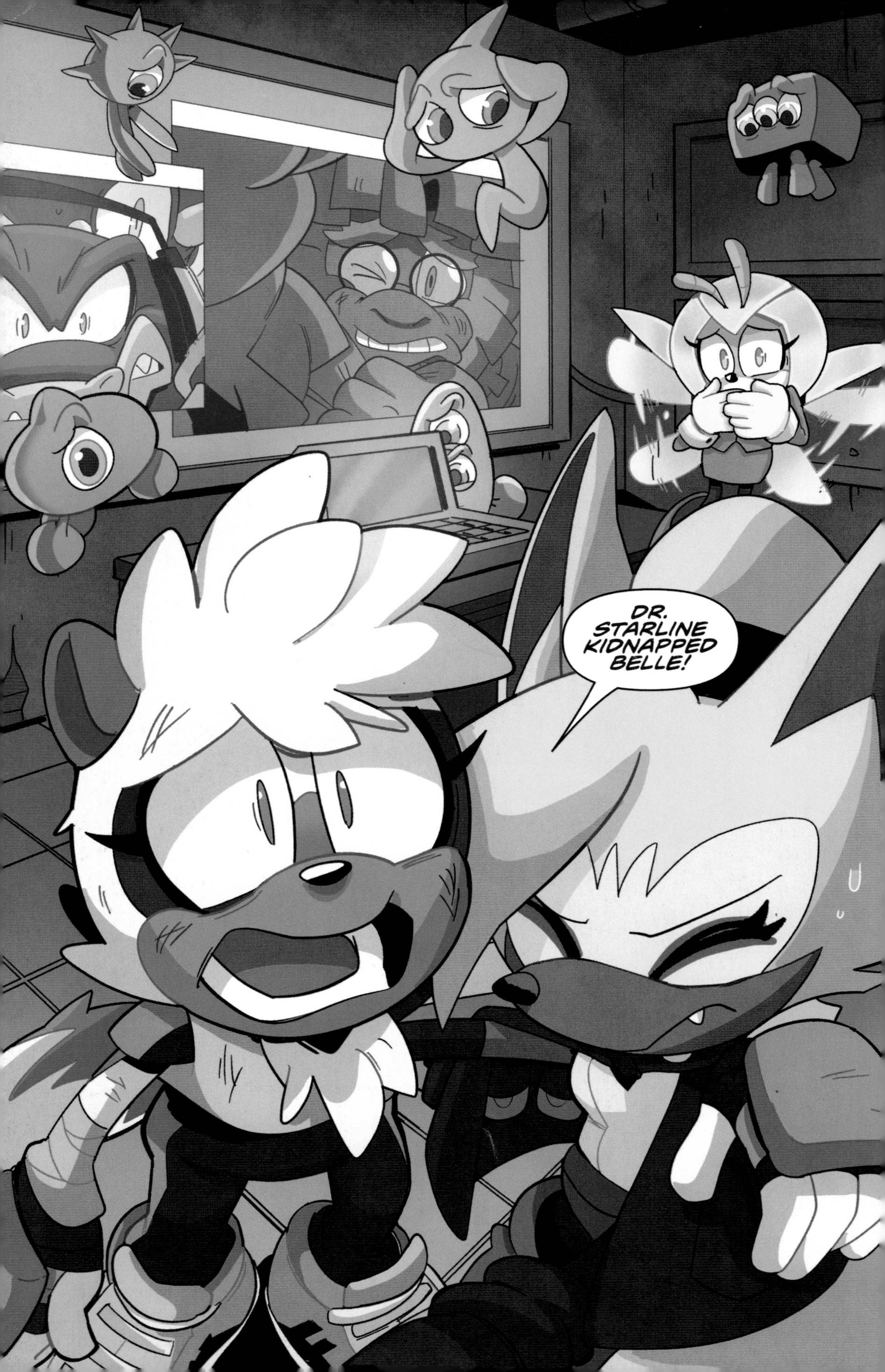
DR. STARLINE KIDNAPPED BELLE!

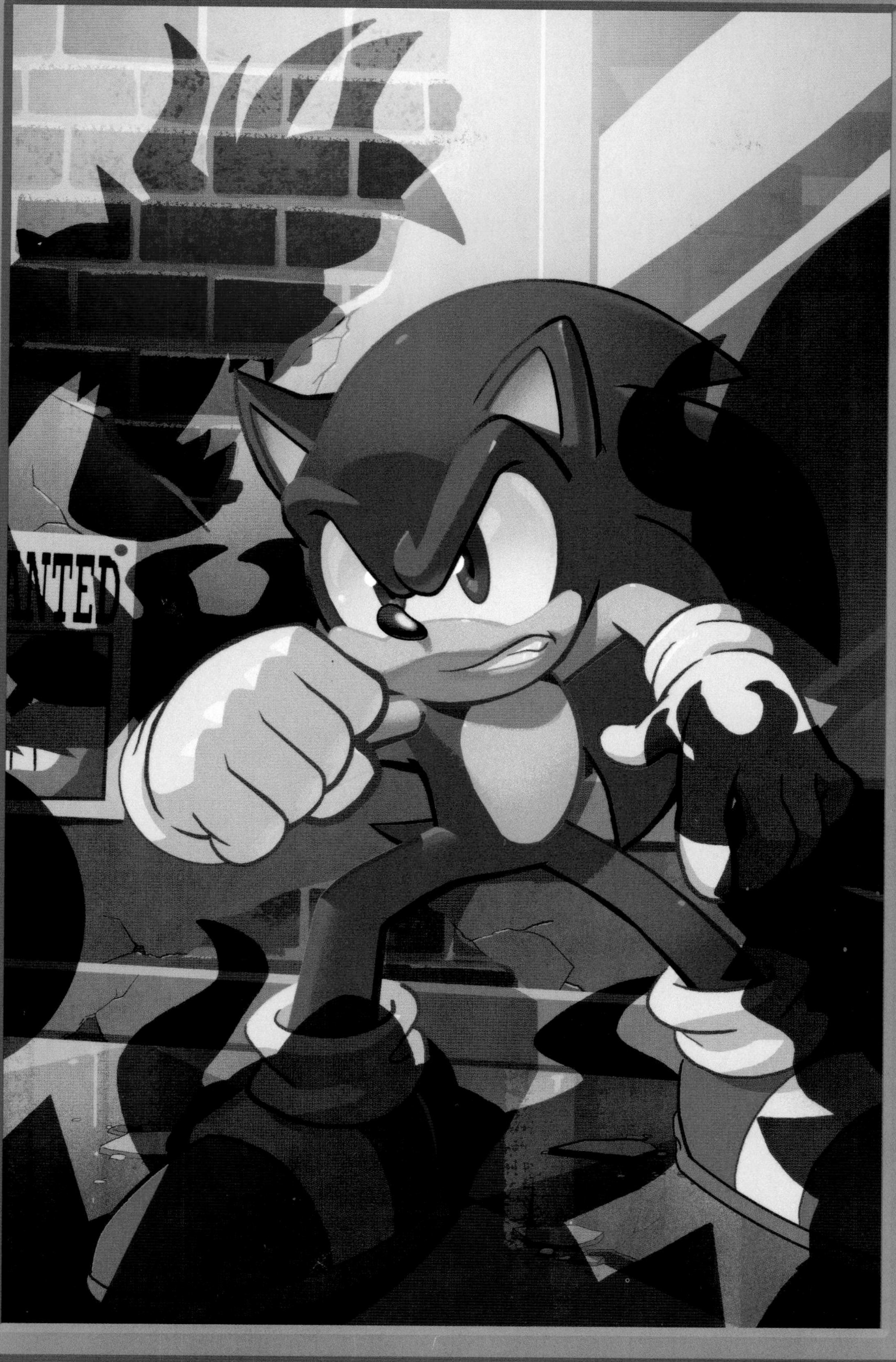
ANTED

ART BY **MATT HERMS**

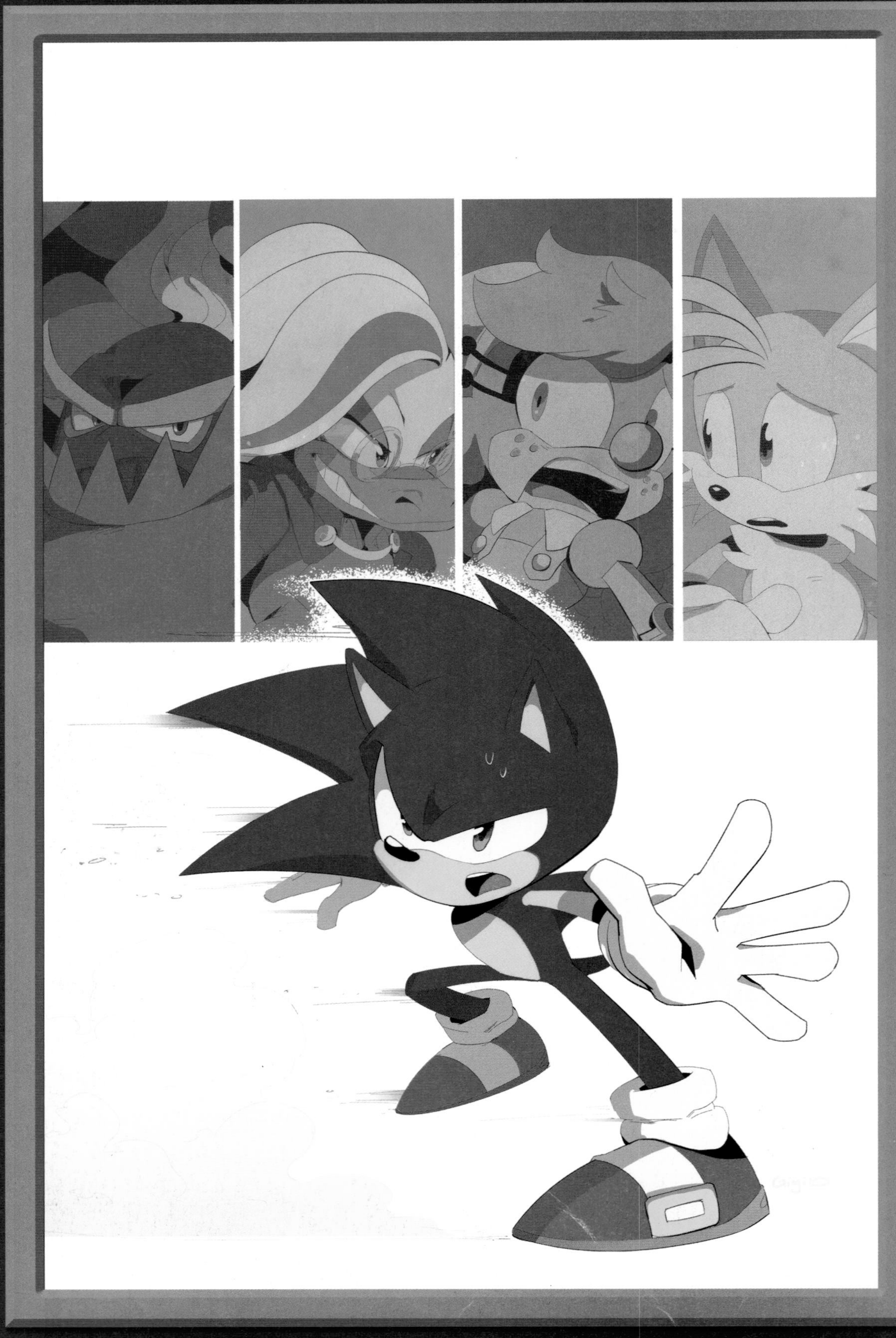

ART BY **GIGI DUTREIX**

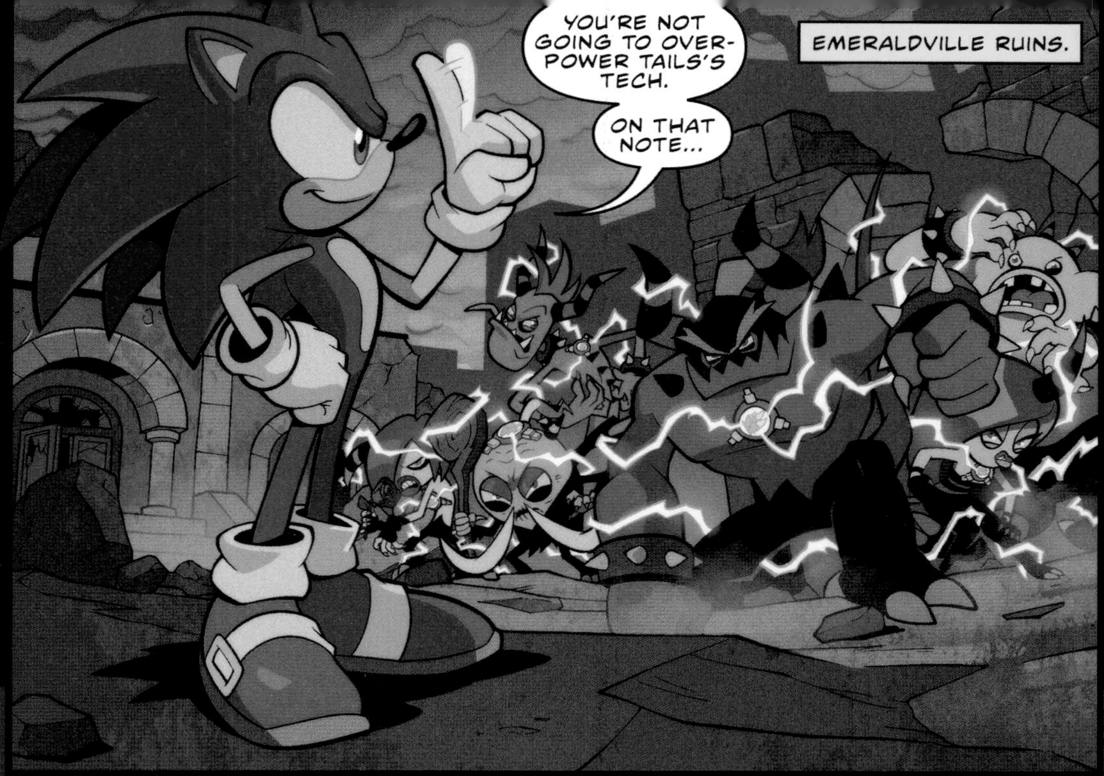
EMERALDVILLE RUINS.
YOU'RE NOT GOING TO OVER-POWER TAILS'S TECH.
ON THAT NOTE...

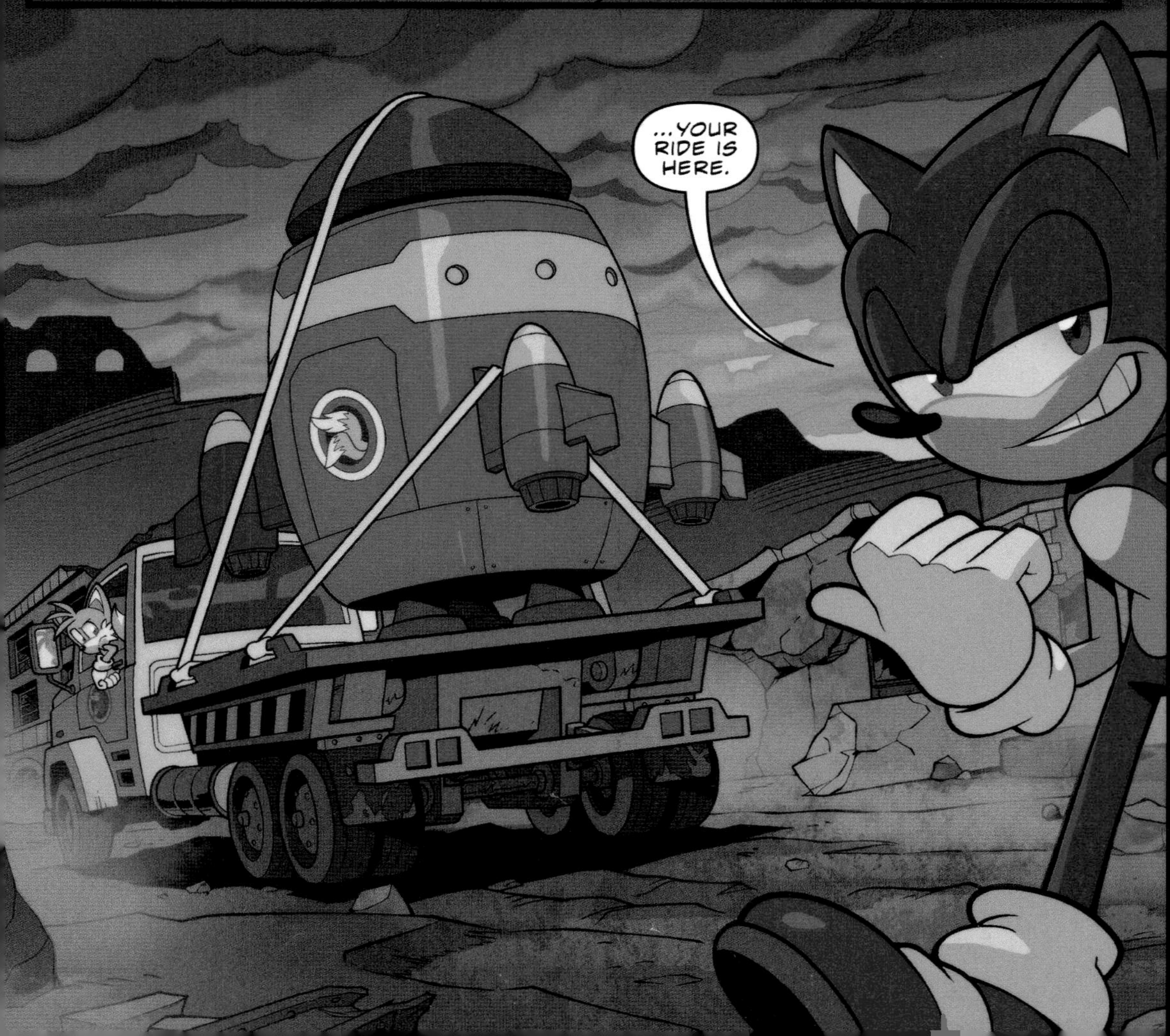
...YOUR RIDE IS HERE.

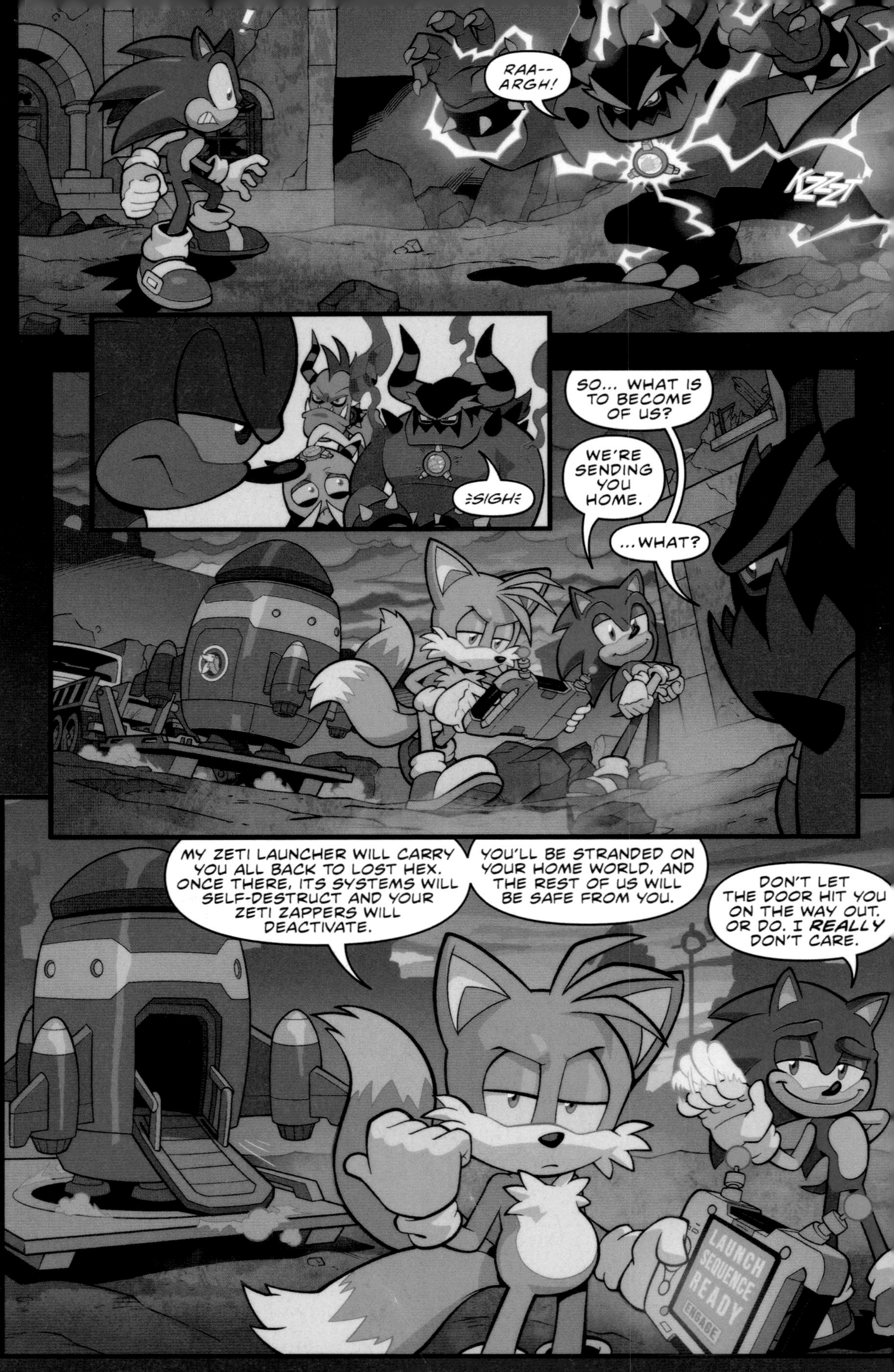
!
RAA--ARGH!
KZZZT
≷SIGH≶
SO... WHAT IS TO BECOME OF US?
WE'RE SENDING YOU HOME.
...WHAT?
MY ZETI LAUNCHER WILL CARRY YOU ALL BACK TO LOST HEX. ONCE THERE, ITS SYSTEMS WILL SELF-DESTRUCT AND YOUR ZETI ZAPPERS WILL DEACTIVATE.
YOU'LL BE STRANDED ON YOUR HOME WORLD, AND THE REST OF US WILL BE SAFE FROM YOU.
DON'T LET THE DOOR HIT YOU ON THE WAY OUT. OR DO. I REALLY DON'T CARE.
LAUNCH SEQUENCE READY
ENGAGE

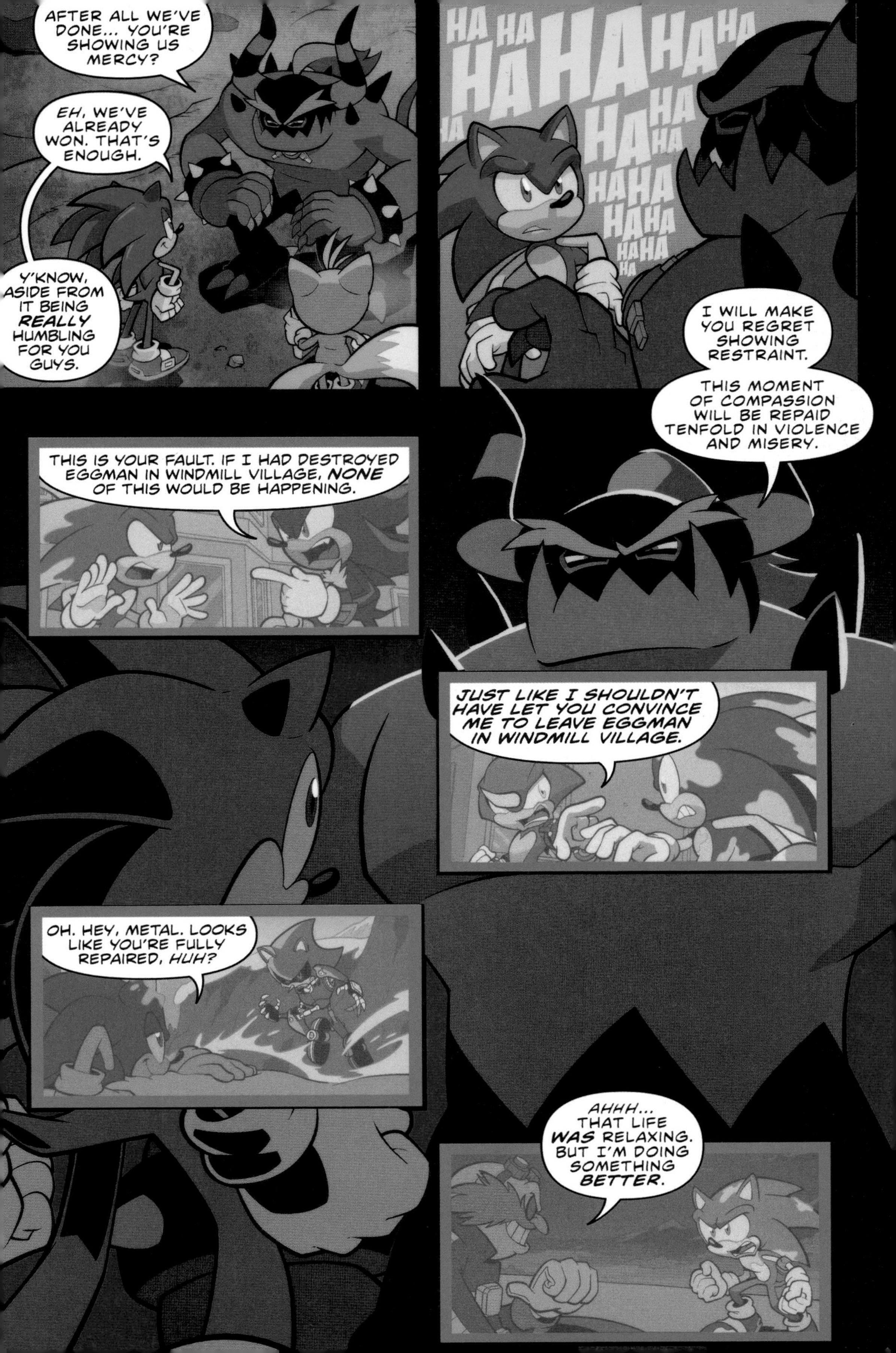
AFTER ALL WE'VE DONE... YOU'RE SHOWING US MERCY?
EH, WE'VE ALREADY WON. THAT'S ENOUGH.
Y'KNOW, ASIDE FROM IT BEING REALLY HUMBLING FOR YOU GUYS.
HA HA HAHAHAHA HA HAHA HA HA HAHA HAHA HAHA
I WILL MAKE YOU REGRET SHOWING RESTRAINT.
THIS MOMENT OF COMPASSION WILL BE REPAID TENFOLD IN VIOLENCE AND MISERY.
THIS IS YOUR FAULT. IF I HAD DESTROYED EGGMAN IN WINDMILL VILLAGE, NONE OF THIS WOULD BE HAPPENING.
JUST LIKE I SHOULDN'T HAVE LET YOU CONVINCE ME TO LEAVE EGGMAN IN WINDMILL VILLAGE.
OH. HEY, METAL. LOOKS LIKE YOU'RE FULLY REPAIRED, HUH?
AHHH... THAT LIFE WAS RELAXING. BUT I'M DOING SOMETHING BETTER.

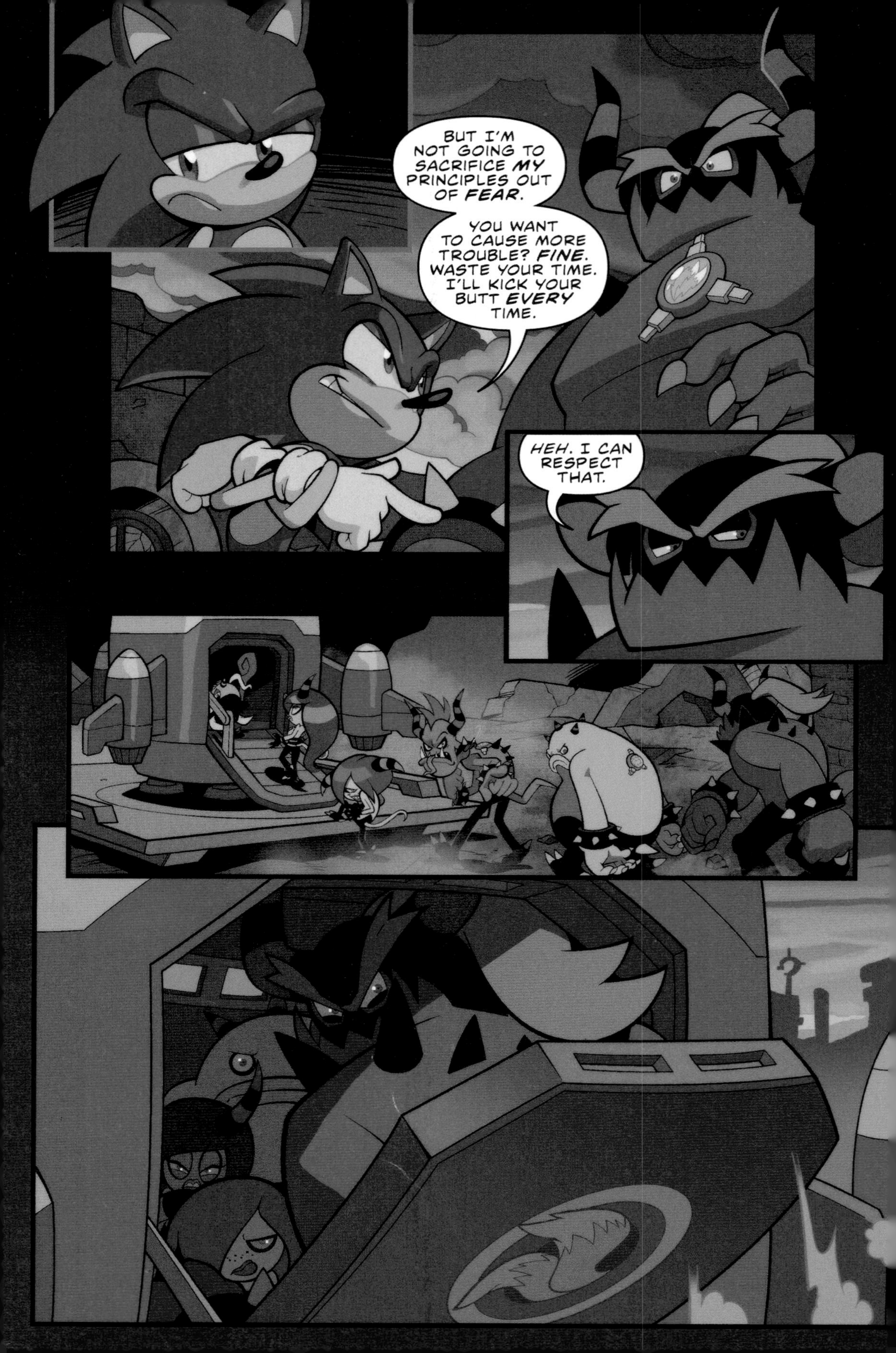

BUT I'M NOT GOING TO SACRIFICE MY PRINCIPLES OUT OF FEAR.
YOU WANT TO CAUSE MORE TROUBLE? FINE. WASTE YOUR TIME. I'LL KICK YOUR BUTT EVERY TIME.
HEH. I CAN RESPECT THAT.

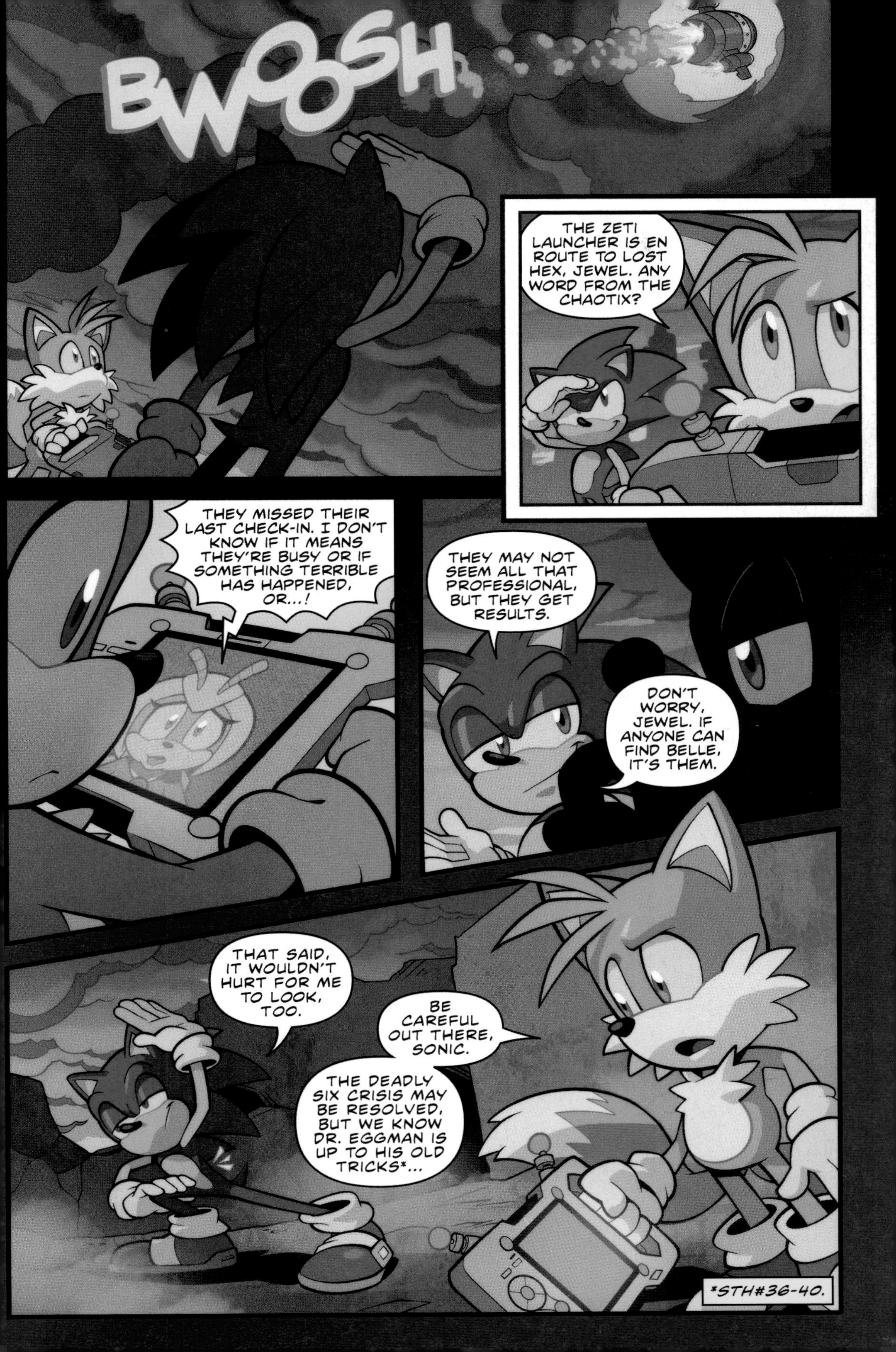
BWOOSH
THE ZETI LAUNCHER IS EN ROUTE TO LOST HEX, JEWEL. ANY WORD FROM THE CHAOTIX?
THEY MISSED THEIR LAST CHECK-IN. I DON'T KNOW IF IT MEANS THEY'RE BUSY OR IF SOMETHING TERRIBLE HAS HAPPENED, OR...!
THEY MAY NOT SEEM ALL THAT PROFESSIONAL, BUT THEY GET RESULTS.
DON'T WORRY, JEWEL. IF ANYONE CAN FIND BELLE, IT'S THEM.
THAT SAID, IT WOULDN'T HURT FOR ME TO LOOK, TOO.
BE CAREFUL OUT THERE, SONIC.
THE DEADLY SIX CRISIS MAY BE RESOLVED, BUT WE KNOW DR. EGGMAN IS UP TO HIS OLD TRICKS*...
*STH#36-40.

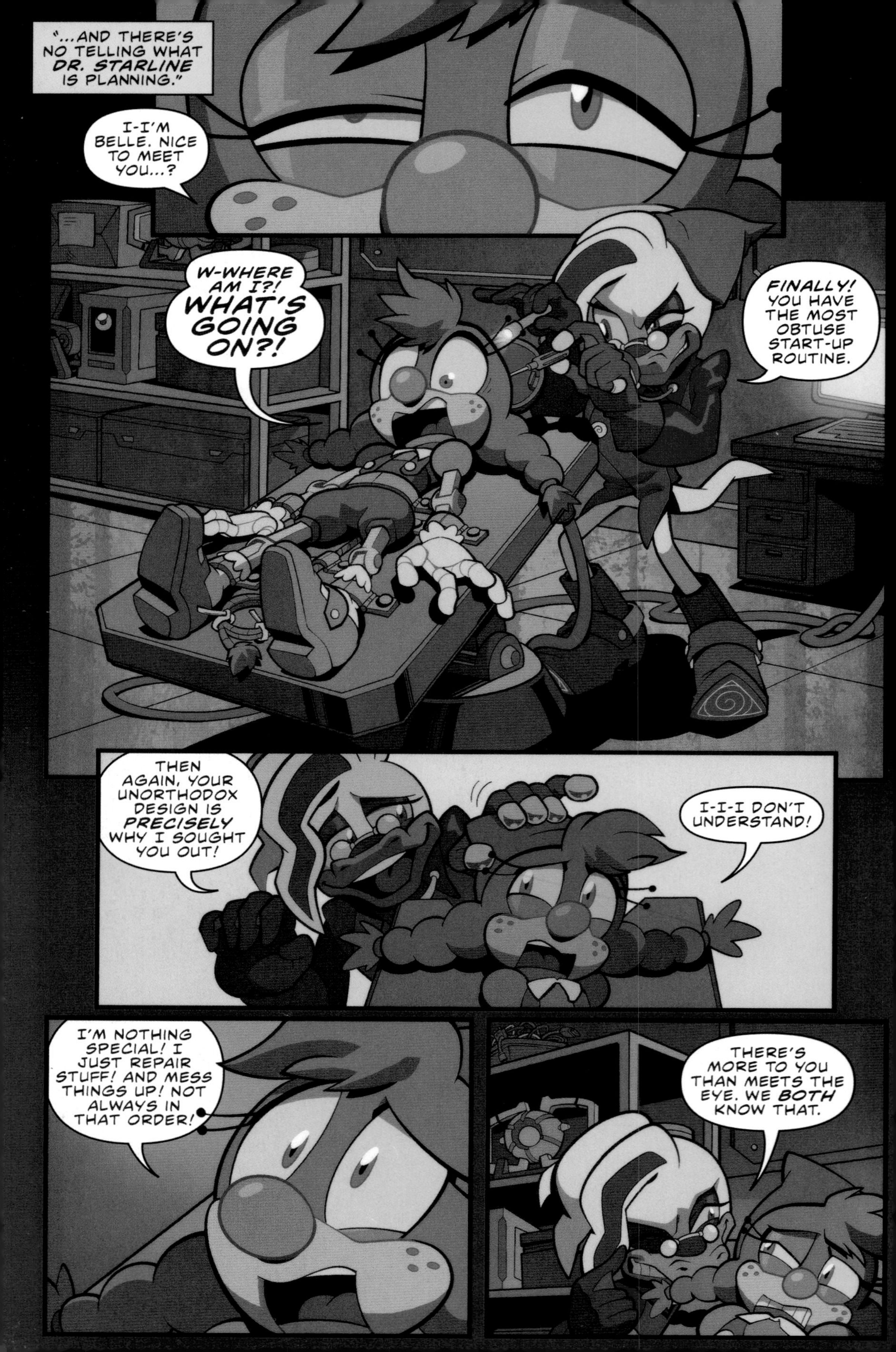

"...AND THERE'S NO TELLING WHAT DR. STARLINE IS PLANNING."
I-I'M BELLE. NICE TO MEET YOU...?
W-WHERE AM I?! WHAT'S GOING ON?!
FINALLY! YOU HAVE THE MOST OBTUSE START-UP ROUTINE.
THEN AGAIN, YOUR UNORTHODOX DESIGN IS PRECISELY WHY I SOUGHT YOU OUT!
I-I-I DON'T UNDERSTAND!
I'M NOTHING SPECIAL! I JUST REPAIR STUFF! AND MESS THINGS UP! NOT ALWAYS IN THAT ORDER!
THERE'S MORE TO YOU THAN MEETS THE EYE. WE BOTH KNOW THAT.

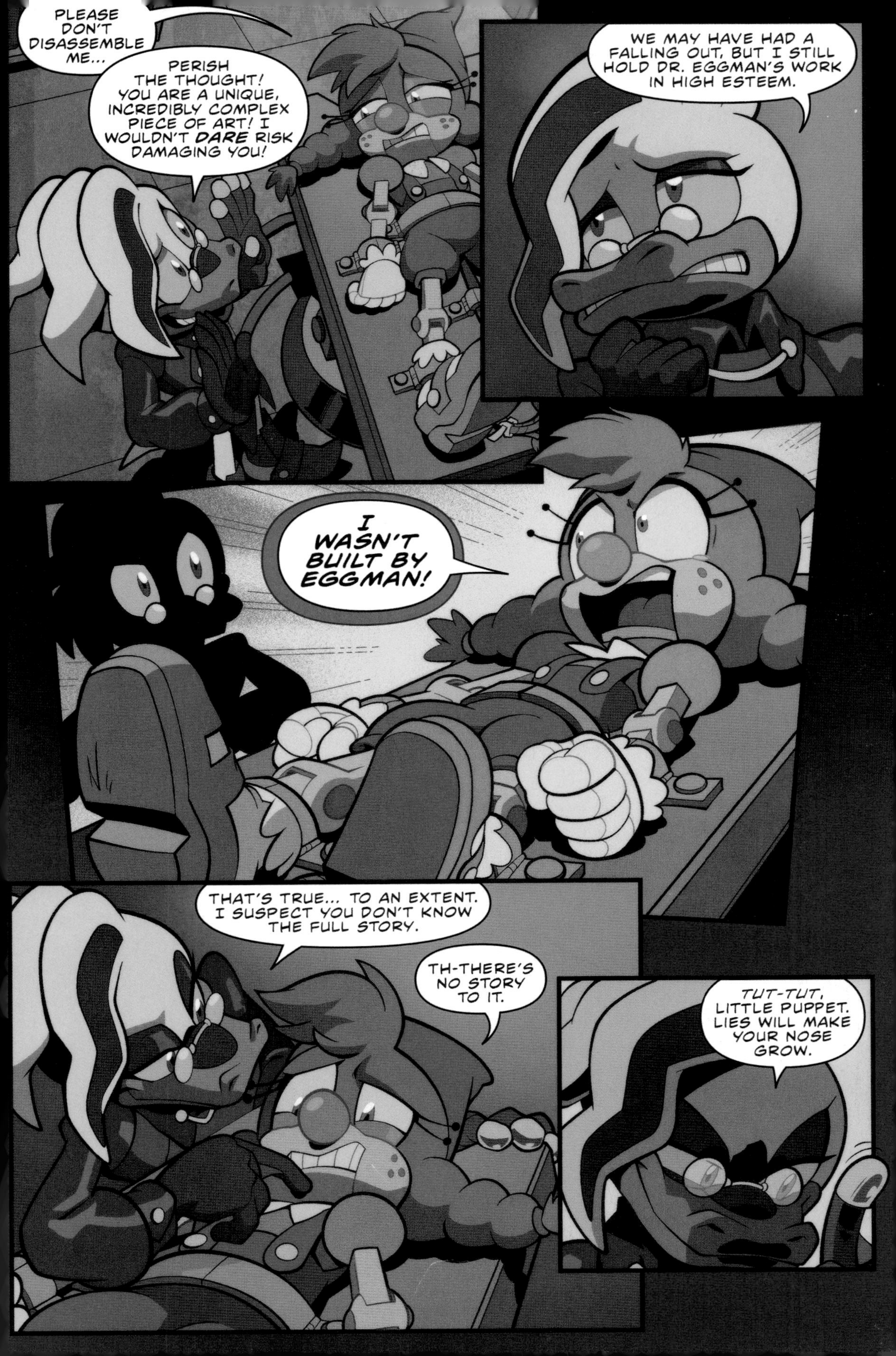
PLEASE DON'T DISASSEMBLE ME...
PERISH THE THOUGHT! YOU ARE A UNIQUE, INCREDIBLY COMPLEX PIECE OF ART! I WOULDN'T DARE RISK DAMAGING YOU!
WE MAY HAVE HAD A FALLING OUT, BUT I STILL HOLD DR. EGGMAN'S WORK IN HIGH ESTEEM.
I WASN'T BUILT BY EGGMAN!
THAT'S TRUE... TO AN EXTENT. I SUSPECT YOU DON'T KNOW THE FULL STORY.
TH-THERE'S NO STORY TO IT.
TUT-TUT, LITTLE PUPPET. LIES WILL MAKE YOUR NOSE GROW.

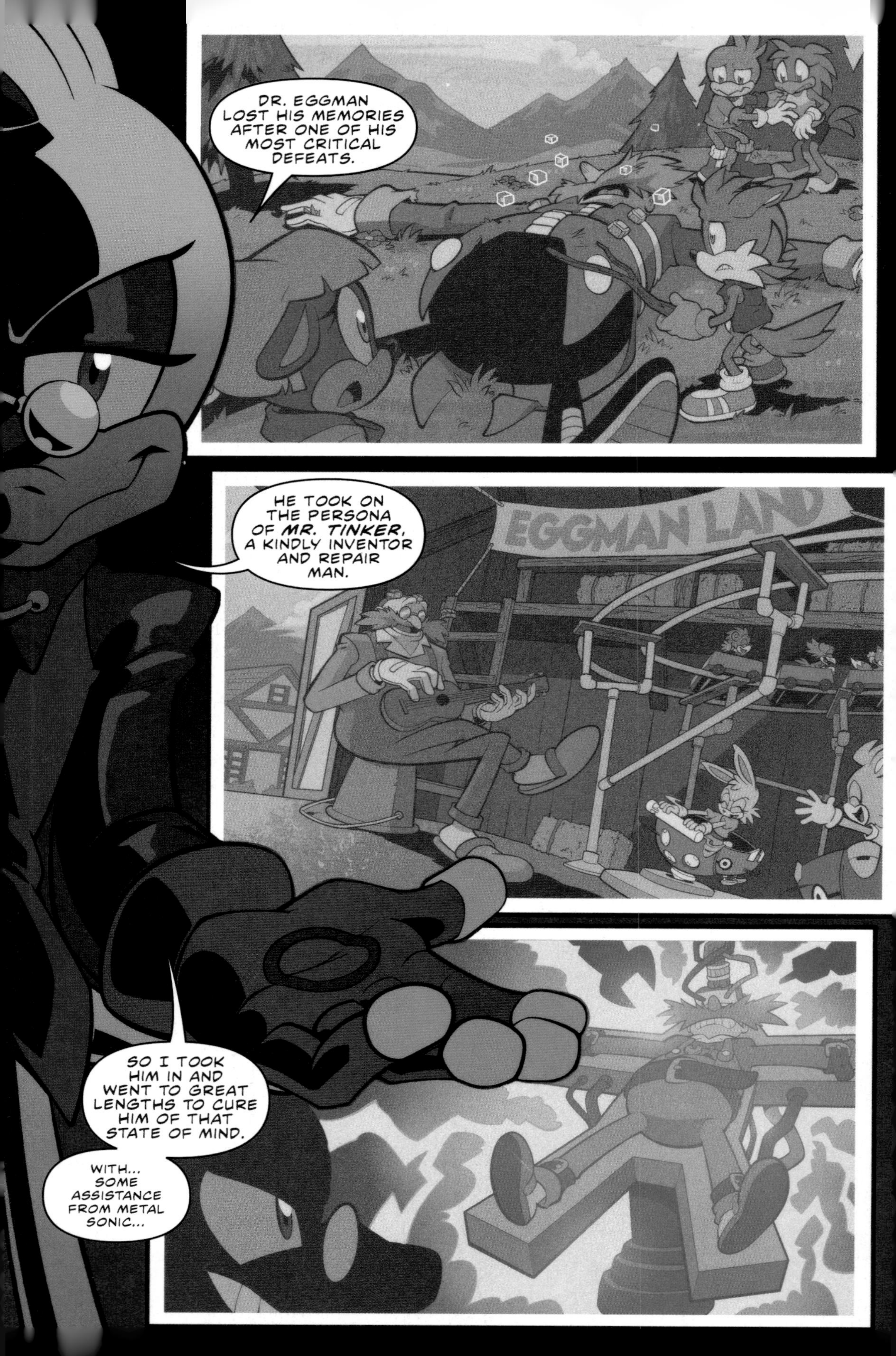
DR. EGGMAN LOST HIS MEMORIES AFTER ONE OF HIS MOST CRITICAL DEFEATS.
HE TOOK ON THE PERSONA OF MR. TINKER, A KINDLY INVENTOR AND REPAIR MAN.
EGGMAN LAND
SO I TOOK HIM IN AND WENT TO GREAT LENGTHS TO CURE HIM OF THAT STATE OF MIND.
WITH... SOME ASSISTANCE FROM METAL SONIC...

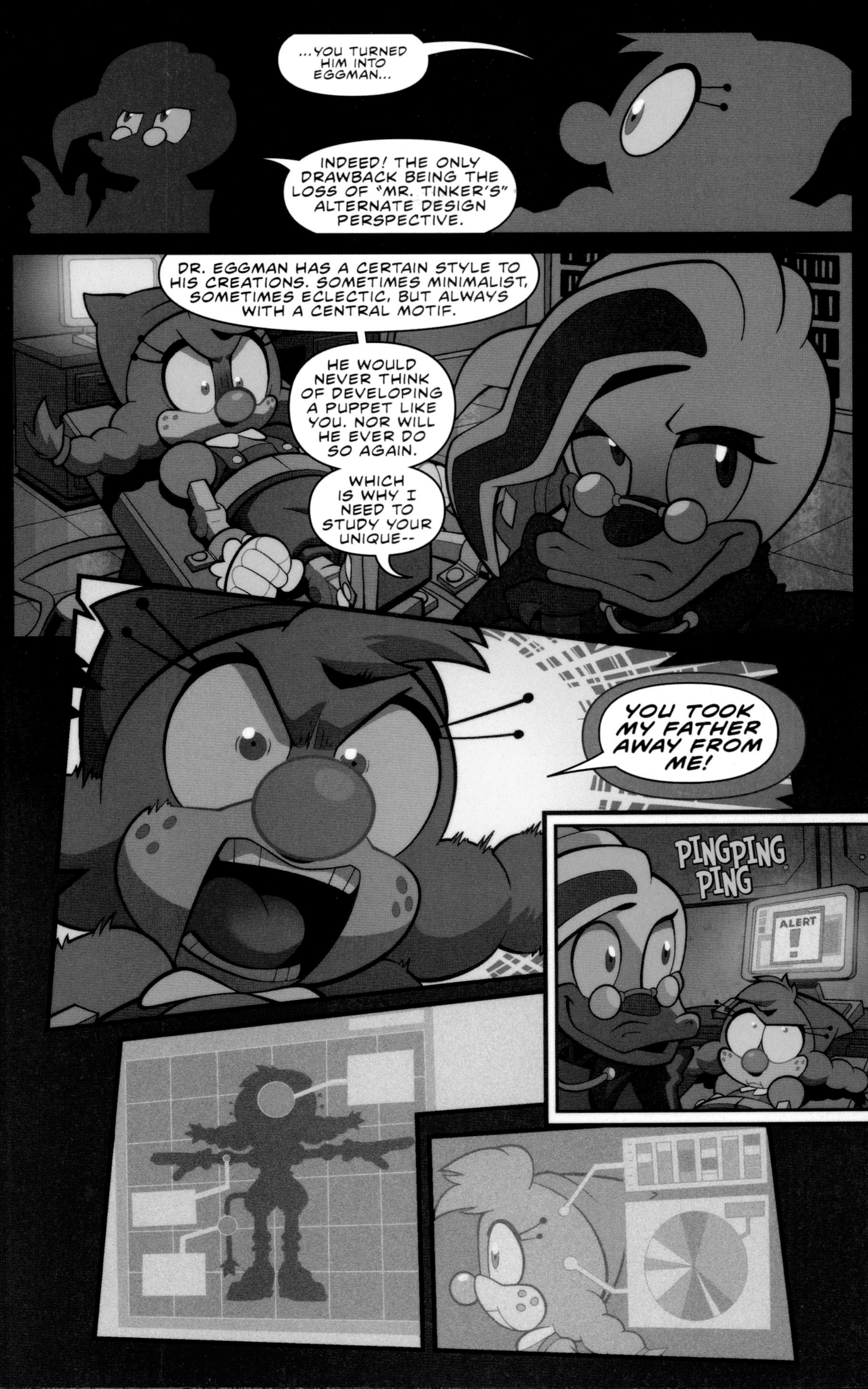
...YOU TURNED HIM INTO EGGMAN...
INDEED! THE ONLY DRAWBACK BEING THE LOSS OF "MR. TINKER'S" ALTERNATE DESIGN PERSPECTIVE.
DR. EGGMAN HAS A CERTAIN STYLE TO HIS CREATIONS. SOMETIMES MINIMALIST, SOMETIMES ECLECTIC, BUT ALWAYS WITH A CENTRAL MOTIF.
HE WOULD NEVER THINK OF DEVELOPING A PUPPET LIKE YOU. NOR WILL HE EVER DO SO AGAIN.
WHICH IS WHY I NEED TO STUDY YOUR UNIQUE--
YOU TOOK MY FATHER AWAY FROM ME!
PINGPING PING
ALERT

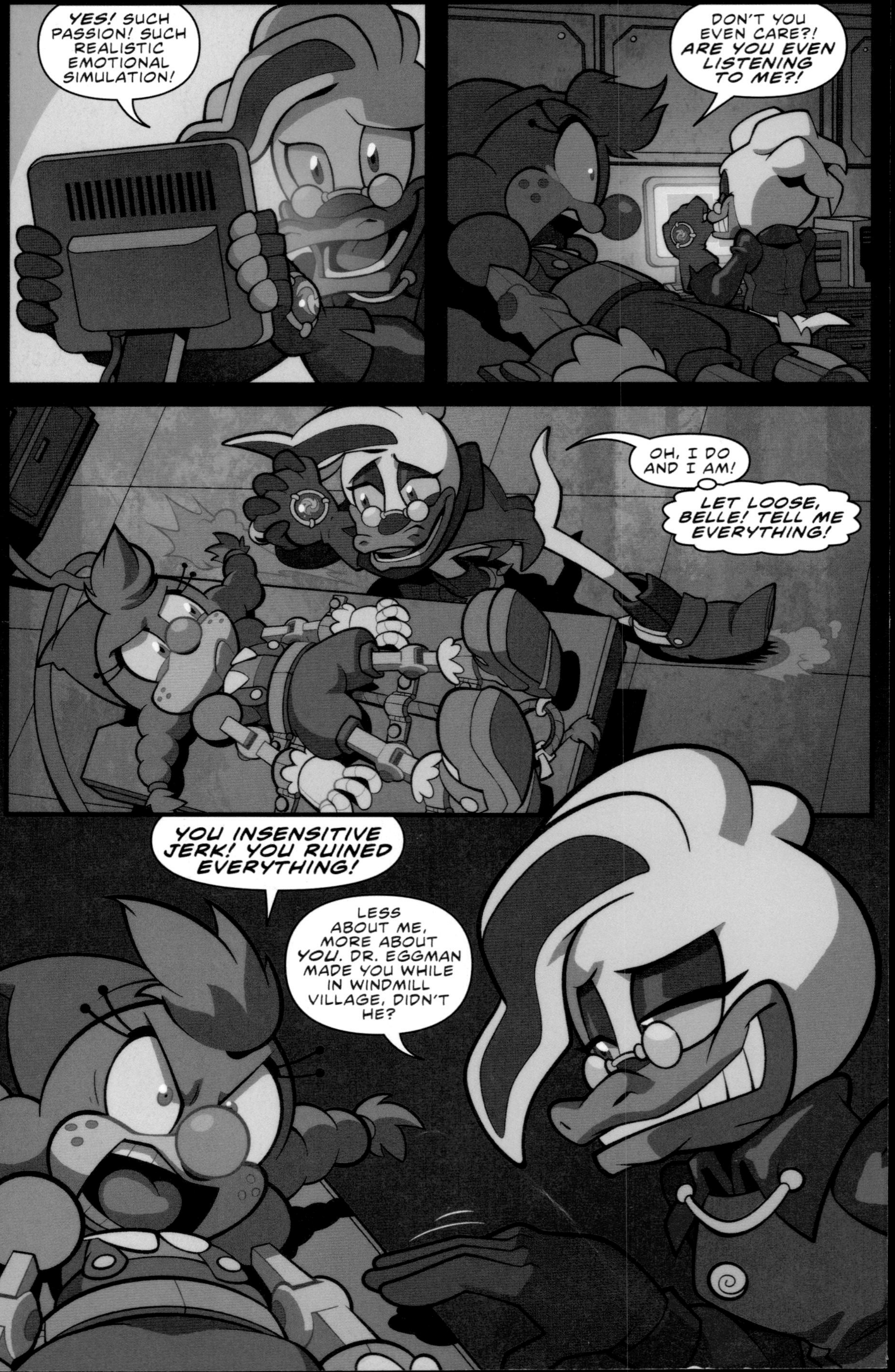
YES! SUCH PASSION! SUCH REALISTIC EMOTIONAL SIMULATION!
DON'T YOU EVEN CARE?! ARE YOU EVEN LISTENING TO ME?!
OH, I DO AND I AM!
LET LOOSE, BELLE! TELL ME EVERYTHING!
YOU INSENSITIVE JERK! YOU RUINED EVERYTHING!
LESS ABOUT ME, MORE ABOUT YOU. DR. EGGMAN MADE YOU WHILE IN WINDMILL VILLAGE, DIDN'T HE?

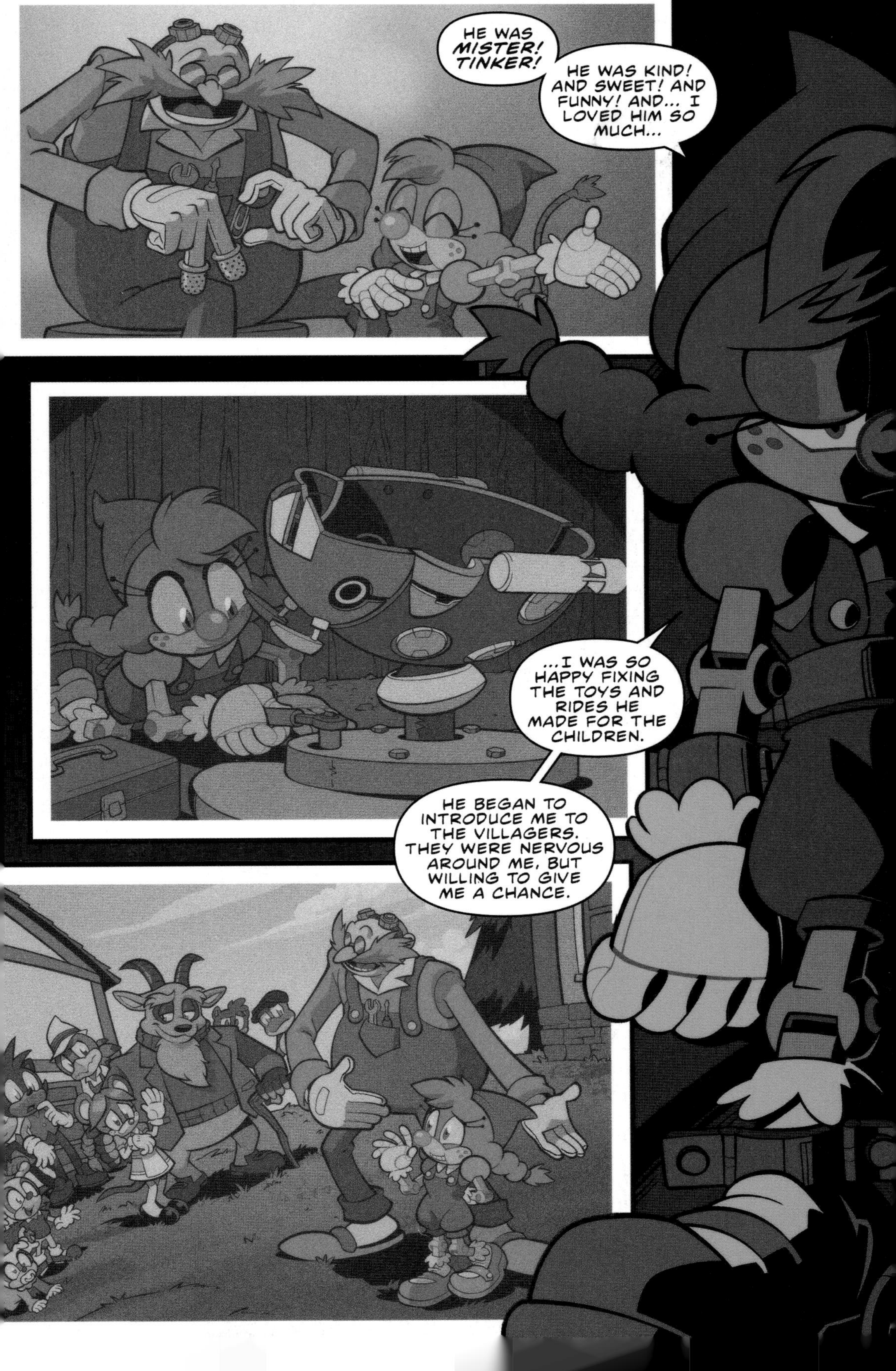
HE WAS *MISTER! TINKER!*
HE WAS KIND! AND SWEET! AND FUNNY! AND... I LOVED HIM SO MUCH...
...I WAS SO HAPPY FIXING THE TOYS AND RIDES HE MADE FOR THE CHILDREN.
HE BEGAN TO INTRODUCE ME TO THE VILLAGERS. THEY WERE NERVOUS AROUND ME, BUT WILLING TO GIVE ME A CHANCE.

"THEN ONE DAY...
HE VANISHED.

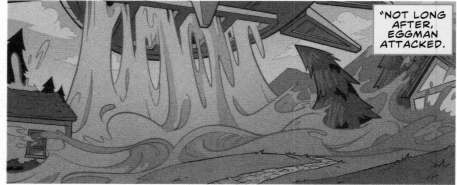

"NOT LONG
AFTER,
EGGMAN
ATTACKED.

"THE METAL VIRUS
DIDN'T AFFECT ME...

"...AND I WAS
VERY ALONE."

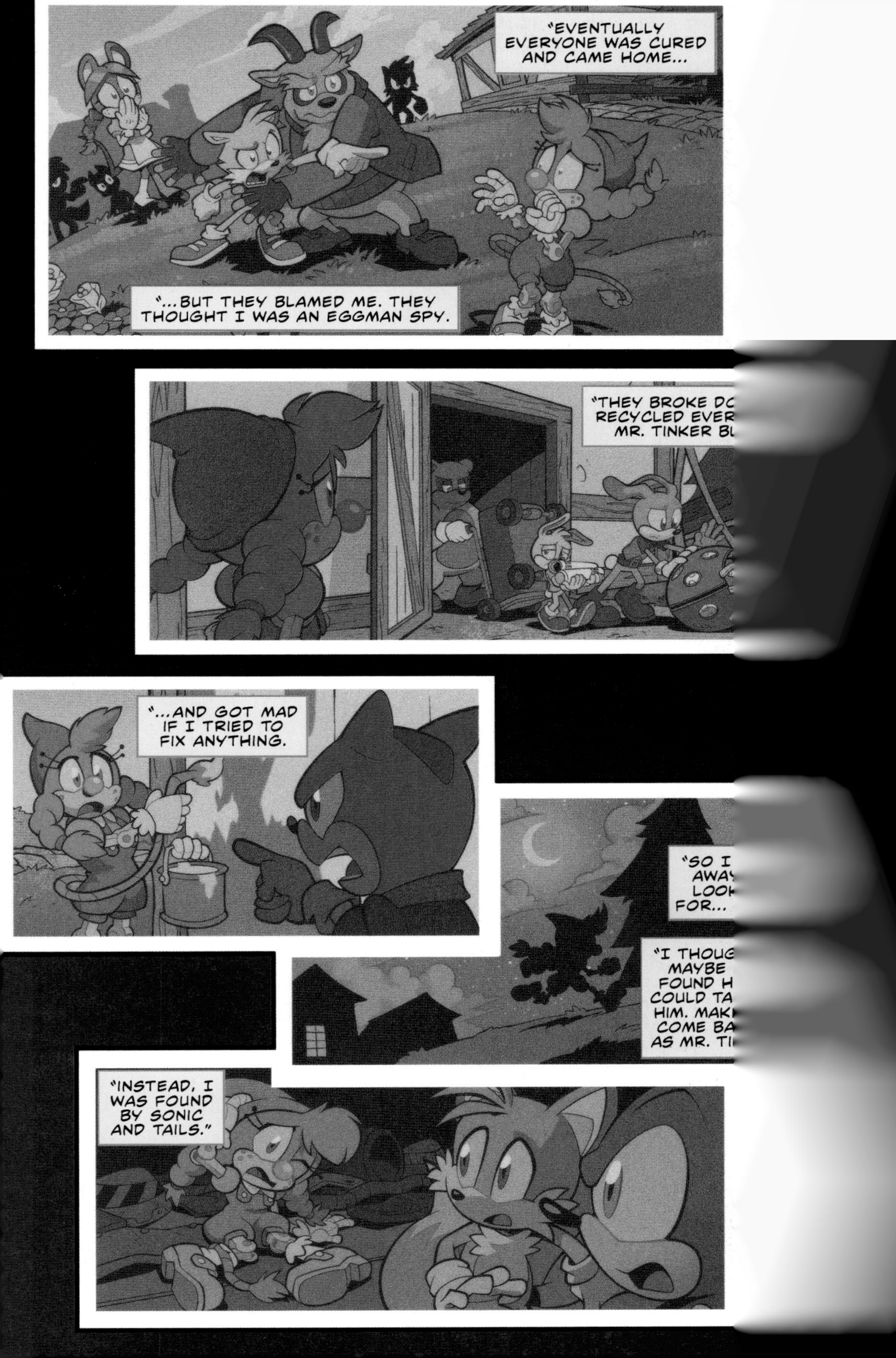
"EVENTUALLY EVERYONE WAS CURED AND CAME HOME...
"...BUT THEY BLAMED ME. THEY THOUGHT I WAS AN EGGMAN SPY.
"THEY BROKE
RECYCLED
MR. TINKER
"...AND GOT MAD IF I TRIED TO FIX ANYTHING.
"SO I
FOR...
"I
MAYBE
FOUND
COULD
HIM.
COME
AS MR.
"INSTEAD, I WAS FOUND BY SONIC AND TAILS."

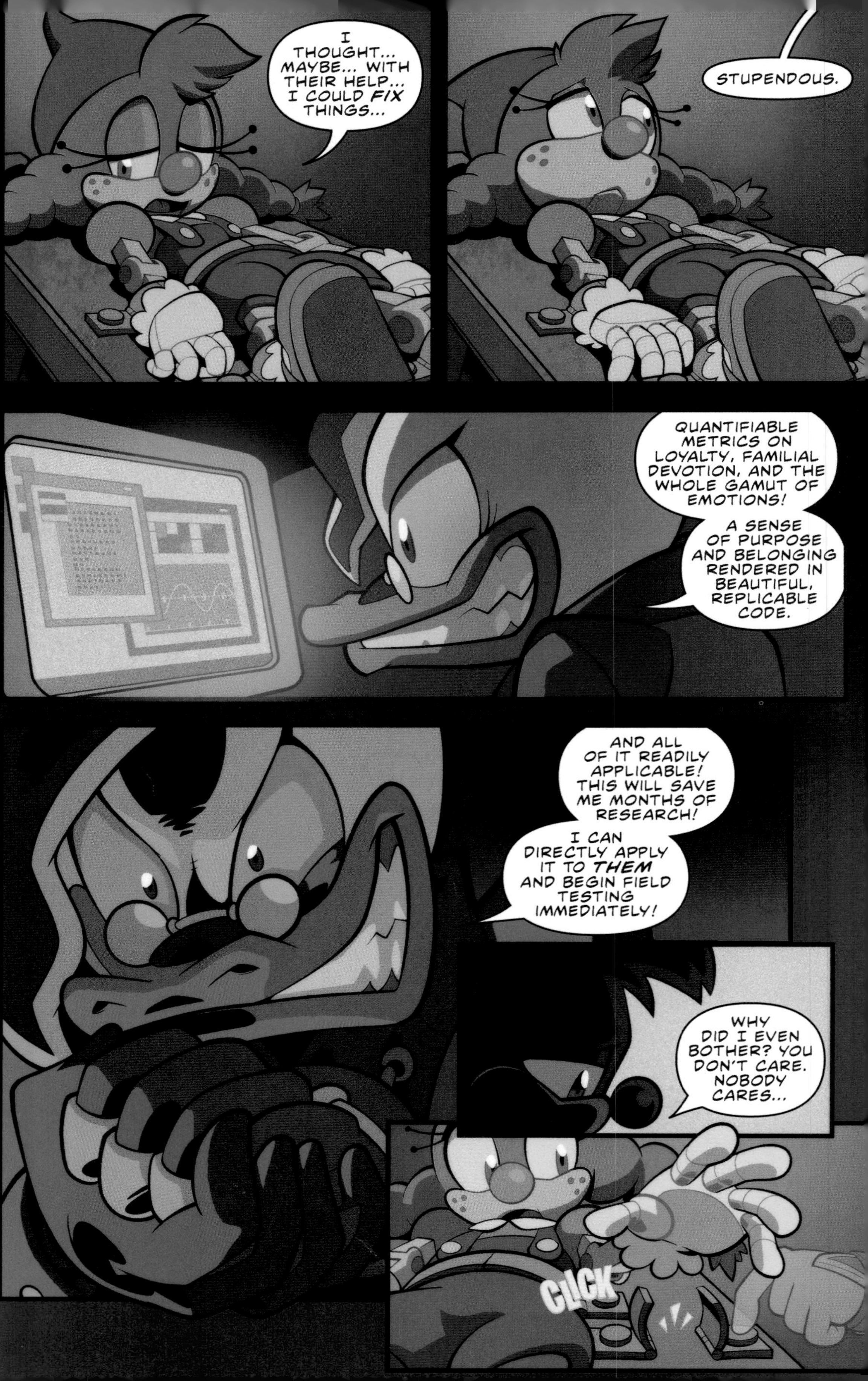
I THOUGHT... MAYBE... WITH THEIR HELP... I COULD *FIX* THINGS...
STUPENDOUS.
QUANTIFIABLE METRICS ON LOYALTY, FAMILIAL DEVOTION, AND THE WHOLE GAMUT OF EMOTIONS!
A SENSE OF PURPOSE AND BELONGING RENDERED IN BEAUTIFUL, REPLICABLE CODE.
AND ALL OF IT READILY APPLICABLE! THIS WILL SAVE ME MONTHS OF RESEARCH!
I CAN DIRECTLY APPLY IT TO *THEM* AND BEGIN FIELD TESTING IMMEDIATELY!
WHY DID I EVEN BOTHER? YOU DON'T CARE. NOBODY CARES...
CLICK

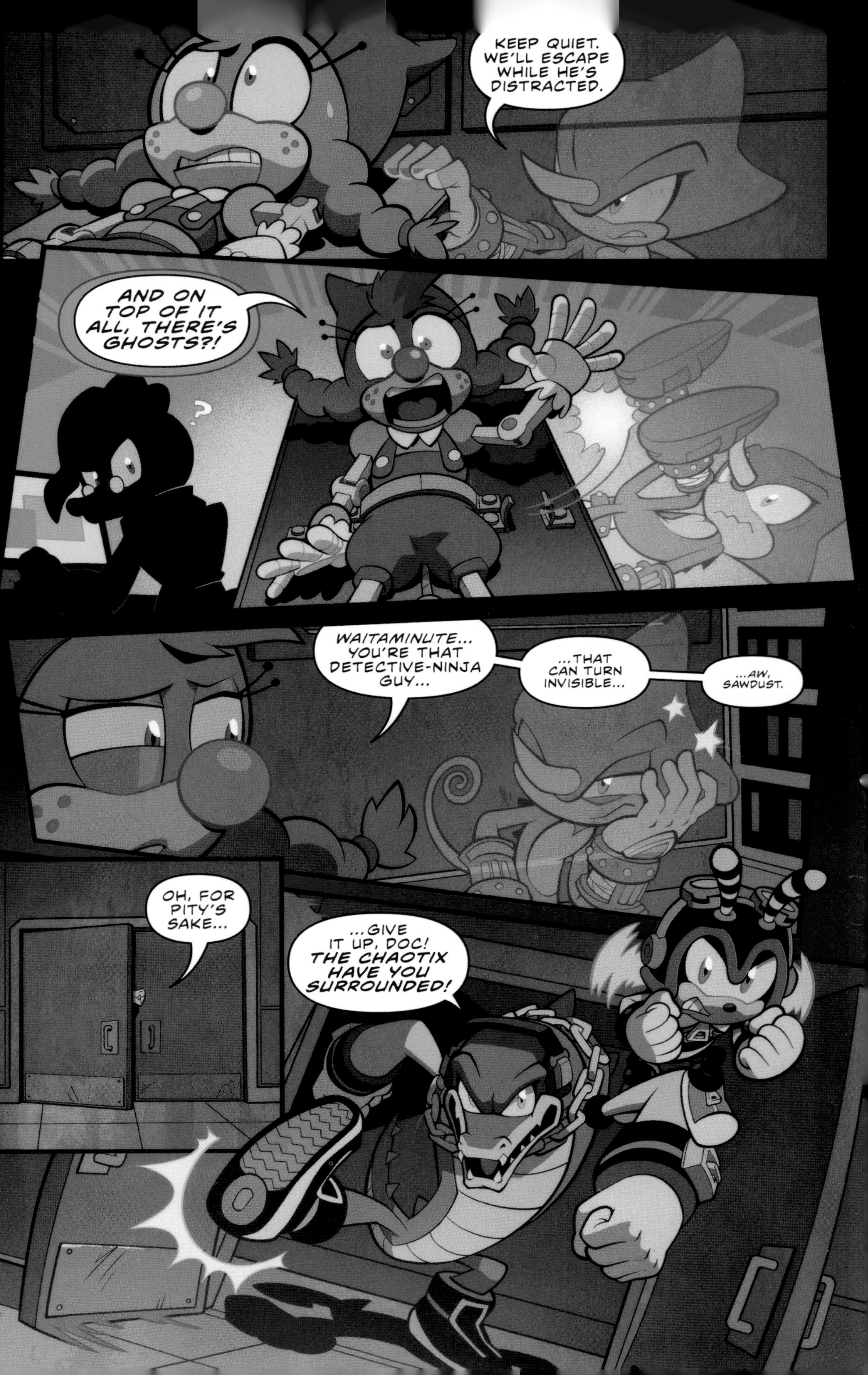
KEEP QUIET. WE'LL ESCAPE WHILE HE'S DISTRACTED.
AND ON TOP OF IT ALL, THERE'S GHOSTS?!
?
WAITAMINUTE... YOU'RE THAT DETECTIVE-NINJA GUY...
...THAT CAN TURN INVISIBLE...
...AW, SAWDUST.
OH, FOR PITY'S SAKE...
...GIVE IT UP, DOC! THE CHAOTIX HAVE YOU SURROUNDED!

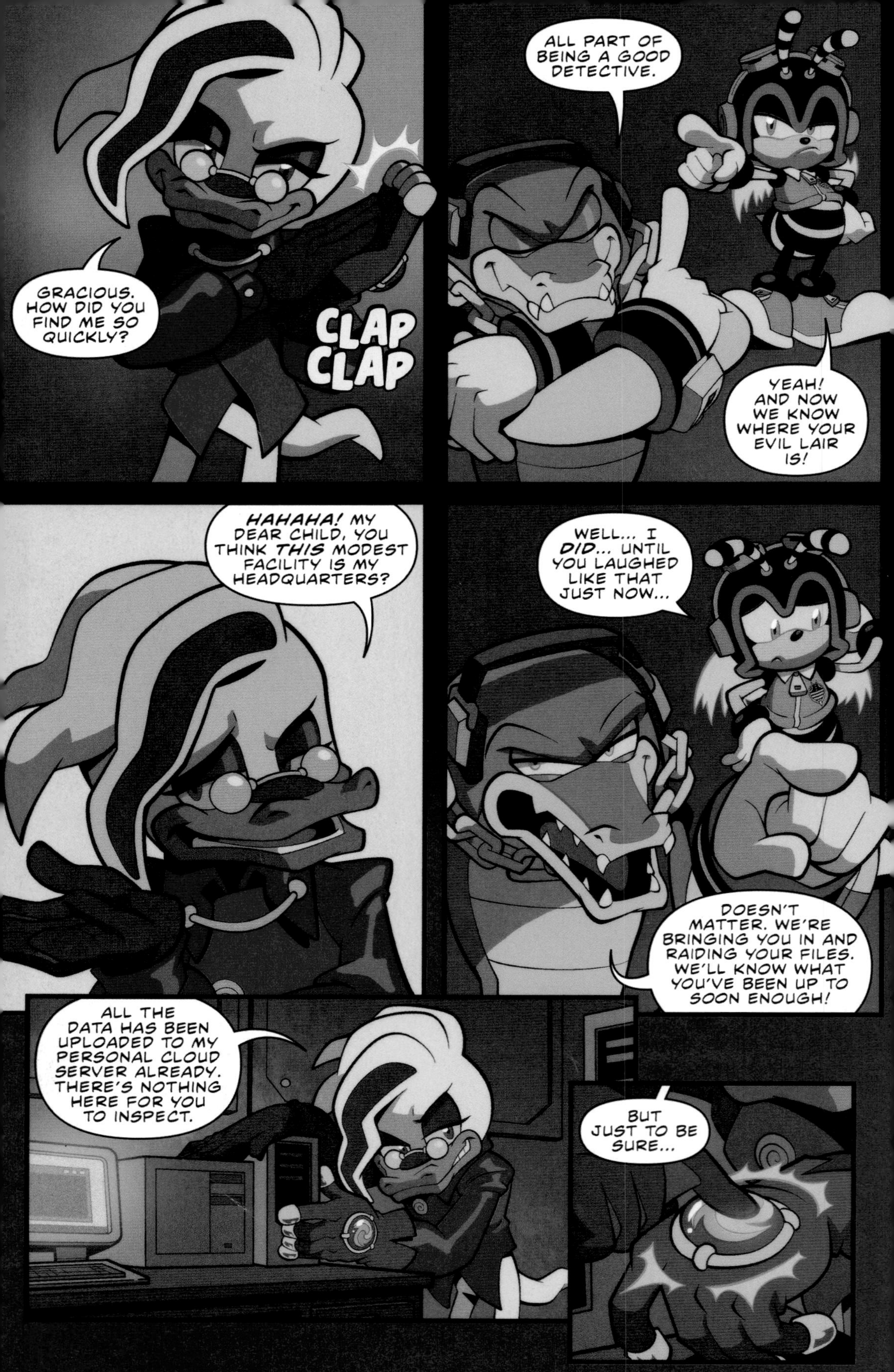
GRACIOUS. HOW DID YOU FIND ME SO QUICKLY?
CLAP CLAP
ALL PART OF BEING A GOOD DETECTIVE.
YEAH! AND NOW WE KNOW WHERE YOUR EVIL LAIR IS!
HAHAHA! MY DEAR CHILD, YOU THINK *THIS* MODEST FACILITY IS MY HEADQUARTERS?
WELL... I *DID*... UNTIL YOU LAUGHED LIKE THAT JUST NOW...
DOESN'T MATTER. WE'RE BRINGING YOU IN AND RAIDING YOUR FILES. WE'LL KNOW WHAT YOU'VE BEEN UP TO SOON ENOUGH!
ALL THE DATA HAS BEEN UPLOADED TO MY PERSONAL CLOUD SERVER ALREADY. THERE'S NOTHING HERE FOR YOU TO INSPECT.
BUT JUST TO BE SURE...

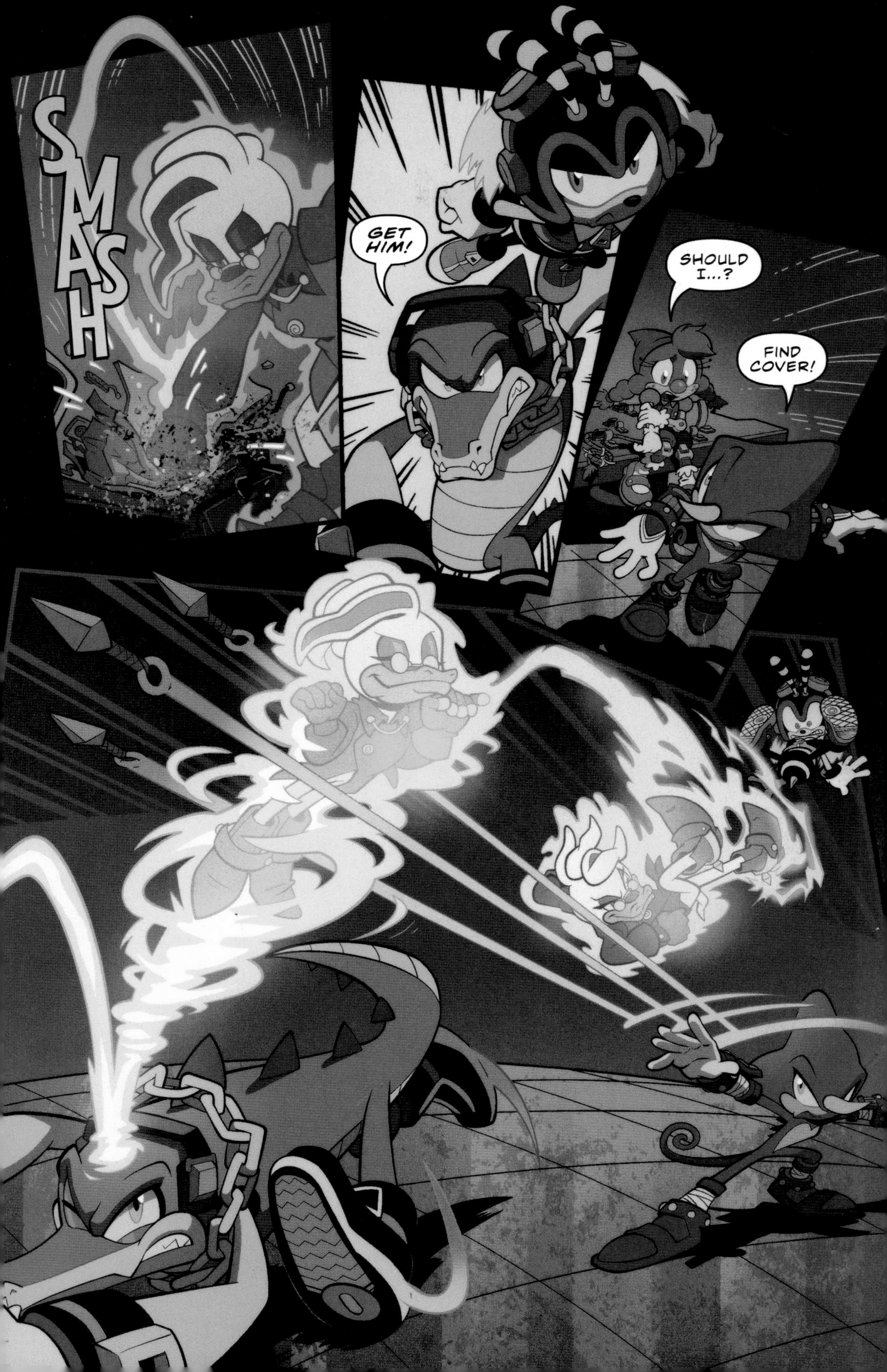
SMASH
GET HIM!
SHOULD I...?
FIND COVER!

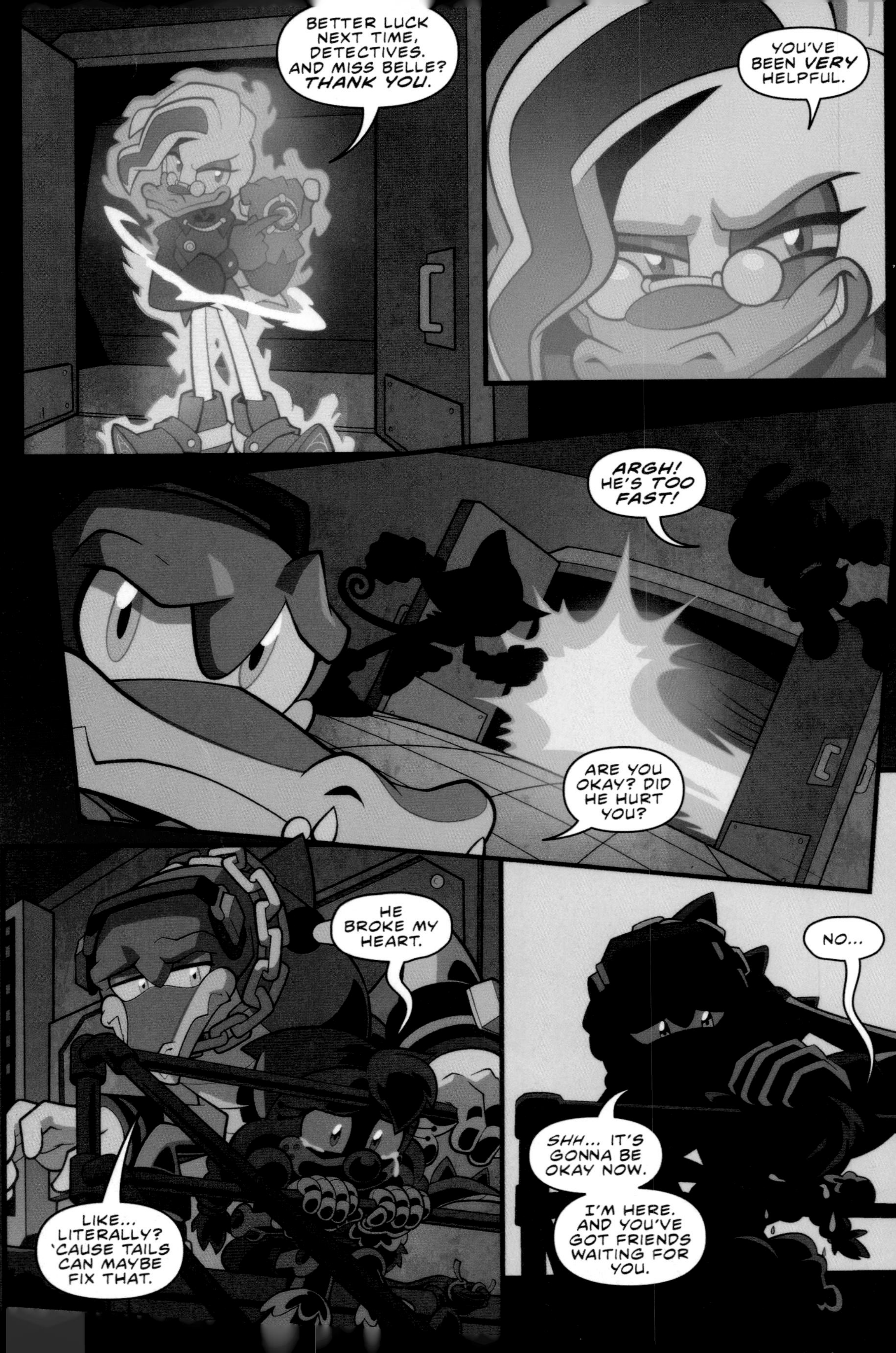
BETTER LUCK NEXT TIME, DETECTIVES. AND MISS BELLE? THANK YOU.
YOU'VE BEEN VERY HELPFUL.
ARGH! HE'S TOO FAST!
ARE YOU OKAY? DID HE HURT YOU?
HE BROKE MY HEART.
LIKE... LITERALLY? 'CAUSE TAILS CAN MAYBE FIX THAT.
NO...
SHH... IT'S GONNA BE OKAY NOW.
I'M HERE. AND YOU'VE GOT FRIENDS WAITING FOR YOU.

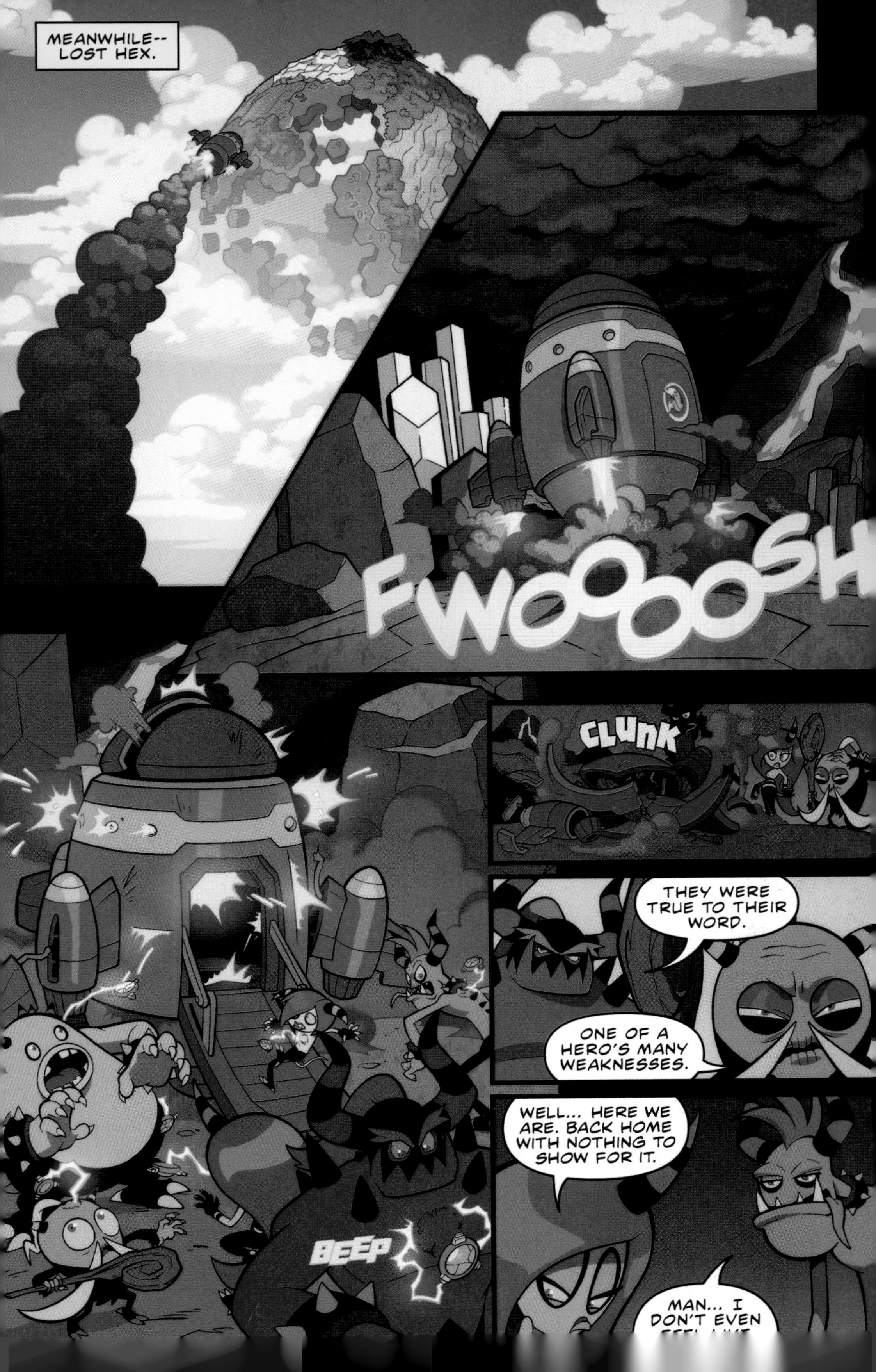
MEANWHILE--
LOST HEX.
FWOOOOOSH
CLUNK
BEEP
THEY WERE TRUE TO THEIR WORD.
ONE OF A HERO'S MANY WEAKNESSES.
WELL... HERE WE ARE. BACK HOME WITH NOTHING TO SHOW FOR IT.
MAN... I DON'T EVEN

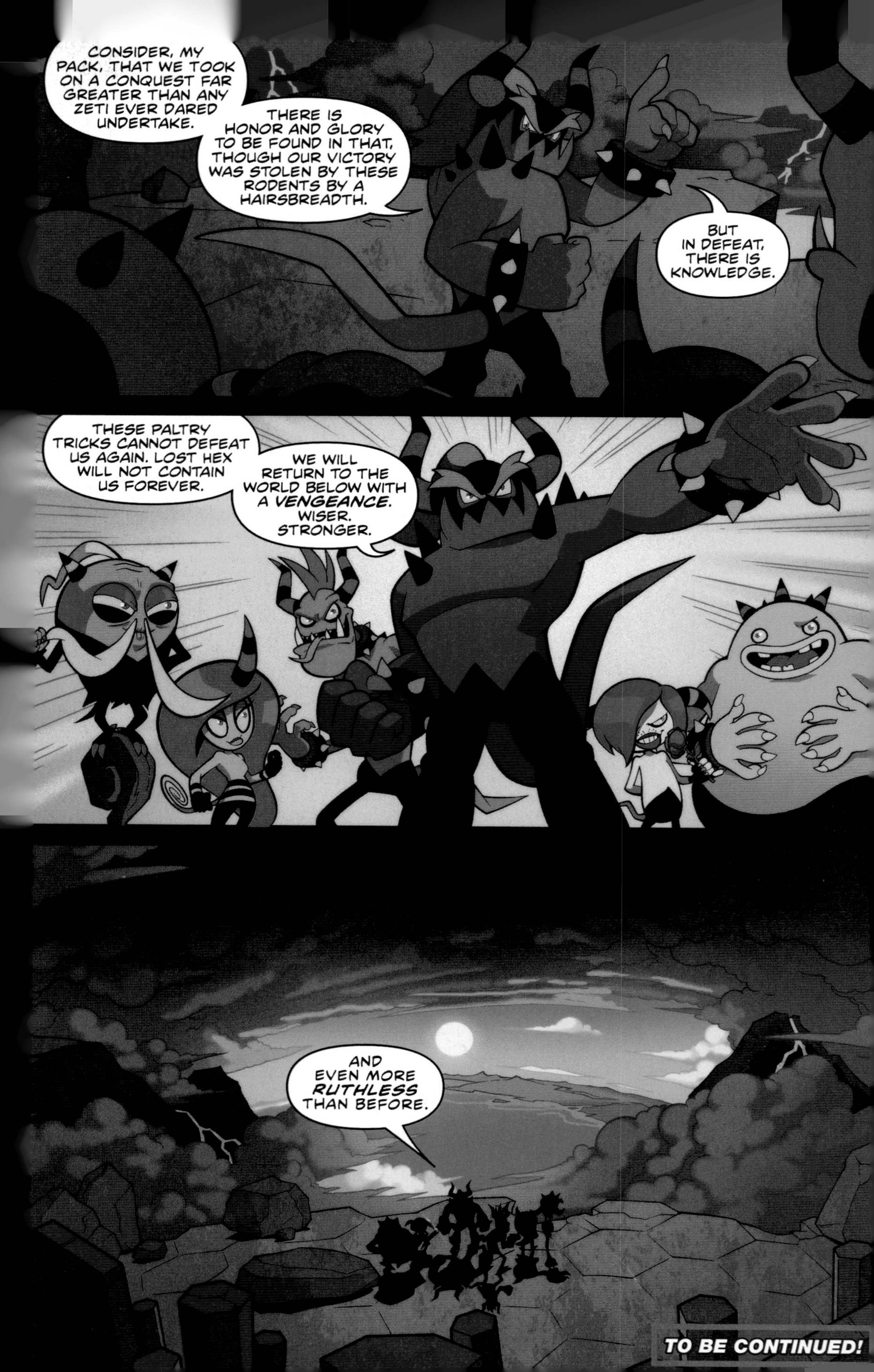
CONSIDER, MY PACK, THAT WE TOOK ON A CONQUEST FAR GREATER THAN ANY ZETI EVER DARED UNDERTAKE.
THERE IS HONOR AND GLORY TO BE FOUND IN THAT, THOUGH OUR VICTORY WAS STOLEN BY THESE RODENTS BY A HAIRSBREADTH.
BUT IN DEFEAT, THERE IS KNOWLEDGE.
THESE PALTRY TRICKS CANNOT DEFEAT US AGAIN. LOST HEX WILL NOT CONTAIN US FOREVER.
WE WILL RETURN TO THE WORLD BELOW WITH A *VENGEANCE*. WISER. STRONGER.
AND EVEN MORE *RUTHLESS* THAN BEFORE.
TO BE CONTINUED!

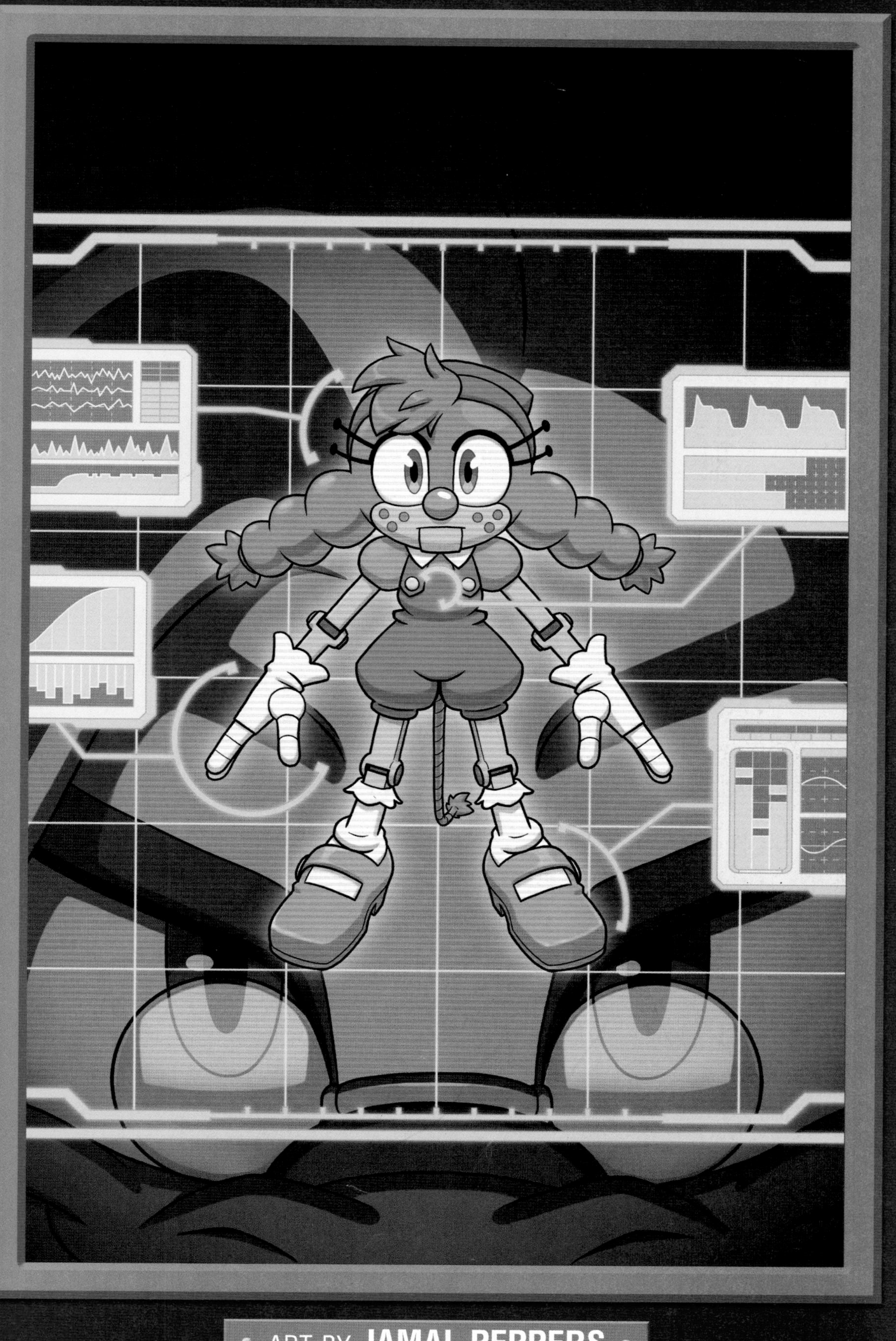

ART BY **JAMAL PEPPERS**

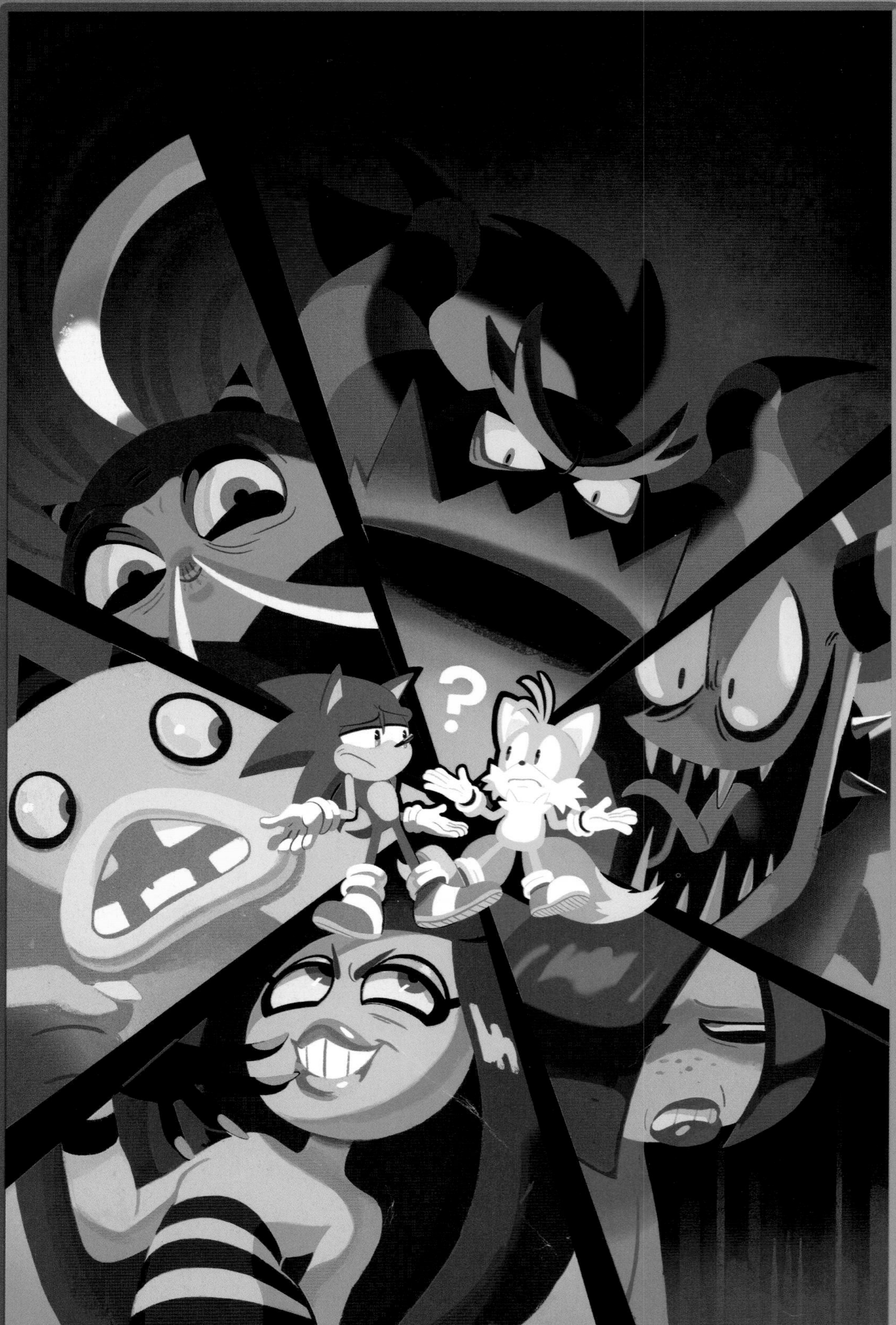
?

ART BY **NATHALIE FOURDRAINE**

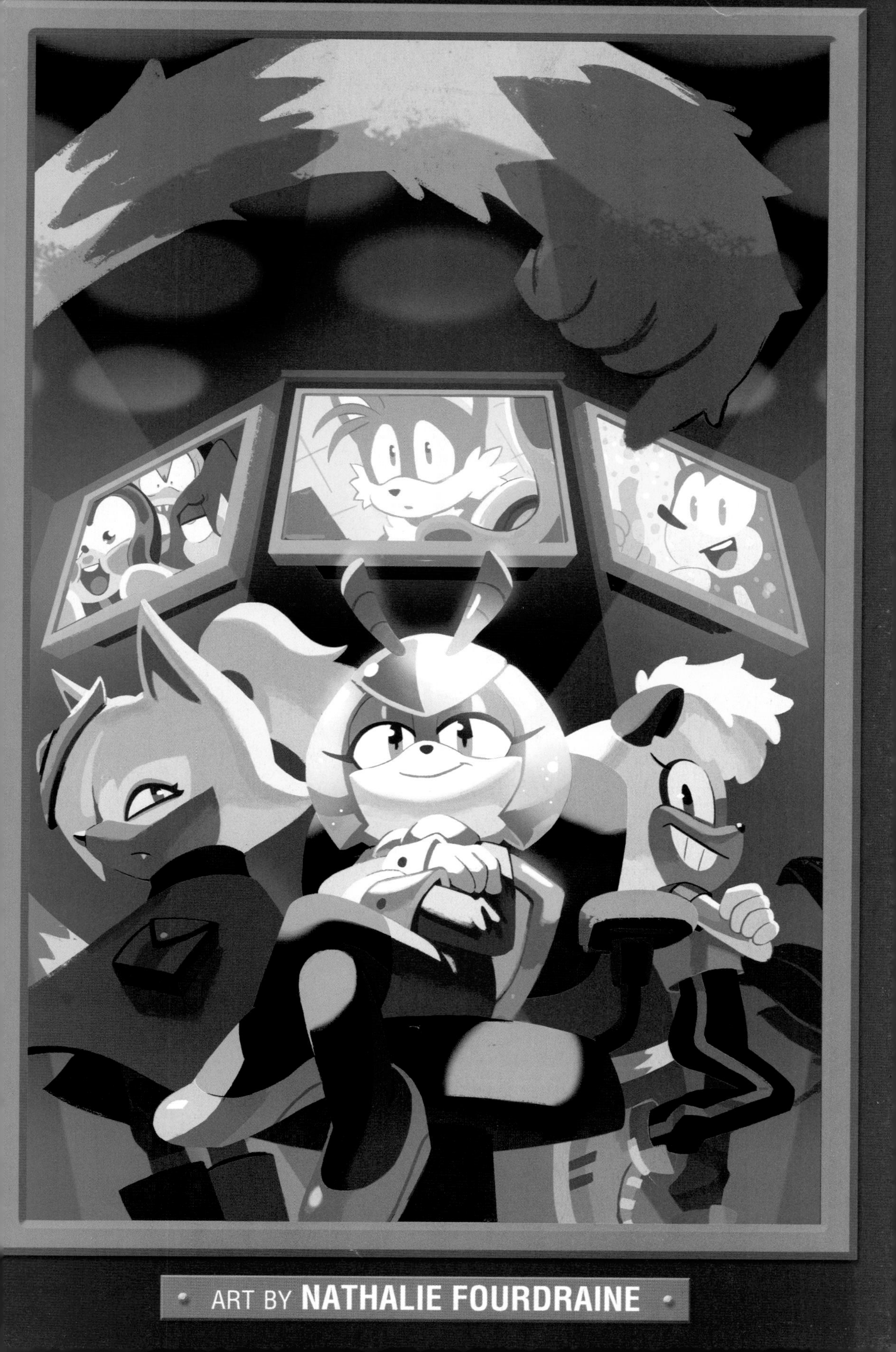

ART BY **NATHALIE FOURDRAINE**

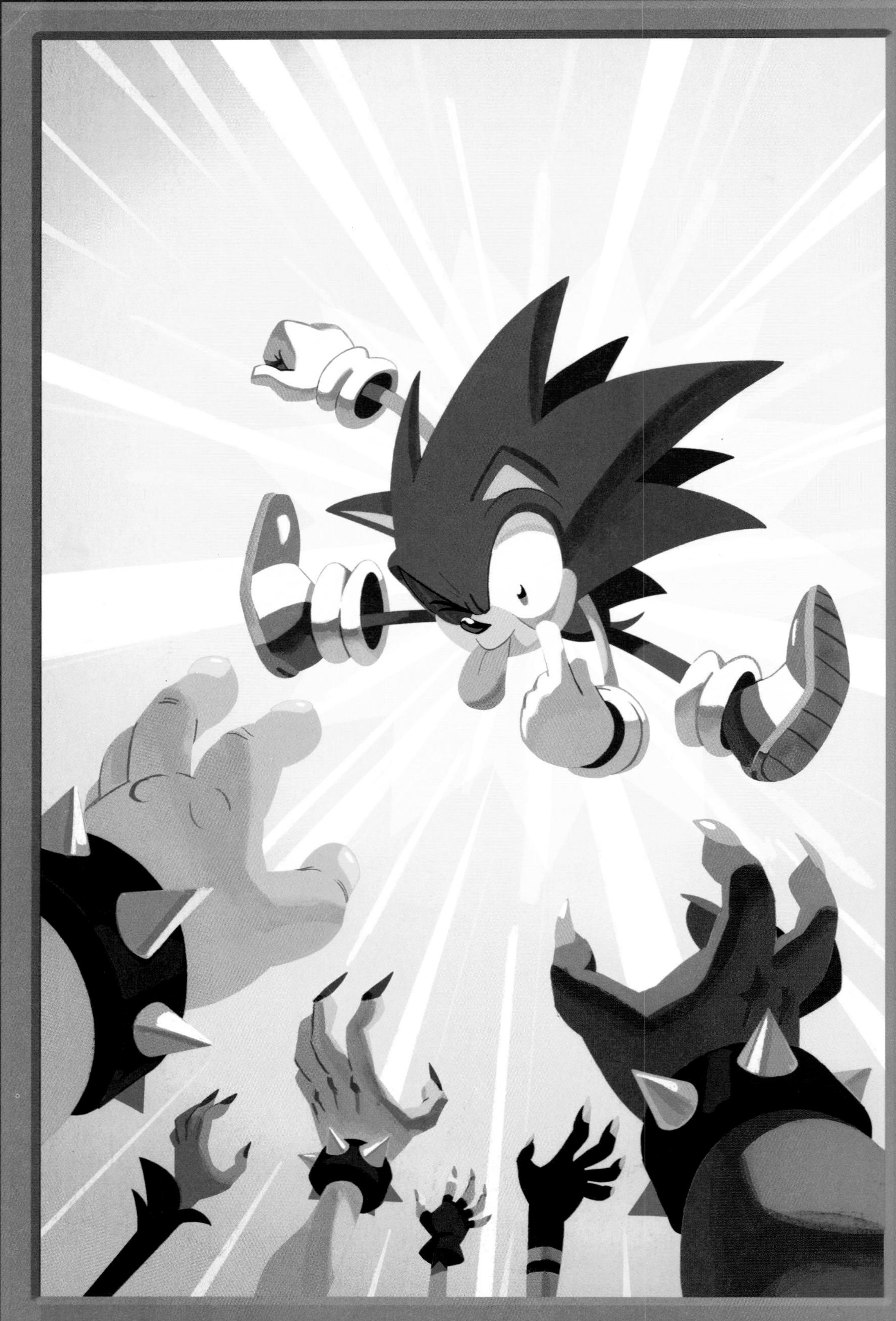

ART BY **NATHALIE FOURDRAINE**

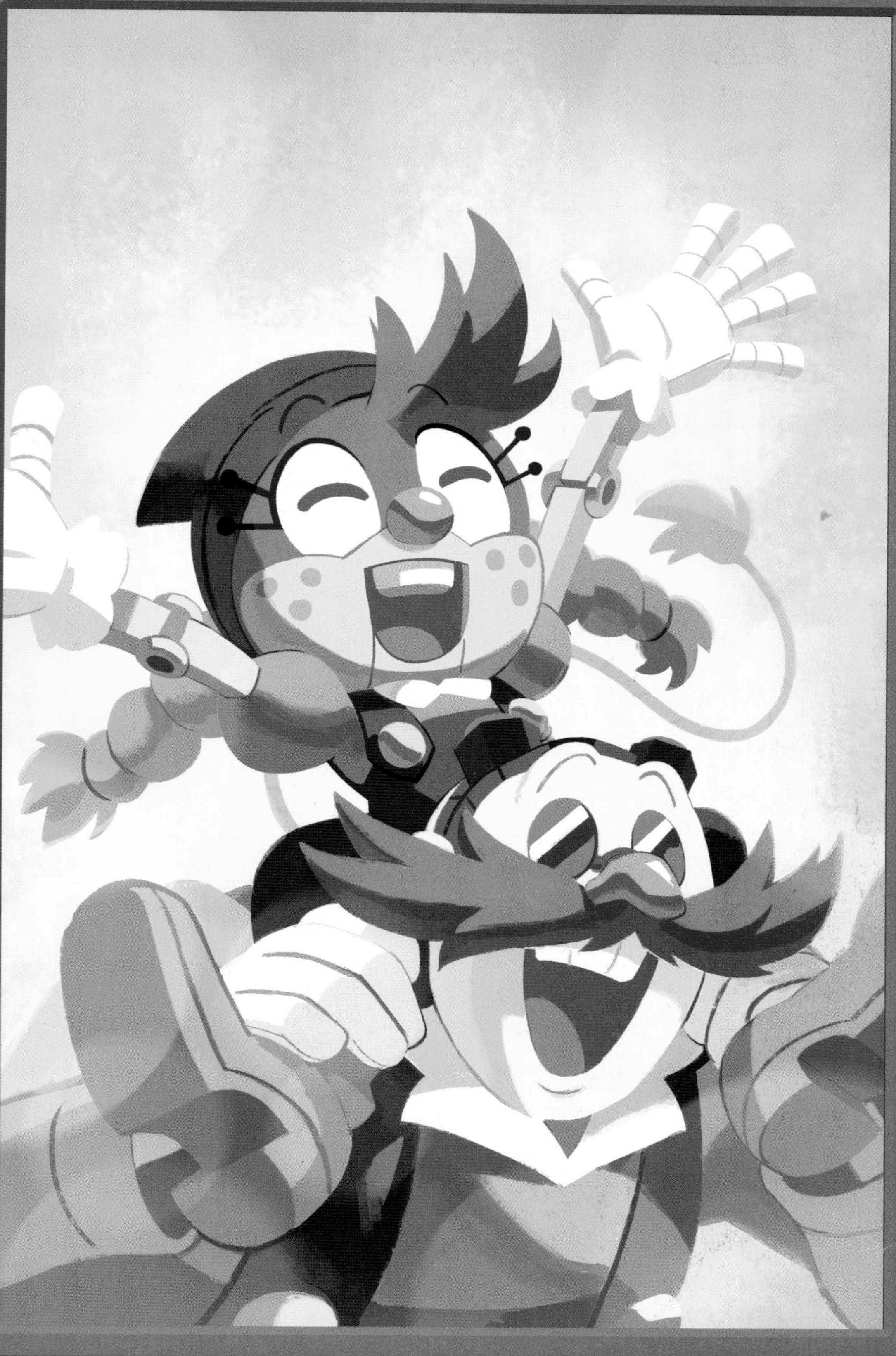

ART BY **NATHALIE FOURDRAINE**

SONIC™
THE HEDGEHOG

ZETI HUNT!